UNDER CUBA

CHAP HARPER

This is a work of fiction, and is produced from the author's imagination. People, places and things mentioned in this novel are used in a fictional manner.

ISBN: 978-1-7348196-4-9

Library of Congress Control Number: 2017938567

Acknowledgments

Fiction writers spend a great deal of time and effort researching the sparse truth that exists in their stories. I am no different. Maybe it's a feeling of guilt or just compensation for making so much stuff up. In one book, I spent a great deal of time researching the placement and description of the rank and corresponding stripes on the uniform of a naval officer in the Dominican Republic. I wonder who cares.

Once I placed the number 52 as a runway number on an airstrip in the Congo in a story. Thankfully, someone (a former air force officer) told me that runways were all compass headings and therefore they didn't go that high. I pulled out the picture of the runway and realized I was reading it backwards. It should have been 25. Who would have cared? Possibly no one except pilots and the people who expect writers to at least present those small nuggets of truth in an accurate manner.

I would like to thank all the nonfiction writers who slave over facts. I will continue to read your books, essays, journals, and yes, your Wikipedia entries. Writers need real bones to build a great story. I will continue to come to the bone pile many times in the future.

Chap Harper
May, 2017

Dedication

I doubt this novel will be on any reading lists in Cuba for a long time. It may not be allowed to be sold there since most of the books sold in Cuba have the late Fidel Castro's picture on them. Nevertheless, I am dedicating it to those Cuban citizens living in their country, and to the Cubans fortunate to have found a home in the United States and other countries.

Cuba is a beautiful country, rich in architecture, with beautiful beaches, lots of palm trees, and forested mountains. The people are friendly with warm hearts. There will be struggles for those Cuban citizens moving towards a market economy. I wish them well as they start businesses and provide services for the growing tourist industry. Like most Americans, I dread the first McDonald's or Burger King that will be wedged in between Spanish colonial buildings.

We all wish Cuba could remain a place that resembles an old movie set. But it must grow and provide jobs with the new private enterprise expansion. More than anything, they must keep the beautiful old American cars. Cubans already know that we love them as much as they do. It is a strange economy, however, when a Cuban providing a tour in a 55 Chevy could easily make several times the monthly income of a Cuban doctor in a single day. It's the old Cuba laid next to the new emerging Cuba. It should be an exciting time for the Cuban people.

Prologue

One wealthy US family hurried out of town as Fidel Castro and his rebel army entered Havana. They left their car at the airport, keys inside. Later, Fidel's forces used metal detectors to find valuable treasures sealed in the walls of the Americans' large home. Sterling silver servers and gold-plated dinnerware were cleverly hidden away. The rebel newspaper *Revolucion* displayed pictures of Cuban officials holding metal detectors next to piles of silver bowls and tea sets.

Similar discoveries happened all over Cuba. Many of the valuables were found, but most everyone believes other riches are waiting to be discovered, even after being hidden for over fifty years. It could very well be that the Americans who fled in 1959 passed along to family members the knowledge of exactly where their treasures were stored away. Now their heirs might be waiting for the right time to dig up something that lies under Cuba. Cuba, however, will be watching.

Chapter One

Hotel Nacional de Cuba, Havana, December 22, 1946

Bernie Swartz and Carmine Spada distanced themselves from the important mobsters who sat at a long table in a conference room on the National Hotel's first floor. Salvatore "Lucky" Luciano had just broached the subject of "the boss of bosses" and Vito Genovese and Albert Anastasia told him they agreed that Luciano should remain the boss even though he had been expelled from the United States and sent to live in Italy. It pleased him greatly to find that he didn't have to fight for a position he believed he deserved anyway. They discussed the issue of Bugsy Siegel and voted to punish him for the losses incurred on the Flamingo project in Las Vegas. Meyer Lansky wasn't able to vote since he wasn't pure blood Italian. He was Jewish, as was Bugsy, yet he spoke up for Siegel and pleaded for the council to wait for the grand opening of the casino, which was only a few days off. They agreed. But Lansky also stated that should the new casino in the desert not be successful, "he would be dealt with." The entire room knew what that meant.

Bernie and Carmine were low-level mobsters—hardly even mobsters. They jointly owned the Caribe Shores, a small-potatoes casino and nightclub in a seedy outlying district of Havana's Malecon. Actually, the front of the casino was a restored two-story colonial building across the street from the main waterfront with a view of Moro Castle, which stood high on a bluff with cannons trained down to ward off pesky pirates. The Caribe Shores was very nice inside and out, but a few paces away from the parking lot was a neighborhood crawling with thieves and dope heads. Yet in spite of its out-of-the-way location, the casino was a wildly successful property. The building was paid for, the nightclub had a great reputation, and the entertainment and meals were top notch. Guards were posted in the parking lot and actual run-ins with local thugs were rare. The two owners were not high on the pecking order at the gangster convention underway at the National Hotel and Casino but were well-respected. As they sat some distance from the big Mafia table, those leaving for the restrooms and smoke breaks would stop and talk to the partners. Meyer Lansky was always friendly, especially to his Jewish friend Bernie Swartz; he placed a hand on Bernie's back as he headed out of the conference room.

"Bernie, can you believe we have rented the whole goddamned hotel for this meeting? It's wacky! Be glad you're not at the main table deciding who is going to be left alive to rule the earth," Meyer said, sporting a big grin.

"Meyer, you and I are the accountant types and not meant to run the show. We do a hell of a job counting the money, though," Bernie said. Meyer laughed and headed for the exit.

All the casinos in Cuba were surging as they recovered from the war years. Carmine Spada had served in North Africa where he almost lost his foot under a half-track in the desert. He dodged amputation but would always limp as too many bones were broken to ever heal properly. He was discharged in 1943 and shortly after he returned, he saw Bernie leave for Europe as an army air pilot. Bernie flew missions as a P-51D Mustang pilot and escorted bombers on their flights over Germany.

Both were US citizens who had permits to operate a business in Cuba. Fulgencio Batista, who was usually the president of Cuba (and when he wasn't, he still was), had offered to match casino investments, dollar for dollar, up to a million, to attract investors in his largest city. A typical in-depth background check was waived. All casinos were hurt during the war, but most survived as GIs on leave and other fun-seekers took the ferry, which ran only a couple times a week, from Miami to Havana. Now it ran two times a day during the week—three times on the weekend. 1946 was the rebirth after all those bleak times.

There were Christmas parties at the hotel, and Bernie and Carmine made appearances if they got a phone call asking them to show up. The coveted invitation was for Frank Sinatra's performance.

Of course, the Caribe Shores owners attended and sat among the largest concentration of Mafia, gangsters, Cosa Nostra, and mobsters ever assembled in one place. People would like to think that the singer was naïve about his audience, but he grew up with a lot of these guys back in New Jersey. Many were his friends and always would be. The Italians loved their golden boy, and he returned the affection. The parties started breaking up right after Christmas, and the hotel began to receive their normal wealthy guests from all over the world. Bernie and Carmine went back to their club where Carmine booked the shows, hired and managed the staff, while Bernie massaged the books and supervised the gaming operations.

Carmine lived nearby in a good neighborhood in a large Spanish Colonial house. He had a lovely wife and two beautiful young daughters, Suzanne, age 8, and Liza, age 9, who attended school back in Boston. His wife Betty traveled back and forth to look after them. Their summers were spent in Cuba, Europe, and on vacation with their dad. Carmine knew he couldn't hold on to them forever since it wouldn't be long before they discovered boys. The girls were in Catholic elementary boarding school and were only a little more than a year apart in age. Betty had relatives nearby in Cambridge, so there was always family close by. Carmine had married at twenty-one and now was 32 years old—five years older than Bernie. He took on the role of older brother much of the time, yet both were really young to be in the casino business. Betty found out right after the big hotel assembly that she was pregnant again. It wasn't planned, but the surprise was really welcomed. The girls were away in school so much of the time, she would now have a baby to occupy her time. The girls were also excited and looked forward to a new sibling.

Bernie was also married. He had met a British nurse named Connie after he sustained some flak wounds on a mission deep in Germany's heartland. She was blonde, sexy, and required a lot of attention. They had an apartment near the US embassy on the other end of the Malecon and a horse farm on the Isle of Pines. Their land contained almost three miles of coastal waterfront, including a nice beach, a house on the water, and a separate large boathouse for Carmine's 43-foot cabin cruiser named *Caribe Queen*. In order to get to his farm, Bernie kept a well-maintained twin-engine Beechcraft Model-18, which he picked up as an Army Air Corps surplus trainer and kept at a rented hangar at the Havana airport. The flight took less than an hour, and he made the trip a couple times a week. Connie was six months pregnant with their first child during the big National Hotel meeting. She was never comfortable around the Mafia types— but who was? The free-flowing money and all that it bought suited her just fine. She thought about sending her unborn daughter to boarding school when the child was older. She wanted to keep her children as far away from the mob as possible, and hoped it was a long time before they understood what their father did for a living. They would eventually find out, but the parents delayed revealing this disturbing secret as long as possible. Since she and Betty were pregnant at the same time, the two shared a common bond and became close friends.

The years after 1946 were successful beyond their dreams, but rather than expand the business, the two owners refurbished the Caribe Shores. After Fidel Castro attacked some of Batista's barracks on July 29, 1953, in Santiago, Cuba, in what was a losing battle, the two men withdrew most of their money from the National Bank of Boston and Chase Bank in Havana. They worried about the future.

"Carmine, it's not just Fidel and his little rebel band of fuck-ups that worries me. The tone of the country is that Batista has to go. The takeover will be military, and the leader will act as a dictator, most likely. I've heard Fidel say that the casinos are part of the corruption of the government. We need to be ready," Bernie said.

A secret location below the boathouse at Bernie's place, under several feet of concrete, was the depository of enormous profits. On several occasions, they discussed building an airfield on Bernie's land for emergency flights. Fidel's attack had been a complete ass-whipping, but Bernie and Carmine knew the pulse of the people and the tenacity of Fidel's rag-tag rebels. They believed that if Fidel didn't survive the war, another military leader would arise to defeat the increasingly unpopular Batista Regime. Neither could imagine a communistic Cuba since the rebels said they were against a soviet-styled government. But a new dictator might outlaw the casinos with whatever brand of government they put in place.

Bernie and Carmine had sons born just six months apart in 1947. Bernie and Connie named their son Moses Franklin Swartz, and Carmine and Betty Spada came up with the name Roman Nico Spada. At least once a week, one couple would babysit the other couple's child; this gave both couples an opportunity to take in a movie or to visit the Tropicana nightclub and casino. Victor de Correa and Martin Fox always had a special table for them at the Tropicana, and the favor was returned to them at Carmine and Bernie's Caribe Shores.

Every so often Bernie and Carmine would load up the families and fly to the Isle of Pines where Carmine kept his big Chris-Craft moored at Bernie's dock. While the wives were at the beach or otherwise occupied, the two casino owners would pull a big rug back in the interior of the furnished boathouse, raise a trap door, and descend down into a small room. There was a table for sorting items, a couple of rattan chairs, and a huge walk-in safe. The boathouse had been built over the safe by American contractors. No native Cubans were allowed near the area when it was built, and as a further precaution, the contractors were from Washington State. They didn't want anybody who could jump in a boat and nose around, looking to bust into the safe. Not that it would have been easy to do. The sides were made of reinforced concrete and were three feet thick. The ceiling was four feet thick, reinforced with metal rebar, but the steel rods were only placed in the lower part of the ceiling so a metal detector couldn't pick them up from above. Metal detectors were becoming very popular in law enforcement, and Bernie and Carmine had tested them over the safe. Not a single ping. However, the stairs and the trap door were made of metal, so they had to go. Plans were in the works to rip them out and replace them with either wood or the new hard plastic models that started being used after the war.

Carmine made it a point to attend the Miami boat show every year. On one of these trips, he boarded a brand new blue water sailboat and found a hatch cover and steps made from a hardened plastic.

The sales person remarked, "This plastic isn't affected by salt water, won't rust, needs no treatment, and is as strong as metal or wood. The gangway and hatch are an option, so they can be ordered and shipped to Havana for you to pick up."

Carmine was about to leave when the salesman stopped him.

"Sir, we do have one of the units in stock. It has an extra-long ladder and won't fit any of the boats we have in stock. If you want it, I'll let you have it for the price of the shorter one."

Carmine smiled at his good luck and bought it. Once they installed it, the metal detector didn't make a sound when it was passed over the hatch. The hatch was recessed about six inches so concrete could be poured over it, sealing it from anyone. Bernie always had sacks of quick-drying cement stored near the boathouse.

Bernie had always liked gold coins and bars. It was illegal at the time to own them in the states, so he kept his collection in the big safe. Carmine owned a few but wasn't a real enthusiast like his partner. Some were in bags, but the ones with numismatic value were mounted on cards with their assigned grade listed. President Roosevelt's Executive Order 6102 in 1933 restricted the ownership of gold and only allowed individuals to own a few coins unless they were collectors of rare coins. Jewelers could have only enough gold for making products. If you fell under one of these classifications and registered, the treasury agents would be by to check on you. One slip-up and they would confiscate your coins, your gold, and put you in jail for up to ten years.

***

On one of these trips to the Isle of Pines in the summer of 1955, Bernie and Carmine drove their Jeep roadster into town to pick up some groceries. They left their wives behind at the beach house, along with Carmine's two daughters, Suzanne and Liza, who were now 17 and 18. His son Roman and Bernie's son Moe, both 8 years old, were also at the house. It was over twenty-five miles from Roja Beach on gravel and dirt roads to the main town Nueva Gerona, but it gave them time to talk about the future.

"Bernie, we need to plan exactly how to escape this place in case one of the rebel factions overthrows that asshole Batista. So far most of these guerilla attacks have been ill-planned and poorly executed. But I'll tell you what's going to happen: Batista's troops are going to be lured up the sides of those mountains where the rebels hide and then they'll pick them off one by one—steal their guns—and do it again. We can't be caught with our pants down," Carmine said as he rose up in his seat spotting a pothole he knew Bernie would hit dead on.

"You and I have this fucking conversation every time we're away from the wives—the very damn reason we built the safe," Bernie said. "So far, we've been putting from one-to-two million dollars a year in that damn thing—not counting the gold. We have a compartment in the plane and the boat to carry some out, but most we'll have to leave until later. I'd feel better if I had an airstrip near the house. Right now the airport is about thirty fucking miles away. A lot could happen in thirty miles."

As they entered the outskirts of the small town of Nueva Gerona, they observed the traffic was unusually thick. A huge crowd stood transfixed while a man standing in the bed of a pick-up truck spoke. The two men stopped and got out of the Jeep to hear what he was saying.

"I am thankful to be out of prison, but will not stop my struggle for the people of Cuba. Also with me is my brother Raul." Fidel Castro reached out and helped his brother into the back of the truck. They all joined hands as the crowds roared "Fidel! Fidel!" When they saw some soldiers approaching, the two men jumped off the truck and disappeared into the throng of onlookers.

Bernie frowned at Carmine. "Why in the hell did they let those thugs out of prison? I had even forgotten he was on the Isle of Pines in the Presidio Modelo. Mark my words: they will be back and with a vengeance. Word is that Fidel is getting money from the communists. He denies it, but I have seen pictures of him with Russian operatives. What he doesn't realize is that socialism will make everyone poor. Look at East Berlin and West Berlin. Capitalism may not be perfect, but it's better than that commie shit. And, for those that work hard, most can rise above the lazy assholes of the world," Bernie said.

"Hey, you don't have to sell me on capitalism—I'm sold. The communist, socialist or whatever crap they call themselves will never let the casinos stay. We must be prepared. Let's talk about that airstrip by your house. I bet you want me to chip in on the cost?" Carmine said.

"Carmine, only if you want to land your ass there with me someday."

Chapter Two

The Airstrip

A bunkhouse had to be built first for the airstrip construction workers. Bernie didn't really want the workers staying in his home or in the boathouse, even though it had two beds and a loft. It was too risky because they might find the safe. A couple of tents and cots were used while the Western ranch style building was erected. After it was completed, work could start on clearing a level strip of land between the shoreline and a ridge of marble encrusted hills. Finely crushed gravel would work okay as long as it was well packed—so well packed that it wouldn't give when a 6,700-pound airplane set down on it.

Connie and Betty took turns helping their maid to provide meals for the workers. Once the bunkhouse was completed, they would have a generator and a refrigerator for their small kitchen. Even though most of their meals were beans and rice, they would cook meals and fix sandwiches. The Swartzes and Spadas would supply the food and occasionally provide beer and rum.

Bernie and Connie had a live-in maid and gardener; they were an older married couple and worked at the house full time, staying in a bedroom that had outside access. They spoke some English and could be trusted to keep the large house in order. Alberto and Rosa (Rosy as she was called by the group) Diaz had been raised in Havana but had relatives who were working in the grapefruit orchards on the Isle of Pines and knew they could get work. They came with a family of six many years ago, went to work, and put their kids through school on the island. All but two had moved away, some to the states and the rest to Havana. Even so, they had ten grandkids on the island,

and there were many times when several of them showed up to swim in the beautiful waters around the home. Connie adored them, and when Moe and Roman were visiting they asked for Rosy to go get their friends. Connie would load the boys in the Jeep with Rosy riding shotgun until they found enough of Rosy's grandkids for them to play with. They would stay over for a day or two if school was out and then Connie would take them home. When the Spada girls also came along and a full complement of Rosy's grandkids were in attendance, meals were served, weather permitting, on two or three picnic tables pushed together close to the beach. The Swartz and Spada kids learned Spanish, ate great Cuban food lovingly fixed by Rosy, and learned to fish at the capable and patient hands of Alberto (Grandpa Alberto, as all the kids called him.)

Bernie had a few horses which the kids all rode when they were there. It cost him a small fortune to keep them since local horse ranchers had to be hired to brush them and make sure they were shoed properly, plus they had to be seen by the vet on a regular basis. The kids loved them, and Alberto taught all of them to saddle horses, care for the tack, and rub them down. It was a happy place, and wonderful memories were planted for all the kids. They had little to worry about. For the adults, it was another matter.

***

The Tropicana was busier than normal because it was New Year's Eve. On this night, December 31, 1956, bombs would go off in more than a dozen places throughout Cuba. Two women were seriously wounded in a casino as a terrorist had chosen to detonate his hideous device at the most popular nightclub in Cuba. The Tropicana would quickly recover, but one of the women would have an arm amputated because of the injury.

Fidel Castro had re-entered the country on December 2, 1956 after his stay in Mexico and hid out in the Sierra Maestra Mountains with his small army of revolutionary soldiers. At no time did Fidel have more than 1500 forces under his command. And at no time did Batista have less than 40,000 troops set to repel him. There were other independent gangs around, and they all listened to Fidel's radio broadcasts. During this time, Batista actually assisted his own downfall by letting Castro freely broadcast his propaganda on the radio and in the press. Even though Batista was drowning in corruption, strangely, he still held to the tenets of democracy and the 1940 Cuban Constitution. Also, his army rarely pursued the Castro group into the mountains. So many times Batista would counteract the decisions of his generals until the Cuban Army seemed to be without leaders.

Carmine and Bernie toured the damaged casino as had all of the other club owners in Havana. They pledged to Martin Fox any help he might need to fix the damage. But, as he had told Meyer Lansky and Santos Trafficante, "Thanks for the offer, but I will rebuild within the month—double my guards and search my customers as they come in. We will not let this happen again."

On their short drive back to the Caribe Shores, Bernie remarked, "If the election next year doesn't produce a strong leader who is willing to take on these idiots, then we need to be packed and ready to go."

"If that's the case, where do we go, Bernie? My girls are in college in Boston, but that place is too fucking cold for me. We have to work someplace. We're too young to retire. Vegas maybe? We both have 11-year-old sons in boarding school on the East Coast. Maybe Florida?"

"I really don't know, Carmine, but we need to take enough money with us so we can buy into a place. Vegas is new. You and I know there will be owners who screw up because they don't know how to run a casino—the places go bankrupt—we buy one for a song and run it the right way."

"We got money. My girls are going to want to get married at some point, have kids—grandkids—and I don't want me and Betty to be embarrassed by what we do for a living. I'm thinking about a legit nightclub in Miami. Still can make some money—warm climate—I can take my boat to the Bahamas—maybe get a place there too," Carmine said.

"Okay, Vegas and Miami sounds good. We had better start looking for places this year because our time here is limited. Hope I'm wrong— but it don't look good."

***

August 30, 1958

Bernie landed his plane on his private packed-gravel runway and surprisingly didn't spray small rocks all along the fuselage as he had done in the past. The new layer of adhesive oil really seemed to work, even though it wasn't cheap to install; it was just sticky enough to bond the small marble chips together. When the big twin engine plane touched down, Rosy and Alberto drove the Jeep to the plane and helped everyone with their luggage. On this trip, it was just Bernie and Connie, but someone from the states was flying in later in the day.

Meyer Lansky was flying to Cuba's Isle of Pines to talk to Bernie and Connie about a venture in Las Vegas. Later that afternoon, the couple welcomed Meyer and his pilot as they stepped off his beautiful twin engine Cessna 310. After a few drinks, discussions began about an opportunity at the Thunderbird Casino. The unique property had opened a few years back and was doing a great business. The casino's big pull was the great entertainment presented there, including nearly nude ice skaters. The Thunderbird even provided a trailer at the back of the nightclub so Nat King Cole had a place to stay. Segregation laws prevented him from staying in any of the hotels.

"What are you offering, Meyer?" Bernie asked.

"The Thunderbird's license was suspended last year because me, my brother Jake, and George Slado had invested in the business. It went to court, and the casino won the case. They suggested we sell our interest, and we asked if there would be a problem with the gaming board if you bought us out. The board checked your background and found you squeaky clean. I used your name because you called and asked if there was a casino you could buy into. I hope that was all right?" Meyer asked.

"Yes, I was interested when I called you and I still am," Bernie said.

"Also, the principal owners, Cliff Jones and Marin Hicks, would love to put you to work as the in-house accountant and CFO of the gaming operation. You don't realize what a great reputation you have among your peers," Meyer said.

"Three things: how much will it take to buy you guys out? How much will I be paid as CFO, and how are the profits paid out to the investors?" Bernie asked.

"Two hundred fifty thousand dollars cash. Twenty thousand dollars a year for the job plus bonuses. All profits shared equally with the investors according to their percentage of investment. You would have 14.2 percent ownership," said Meyer.

Bernie got up and walked to the kitchen and talked to Connie. They looked at each other and smiled. He took her hand and kissed her cheek. She nodded. The business was what Bernie knew, and he was damn good at it. She knew if things started going south, he would be the first to know and would bail out. Their son Moe would go to school in Newport Beach, California where they would maintain a home. They had decided this weeks before and had made one trip to look at houses and schools. Bernie would fly home and join her a couple days a week, and they would spend the summer on vacation or at a home in Vegas.

"You on board, dear?" Bernie asked.

"Yes. We'll need a few months to get everything in place, but I think it's a great opportunity for us," Connie said.

Bernie and Connie walked back in the dining room where Meyer was seated and noticed he had paperwork spread out on the table. His pilot was sitting in a wingback chair away from the action, nursing a drink that Connie had prepared for him, and reading a Miami Herald newspaper.

"Connie blessed the deal, Meyer."

"Good! Do you have the cash here at the house?" Meyer asked.

"Yes, let's get the paperwork out of the way, and I'll retrieve the cash."

Once all the papers were signed, Bernie excused himself and walked down to the boathouse with a duffel bag, retrieved the money, and walked back to the house. On the way, he stopped and looked at the two-story Spanish Colonial style home. It was painted pastel yellow with green shutters. It looked fabulous with the blue Caribbean Sea lapping at the shores behind the house. He would never have a home like that again. Cuba had been good to him and his family, but the change coming would be bad for everyone except those in charge.

"Thank you, Bernie. I believe this will be good for all of us. I can't promise you won't have your work cut out for you at their casino, but you are the man for the job."

"Thank you, Meyer, for putting together this deal. Things are not good in this country. Last month Batista's forces of a few thousand men had Castro rebels against a wall—could have wiped his ass with them. Castro asked for a cease-fire, and while the Cuban army was negotiating with Fidel all of his men escaped unharmed. The Cuban army isn't motivated; it has stupid leaders and will refuse to put their lives on the line. Destined to fail. One of Fidel's right-hand men, Che Guevara, rode a motorcycle through most of South America and saw a lot of poor people. He has decided that by taking the rich people's property and dividing it with the poor, he will have a utopia," Bernie said.

"If you like standing in line for bread, having no voice in who your leaders might be, and don't mind losing of all your personal freedoms, then you should be happy," Meyer said. "Don't forget I have some ownership in the National Hotel Casino, and my new Capri has just opened. I stand to lose a fucking boatload of dough if Cuba goes red."

"Well, Batista just built a Hilton Hotel right down the beach from us here. He calls it the Colony. It has a nice little casino. I hope for everyone's sake that Fidel somehow gets his butt kicked," Bernie said.

Everyone stood up from the table and Meyer placed the signed documents in his briefcase.

"Meyer, we have a guest room for you and your pilot, and Connie will cook dinner for you."

"Can't stay. I have a meeting tonight in Miami. Connie, it was great to see you again. You're as beautiful as the first time I saw you at Sinatra's concert in 1946. Good luck to both of you with the new venture."

Alberto opened the door of the Jeep and gave the two men a short ride to their airplane. In a few minutes, they were airborne towards Florida.

Carmine and his family were coming over in a few days. It was time to seal the vault.

Chapter Three

Cuba Falls

The tradition had been for everyone to spend Thanksgiving at Bernie's on the Isle of Pines. Bernie flew to Miami a few days before to secure a couple of turkeys and everything else that wasn't available in Cuba for the big feast. Rosa picked up her grandkids, Clara and Wendy, from her son, Joseph Diaz. They were Moe and Roman's age and had been friends for years. Although they weren't identical twins, they were twins nevertheless and very pretty. They were twelve years old, and the boys were eleven. The explosion of the onset of puberty had begun with the girls, and they felt awkward as the boys stared at them (since they were starting to look like women). The boys would kid them about their new breasts and how tall they were getting.

Rosa also had grandsons who were just a year or so younger than Liza, who was twenty, and Suzanne, who had just turned twenty-one. Both girls were attending Boston College. Rosa's grandsons from her daughter Yanez were Brian and Alian Artigas, and they were handsome pre-law students at Havana University. They had also been friends with Carmine and Betty's girls for about ten years. All these kids had grown up together because of their frequent visits to the beach house. The older group talked about music and their favorite rock and roll bands. Rarely would they tackle politics, but it did come up. The younger group discussed TV programs, music, and movie stars. TV reception on the island was spotty and Batista censored what could be seen. There was a local movie theater, and American movies were the most popular. Radios worked well, and the American rock stations ruled the airways. Mainly, they all liked to swim and fish. It didn't take long for them to get their swim suits on and hit the water.

Alberto watched them while he fished nearby. Occasionally, he could be caught eyeing Liza and Suzanne in their two-piece swimsuits. He had a good eye as they were nicely put together.

Inside the house, Connie, Betty, and Rosa prepared the meal. Carmine always loved oyster dressing and made sure Bernie didn't forget them on the Miami run. After cooking up a feast, Rosy took snacks and soft drinks out to a picnic table near where the young people were swimming. She noticed Alberto watching the older girls walking to the snack table.

In Spanish, she let him have it: "Alberto, you dirty man, do not stare at the girls!"

Immediately he jerked his head around and looked intently at the fishing line he had strung out in the water. All the kids laughed. At this point in their lives, all of them knew enough Spanish to translate what she said.

The two Artigas boys looked over at the older girls, and Brian said, "I don't blame my grandfather. You girls are beautiful."

"Shut up and eat your snack. All men are the same--horny dogs!" Suzanne said. She smiled and looked at her sister, who was striking a photo shoot pose.

After swimming most of the day, it was time for dinner. The big colonial house had seven bedrooms and the same number of bathrooms; however, four outside showers were on the path to the house, two on each side, with changing rooms and plenty of towels.

Bernie's house had two beauty shop hair dryers and there now was a fight for who would use them first. The girls didn't want to show up at the dinner table with wet hair. The boys had racked the balls on a pool table and held cue sticks as though they were experts. Maybe they weren't, but all had played on this pool table since they were very young.

Shortly after, Connie and Betty called everyone to the long mahogany table which had all the leaves in and was extended to seat fourteen people. Rosy said grace in Spanish, Connie in English. The men were quiet. Wine flowed freely and the Cuban kids sampled turkey and dressing, which was customary. No one said it, but there was a feeling of finality and sadness during the meal. More and more reports were broadcast on the radio of Fidel and other independent rebels moving around on the main island of Cuba. The word-of-mouth reports were even more startling. Even though Batista was hated, not everyone was sure any of the rebel factions would be any better. An election had taken place and Batista had nullified the results, so the US had severed ties with him. The air was thick with anticipation and dread at the same time.

After dinner, the men smoked cigars and drank rum in the den. The ladies cleaned up the kitchen while the young people played cards and pool. Rosy's grandkids would spend the night as they usually did. Suzanne and Liza would be in bedrooms next to Brian and Alian. At a designated time Suzanne would sleep with Brian, and Alian would move to the bedroom where Liza was waiting. The girls had lost their virginity to these handsome Cuban boys a few years back. Neither girl would linger with the two young men more than an hour, and both treated sex as a special dessert. Each young lady had a serious boyfriend on the East Coast, but quick sex with Cubans boys just didn't count and certainly was not worth reporting to their American lovers. Thanksgiving had become one of the foursome's favorite times of the year. The younger group had done some basic making out but had not moved to full-blown sex. Given time, there was no doubt they would follow the actions of the other couples.

On this night, Bernie and Carmine went to the boathouse with a bottle of 7-year-old Havana Club rum and started to work on sealing the vault. It wasn't a difficult task. Bernie pushed a wheelbarrow with a bag of quick-mix cement into the boathouse's main room. Bernie stirred a mixture of cement and water in a big five-gallon bucket. He would rest, have a pull on the big rum bottle with the gold label, and take a puff of a cigar. Then it would be Carmine's turn, and he pretty much followed the same routine. It was obvious that their construction skills were minimal. Casino work was their right calling in life.

On their third bucket of cement, they got on their knees and spread the cement smoothly over the hatch cover with trowels. Dead center of the hatch cover, Bernie pulled a button from his shirt and placed it on the surface. He pushed it just below the surface where someone with a steel brush could uncover it. Bernie asked Carmine to take notes and struggled to find a pencil or paper. Finally, Carmine tore off an inside page of a Life magazine and wrote the dimensions and measurements of the hatch cover from the walls. Both men were drunk when the task was complete.

"Leave the rug off the wet concrete and let it dry. I believe the edges of the hatch cover will have cracks in it when it dries. I'll have to come back and doctor it up. Later, I'm going to use concrete to build some steps down to the water's edge, so suspicions won't be raised about the recent use of concrete. Also, I have a concrete polishing machine, and I'll try to smooth this out, and then paint it gray so the recent work won't show."

"Bernie, you've done a great job. I'm really going to miss working with you every day."

"Why don't we plan to spend time at either Thanksgiving or in the summer each year so our families will stay close?" Bernie said. "You have that offer at the big nightclub, Raimondo's, in Miami Beach so I know where to find you."

"And I fully expect you to turn the Thunderbird into a gold mine."

***

The Caribe Shores was packed for the usual New Year's Eve party on December 31, 1958 when the word came. Fidel had won, and the new government would take over the next day. Bernie and Carmine didn't panic as they had planned for this outcome for a few years. Betty drove to the airport with Roman since the girls were in Boston at a New Year's party. Connie and Moe were headed to the airport as well. There wasn't much to do at the casino. Bernie counted out the night's earnings, left the keys with the floor manager, and said goodbye.

Carmine was emotional and was unable to speak to the staff. As they headed to the Jose Marti Airport a little ways southwest of the city, he began to cry. He loved Cuba, the Caribe Shores, and his many friends in Havana. He composed himself as he walked to Bernie's plane and saw everyone was there loading last minute baggage on the plane. Most of the heavy stuff had already been shipped to both of their new homes. A lot of Bernie's stuff went to their new Newport Beach location with only a few items transferred to an apartment in Las Vegas. He had instructed Rosy and Alberto to take care of the house and move her family there so it would be harder for Fidel to kick them out. Carmine had a waterfront house in South Beach and was toying with buying a place on Bimini. Everything was set. Their cars were shuttled to the night ferry to be taken to Miami. After tomorrow, nothing was for certain.

They landed safely on the Isle of Pines and waited for Alberto to pick up Carmine, Betty, and Roman, while Bernie and Moe stayed on the plane. Rosy was in the Jeep, crying. Connie left the plane and ran to the car to console her.

"Rosy, we love you and hope to see you soon. Send the phone bill and any other bills to us in California. None of us knows how long this will last, but we have put ten thousand dollars under the floor in your room—you know the hiding place. Use it for whatever you need." Connie kissed Alberto on the cheek and helped shut the car door.

"See you in Miami in a few hours," Connie said.

Bernie waited to take off until the big Chris-Craft cabin cruiser started out to sea. It was still dark, but Carmine knew his way around the island, plus he had the latest radar onboard and huge spotlights trained ahead of him.

The lights along the runway had been installed a couple years ago. The whole house was powered by generators that had automatic starters. Some were gasoline and others were diesel, but electricity had been brought to the Colony Hotel up the beach from their location. Batista had approved the extension of the lines to be run to Bernie's house, but they hadn't been turned on yet. It was unlikely they would be turned on anytime soon.

The flight took less than an hour to Miami's airport. It was 4 a.m., and Bernie began to think he would run out of gas before he was given clearance to land. Everyone was getting out of Cuba. Finally, they landed and tied down near a hangar that only a few days ago would have been easy to rent, but Bernie found that the rate for tie space was now at a premium. Going through customs was a breeze since the officials were overwhelmed and seem to let everyone through.

A taxi took them to the ferry terminal, where they sat and drank coffee from a local coffee stand on wheels. Moe laid his head on Connie and went back to sleep. The ferry was four hours late. As daylight broke, the ferry, loaded with people, furniture, cars, and luggage lumbered to the dock. It was a wonder it didn't sink. The men had given the drivers $300 each to make sure the cars got on board, but the cost was worth it since Bernie's '57 Cadillac and Connie's '58 Chevy hardtop were the first to come off. Carmine's '56 Mercedes came off almost an hour later, and by then he was there to pick it up. They had to wait over an hour to find a place to dock the boat and find a taxi. Then the harbor master and customs inspectors were going crazy with so many boats fleeing Cuba. Any other time, Carmine could dock at his own home in South Beach.

Bernie's Jeep would now be Rosy's and Alberto's, with a title in their name. The horses at the beach house had been sold a few years back, so no one had to deal with them. Everyone was together, so they all went to Carmine's house. Once there, they turned his TV on to the news. There was Fidel —standing with Che Guevara and his brother Raul. Fidel announced something just about every day until, in 1965, he declared that Cuba was now a communist country. It surprised no one.

Chapter Four

The Pact—1978

The two families met at least once a year for several years. Carmine and Bernie would always find a quiet spot to have a cigar and a drink. The year was 1978 and the subject of retirement was on Carmine's mind as they sat on the back porch of the Spada residence in South Beach, Florida.

"Bernie, I ain't getting any younger. I can get Social Security next year and might just hang it up and go live in the Bahamas," Carmine said.

"Wish we had the money in the safe," Bernie said.

"That asshole Fidel keeps plugging along, and with Russia giving them billions each year, nothing will change. It looks like fucking Communist Cuba will outlive us. We need to do something for the kids and grandkids about the money."

"Like what?" Bernie said.

"If we hire a law firm, we'll need to know it will be around for the next fifty to seventy-five years. The firm will need to stay in touch with the family and pass along the information regarding the vault to the relatives that are still alive when America reopens the embassy and travel restrictions are lifted," Carmine said, looking in disgust at the ragged end of his soggy cigar.

"You mean like a family treasure map?"

"Sort of. If they're young, it could be a great adventure for them to try to break into the old boathouse and chisel their way into the vault, load it on a boat, escape the Cuban navy, and then smuggle the money into the US," Carmine said. "You do realize that taxes may have never been paid on that money?—we paid the Cuban taxes, yes—but I don't remember if you filed them here."

"Well, as I recall, since I did our tax forms, we wouldn't have received a US tax credit unless we paid our foreign taxes. We did pay the required US taxes—just enough to max out our social security benefits. You forget—we were audited by the IRS. Jesus, did we show him a good time! I may still have those records, not that it matters any unless our adventurers declared the money as legal assets. We do need a lawyer. Who do you trust in Miami?" Bernie asked.

"Goldstein, Capello, and Diaz."

"Because they're Jewish, Italian, and Cuban?" Bernie said.

"They've also been around since the '50s and have two hundred lawyers at the firm. Let's meet with them this week. I'll tell them we need to meet before you go back to Vegas."

Carmine secured an appointment at the firm for the next day in the early afternoon.

***

This year, only the two boys, Moe and Roman, were in attendance at the annual reunion. They were both thirty-one, married and in business for themselves. Moe owned a men's clothing store in Los Angeles and was married with a ten-year-old son, Marty. Roman married a local Cuban model, Charo Reyes, and started his own local night club, the Caribe Americana, with his father's help. He also had a son, David, who was eight.

Liza Spada was 41 and married to a dentist, Mark Bennett, in Boston. She had an 18-year-old daughter, Amanda, who was currently at a rehab facility trying to break free of a serious cocaine habit. Her behavior and addiction had put a strain on Liza's marriage.

Suzanne Spada was 40, had been divorced twice, had no kids, and took her last name back. She was now living in New York City and dating an actor. Five years ago, she had a hysterectomy to remove a small lesion that was cancerous. The prognosis was good. Her marriages had been short and tumultuous, and the word was she didn't really want kids.

***

"Please have a seat in the conference room. I will bring you coffee or a soft drink if you want," the receptionist said. Both men said they would like water. When she walked away, they noticed how tightly her short skirt fit around her pretty rear.

"Damn, Bernie, why weren't we lawyers?"

"Did you forget about the showgirls we had in Cuba?" Carmine said. "Lucky for us our wives never knew about the five brothels we owned in Havana."

"You realize we made more on them than we did on our club. We had the prettiest girls and they would travel anywhere," Bernie said.

"What's this about pretty girls?" asked a young handsome attorney in a three-piece suit. He wore glasses, had a deep tan, and looked to be in his twenties. The receptionist followed him in carrying a tray with glasses of water.

"Just reminiscing about our club we owned in Cuba," Carmine said.

"Oh, I see. My name is Saul Fleischner. How can I be of service to you, Mr. Swartz and Mr. Spada?"

Bernie slid a folder over to Saul. "In there you'll find the deeds to all of our properties in Cuba. I know it means nothing now, but if reparations are ever made in the future, we want our families to have it."

"Uhh…you do realize that people here in Florida hold probably a billion dollars' worth of these deeds? Even if they decide to make concessions in the future, there are three huge oil refineries, about 50 farms of over a thousand acres each, and just about every large business you can dream of. They're all in line ahead of you."

"We realize that, but we won't be here to let them know that we owned them at one time," Carmine said.

"Is that all we're going to be discussing today?" Saul asked, looking confused.

Bernie laid a second folder on the table but didn't slide it to Saul just yet.

"Mr. Fleischner, what we are about to tell you is highly confidential. We'll pay your firm a fee every year to follow our specific instructions. Do you think your law firm will be around way into the future?" Bernie asked, his hand still on the folder.

"The firm began right after the war in 1946. We have almost three hundred attorneys and five hundred total employees. Even though some attorneys leave occasionally to start their own firms, we grow every year."

"We will be blunt," Carmine said. "We hid a shit-load of money in Cuba, and I don't think we will live to see relations normalized so we can go retrieve it."

"You want my firm to get it for you?"

"Hell, no! What we want is for the survivors of our two families to know the location, but only after the flag goes back up at our embassy and travel is allowed back to Cuba," Bernie said.

"How will this firm know where your family members will be at that time?"

"This file has all of the addresses, phone numbers, and work addresses of all of the qualifying relatives. Your firm's job is to track these people at least twice a year, so you'll be able to give them this information when the time comes. Currently, there're only seven eligible family members besides Bernie and myself and our wives. Those seven members don't include their spouses—only blood relatives," Carmine said. "We'll know you're checking when you call us every year. It could be that most of the family has died off before Cuba gets in the good graces of America again."

"I don't know—it seems like if it takes years we might lose track—also I have no idea what to charge for these services," Saul said.

"We'll set up a trust to send your payments from Chase Bank here in Miami. It will have enough money to pay you two thousand dollars each six months for fifty years. All you have to do is call these family members or contact them by certified mail every six months to verify their location. In case they resist giving out information, you can tell them there is a trust fund set up for them in the future. If they ask more questions about the trust, tell 'em you aren't at liberty to share that information," Bernie said.

"Oh, just as a check and balance, the trust company will ask for a copy of your report before your check is sent out," Carmine said.

"I still don't feel good about this," Saul muttered.

"You're being paid four thousand dollars a year for fifty years for doing a little of nothing. Once the flag goes up in Cuba and Americans can go visit, you contact the survivors and call them in to pick up the information which is in this envelope. In it, there'll be expense money for the survivors so they can put some affairs in order and be able to travel to Cuba. It will contain information for the location of the money. There will be a separate envelope which will contain a bonus for the law firm. The trust company will be notified that the settlement has been completed and they're instructed to give any balance in the trust funds to the survivors," Bernie explained.

"So other than set up the file, our firm will not have to do anything until the trust firm requests the location and phone numbers of the people on the list. Is that correct?"

"Yes," both men said in unison.

"I'll be just a moment," Saul said and walked into an office right outside the conference room. The two men could hear him arguing with another attorney. After about five minutes, he came back and sat down at the large table in the meeting area.

"Gentlemen, I'll draw up the paperwork and build you a file for these documents. We'll need an initial fee for setting all this up. Our fee will be five thousand dollars, and in six months the fee will be twenty-five hundred each six months. We realize if someone gets lost on our list we'll have legwork to do. I assure you we will honor this agreement even if it takes fifty years to pass over the last documents. If, however, it takes longer than fifty years, we'll give out the documents at the end of a fifty year period, whether Cuba raises the flag or not. Our personnel will see on the file documents that the survivors are to be notified immediately once relations with Cuba are normalized. I assume the trust will also be instructed to notify us?"

Bernie and Carmine looked at each other, frowned, and both reached for a checkbook. Each wrote checks, splitting the fee.

As they drove back to South Beach, they were quiet. Carmine broke the silence.

"Wouldn't you love to be the fucker twenty years from now who opens that envelope and finds there's $25 million dollars and thousands of gold coins waiting for him on the Isle of Pines?"

Chapter Five

Survivors

Carmine Spada's funeral was celebrated at a South Beach funeral home on a warm spring day in 1997. He died of heart trouble at the age of 83 and had outlived many of the other family members. Carmine's daughter, Liza Spada Bennett, had lost her daughter Amanda in 1981 at the young age of 21 when an overdose of heroin caused a cardiac arrest. Her dependence on drugs and various stays in rehab had triggered a split-up of the marriage between Mark Bennett and Liza Spada Bennett. Liza herself had her own problems with alcohol, and she was killed in 1989 at age 52 in a one-vehicle car wreck. Her blood alcohol reading was twice the legal limit. Carmine had been ripped apart when he lost his wife Betty to breast cancer in 1994 and his only surviving daughter Suzanne Spada, age 57, in 1995 from a recurrence of her ovarian cancer. The only surviving members of Carmine's family were his son Roman, grandson David, and great-granddaughter Gina. It had been 39 years since he motored out of Roja Bay, Cuba, and fled to Florida. Most agreed he had lived a very good life since then.

Roman was at his dad's funeral with his son David and two-year-old granddaughter Gina Spada. Bernie's son, Moe Swartz, and his son Marty were in attendance, but Moe's three-year-old grandson Eli waited outside the chapel with his mother because he was acting a bit wild for this formal ceremony. Bernie and Connie were there. Each had their share of health issues, none serious, just the onset of old age. Both Roman and Moe spoke at the funeral about the great times they experienced on Carmine's boats and their days in Cuba. The old Chris-Craft had been retired twenty years ago and the new fifty-foot Trojan named *Caribe Queen II* had been pressed into service. The

Spada home in South Beach, complete with the dock where the *Caribe Queen II* was moored, was left to Roman.

A reception was held there after the funeral. Roman and Moe asked Bernie about the trust fund since the law firm had been contacting them every six months for years.

"I can only tell you that it will be divided among the survivors after a period of time. Please don't ask me any more questions. Most likely you guys won't see any of the proceeds in your lifetime—possibly Eli and Gina just might get their hands on it."

The two toddlers were ten months apart in age and sat facing each other on the floor surrounded by toys Carmine had purchased for Gina's visits. They played with the toys in front of them and talked with the limited vocabulary possessed by two- and three-year-old kids. They asked their parents about their papaw and Uncle Carmy, and they were told about heaven, which brought up more questions, until the parents eventually told the kids to shut up. Eli and Gina cried when they were separated but had no idea they wouldn't see each other again for another eighteen years.

***

Kelsi Manning opened the door to her Miami apartment holding a bottle of Merlot wine under her arm and two orders of chow mein in a plastic bag wrapped around her fingers. Her live-in boyfriend Josh Vargas was on his laptop. He said "hi" to her and quickly turned the screen away from her view.

"Watching porn again? Why do you guys find it so fascinating when we have a damn good sex life—don't we?" Kelsi asked, not really expecting an answer.

"Research, my dear. Simply want to be the best lover I can be," Josh said.

"Bullshit! You just like looking at porn. Turn on the TV. I want to see the news."

"Okay, but they'll just tell you how many black guys were killed in drive-bys."

"Sometimes it's Cubans or Dominicans caught in drug raids. I have to know this shit," she said.

Josh clicked the remote and tuned to the local NBC news channel. A picture of three elderly men standing in front of a flagpole came on the screen. Kelsi heard the words "Cuba and American Embassy." She put down the wine before the cork was completely out of the bottle. There was the American flag going up the flagpole and behind it was the American Embassy.

"Holy batshit! I have to get to the office!"

"Kelsi, it's Friday night."

"Don't care—gotta go. There's a bottle of wine and chow mein on the counter."

"What kinda wine?" Josh asked.

"Merlot."

"I thought you didn't drink Merlot after the movie *Sideways*?"

"It was half price. I'll call you in a little while and let you know how late I'll be, and you better not be watching porn when I get home. You have a law exam Monday, so study for it."

Kelsi took the elevator to the parking garage and clicked the remote. A white Toyota chirped at her. As she slid beneath the wheel, the Cuban estate case was clear in her mind. For 37 years this case had been given to the newest intern every year. It had become a legend—a mystical, magical case. Who would the intern be that held the document for the buried treasure in Cuba? It was hers—all hers, and there was a bonus involved. How much? Maybe a share of the treasure?

Goldstein, Capello, and Diaz owned the entire six-story building and occupied most of it. There were a couple of restaurants, coffee shops, and a bookstore leased out. A private detective agency had an office on the second floor. Much of their work was for the law firm. Kelsi didn't really have an office—more like a big table on the fourth floor with a couple of drawers in the middle of what looked like a law library. No one in their right mind would go pull one of the books and reference a case or look up a case or do anything with a law book. Everything was online or on a disk or a thumb-drive.

There was a file section with real pull-out drawers. Most everything in them was very old because all new cases were scanned, copied, or imaged onto a computer and stored in a mythical cloud somewhere in the sky—Kelsi didn't know or care which.

There it was—Swartz-Spada Family Trust and Verification file. She trembled as she lovingly took the tattered and yellowed file from the drawer. She opened it and took out the family verification file first and stared at the typewritten words. Listed were the surviving members of the two families and a copy of the preprinted Chase Bank's trust form. It itemized the family members still living, their addresses, and phone numbers. A copy of the payment of $2,500 to the law firm had been filed since Kelsi had last looked at the file in June when she made the calls herself.

Listed by oldest first were, Eli Abraham Swartz, age 20, 281 Lincoln Street, Newport Beach, CA, and Gina Sophia Spada, age 19, 1289 Biscayne Bay Circle, Miami Beach, FL.

She flipped the report back, page by page, and found a detailed report of the deaths of the family members. She read the morbid report carefully, looking for any other survivors.

Bernie Swartz, age 85, died in 2005 (natural causes); Connie Swartz, aged 84, died in 2007 (natural causes); Marty Swartz, age 42, died in 2009 (heart attack); Moses Swartz, age 63, died in 2010 (lung cancer); David Spada, age 44, died in 2013 (murder); Roman Spada, age 68, died in 2015 (liver failure).

Also listed were the family members who had died before the year 2000 (Amanda, Liza, Carmine, Betty, and Suzanne), and a note that stated Eli's and Gina's mothers were still living but were not to share in the trust proceeds. Only the two parties mentioned could be present during the distribution of assets. Kelsi was nervous but picked up the phone to call them before putting it back down. She was getting ahead of herself. She had to work out appointments with them around her law school classes at the Miami University School of Law. She jerked her laptop from her backpack and opened to her class schedule. She had her afternoons free every day except for Wednesday evening when she had a mock trial session. Josh Vargas was opposing counsel, and she was determined to tear his ass to shreds in court. Josh was just plain brilliant and didn't seem to study at all except for porn. He absorbed things—drank in knowledge by merely walking past a classroom—and spoke four languages. It wasn't fair. Kelsi had to work her butt off. On this trial, she had him dead to rights with case law out the ass. Oh, was she looking forward to standing in front of the judge on this case!

She decided to read the trust agreement from Chase Bank. Her enthusiasm lessened when she read a clause that said restrictions to tourism must have been lifted. Now she jumped back to her computer and googled "New Cuba Travel Rules." It clearly stated that the traveler must choose one of 12 reasons to go to Cuba. No one really checked up on the traveler, but they must check a box that said "for educational reasons" or "for research reasons."

Beyond those requirements, *how in the hell did you get there?* Again she banged furiously on her PC until she found a few travel agencies with "People to People" trips. Most travel agencies were feverishly putting together compliant vacations. It was too early yet for most trips. One cruise left from Jamaica and toured Cuba and then headed back to Montego Bay. There were no direct flights to Cuba from the US. Once you arrived it appeared that you would be breaking the law if you wandered away from the groups. *Who was there to arrest you if you just laid your ass on the beach for a week? Canadians go there all the time. Americans look a lot like Canadians, only louder and more obnoxious.*

The wording on the document exchange from the law firm was more liberal. It merely said, "...once the flag is raised over the American Embassy and travel is allowed to Cuba." So Kelsi could give them the documents, travel cash, and the secret envelope. The way she saw it, the law firm had the responsibility to give them those items. The trust funds would have to wait until later, and they would need to see the officers at the main branch of Chase in Miami.

Next week she would inform her supervisors of the meeting and see if they wanted to attend. Now it was time to call and set up the appointment. It was Friday night, but she knew both of them had given their cell phone numbers. Kelsi smiled and dialed the first number.

Chapter Six

Revelations

Kelsi called Gina first. The phone rang several times but there was no answer. Just as the prompt started to ask for a message, Kelsi saw that Gina was calling her back.

"Gina, this is Kelsi Manning from the law firm of Goldstein, Capello, and Diaz. If you remember, I was the one who called you in June to verify your information."

"Yes, I've heard from you guys my whole life. Not many of us left anymore, I guess," Gina said.

"The trust is only one part of the reason for my call, Gina. Your great-grandfather Carmine Spada set some money aside for you outside of the trust. The proceeds were to be given to any survivors of the two families when the flag went up in front of the US Embassy and travel was allowed to Cuba. The trust provisions are a little stricter. It will allow the proceeds of the trust to be distributed once there is unlimited travel allowed in Cuba. Most likely, it will happen soon. I have time next week on Tuesday or Thursday afternoon if either is convenient for you."

"Uhh—who else is a survivor? I haven't really kept up with the family."

"Eli Swartz. Have you had any contact from him lately?"

"Not in a thousand years. I have pictures of us together at Grandpa Carmine's funeral, but we were like two years old."

"I'll call him next. Would Tuesday or Thursday work for you?"

"Either time's okay with me. I don't have class—I'm flexible— summer session is over this week. Eli has to come across the country, so let him choose."

"I'll call you back shortly," Kelsi said as she prepared to enter Eli's number.

It was one of those weird connections where no ring occurs, yet a voice was there, waiting in the dark, to speak out of nowhere.

"Hello, hello?" Kelsi stammered.

"Hello—did you call me?" asked Eli.

"I did, but there wasn't a ring. You're Eli?"

"Yes."

"Eli, I'm Kelsi Manning with Goldstein…."

"The law firm that calls me every month?"

"Twice a year, unless we need to settle a disposition of some assets," Kelsi said curtly as she felt Eli was going to cut off all her explanations.

"You need me to come in and collect some assets?" Eli asked, cutting her off anyway.

"Yes, I have time on Tuesday or Thursday afternoon. The money you receive will cover your travel expenses."

"Gina will be there, too?"

"Yes, fourth floor. Thursday, 2 p.m., okay?"

"Sure. You do know that full non-restricted travel isn't possible yet?" Eli asked.

"We're aware of that, and the full trust funds can't be released until then. The assets we'll be talking about only require the flag to go up and travel to Cuba being possible."

"Thanks. Sorry to be short with you, but I had pulled a little information from my dad and grandfather—not much, but just enough to investigate some myself. My guess is my great-grandfather had to blow out of Cuba just as Fidel and his goons were moving in and left a few things. You don't have to tell me if I'm right. I'll find out on Thursday. Sorry I was abrupt, but I don't like to be played with, even if it's by my dead ancestors," Eli said.

Kelsi hung up without saying goodbye and called Gina to tell her the final meeting time. It was late now and she thought about warming the chow mein, beating Josh in court on Wednesday, and Eli. Maybe he was an asshole, or maybe he was one of those super-smart people who knew everything—like Josh. No—the only time Josh was really an asshole was in the courtroom, and there he ruled supreme.

***

Thursday arrived, and Kelsi got her ass chewed for deciding what to do with the Spada-Swartz case without first conferring with the attorneys who were her supervisors. Several times they reminded her she was a second-year law student and had a real good handle on filing things in a drawer—beyond that, she had better grab a real lawyer.

Attorney Dodi Sanchez reviewed the file before the meeting and took the lead on the interview. They had a little time as Eli's flight from Orange County, California was late. It gave Kelsi time to reflect on the battle she undertook yesterday at the mock trial. It was a murder case, and Josh requested the whole case be thrown out because of errors in the way they questioned him, the lack of warrants, the lateness of the Miranda rights read to him, and the language used to read him his rights since he was Native American. He spoke English, but Navajo was his native language. Also, the murder took place on his reservation but was investigated by the FBI over the tribal police. Josh Vargas argued that the tribal police could have used his native language, which would have helped him to decide if he needed an attorney before discussing the case. It didn't matter that when the authorities arrived, the suspect was passed out drunk in his truck, a few feet from the dead man. The murder weapon was in his hand as he slept with his face buried in the steering wheel. The truck was searched, the gun fingerprinted, the bullet matched and the FBI had their man. All their work was wasted since Josh made the FBI look like the Keystone Cops. He was relentless, brilliant, and had the case thrown out. Kelsi never got to the case because Josh knew he would lose any argument on the actual murder. Kelsi was crushed but learned an important lesson—technicalities matter.

Arriving first and now sitting alone, Gina was quiet and just stared at the envelopes lying on the big wooden conference tables. Dodi and Kelsi had excused themselves and moved to a nearby office.

She was in college at Florida State, majoring in political science, which she hoped to use as a prerequisite for law school. She wasn't sure she wanted to go to school that long. She was tall, model thin, but filled out the bright red cotton sweater she was wearing with breasts much larger than normal for a girl her height. At 5'9", she had long black silky hair and classically beautiful facial features with dark, soft brown eyes. If viewed from certain angles one might think Sophia Loren was sitting there staring at the table. Several of the young male lawyers had attempted to intercede, hoping to take over the case from Dodi and Kelsi, but were rebuffed.

It wasn't too long before Eli Swartz marched into the room. If Eli was Jewish, he wasn't typical looking. His mother was Swedish and passed most of the Scandinavian blood his way. Eli was about 6' 2" and had a mop head of straw-colored hair. He was tanned, blue-eyed, and could have been a poster child for the all-American kid. His muscles bulged from his surfboard T-shirt, yet he was slender and fit perfectly into his faded Levis. When he saw Gina, he flashed a huge grin and met her as she stood smiling at him. He hugged her and gave her a very short kiss on the lips. She seemed pleased and hugged him again.

"Gina, I bet we both wore diapers when we met the last time."

"I'm fairly housebroken now—how about you?"

"If I drink too much, I might piss in a wastebasket, but usually I fit in with humans like myself," Eli said.

"You're looking great. Are you in school?"

"Engineering at Cal Poly. Summer break now. You?"

"Political Science. Florida State—start back in September."

"A lawyer in the making, I bet ya?" Eli said.

"Eli, sweetheart, I've missed you so much since the last time we were together. I've been horny, I guess. So glad you're back in my life." Gina said this without smiling.

Eli looked at her like she had just busted out of a psycho ward. Considering she was two and he was three the last time they were together, he knew neither of them remembered the other, but they had seen pictures on holiday cards since then.

He was shocked that this beautiful, demure, intelligent young woman would have so many screws loose. Maybe it was a warped sense of humor. He hoped so.

"Do you need your medication, dear?" Eli said nervously.

"Shit, no. I like myself this way. You do look handsome. Do you sleep with a lot of girls? I need someone who's really experienced," Gina said, trying to be serious. But this time, she couldn't help laughing because Eli was beginning to disintegrate.

Then Eli joined her laughter as he realized her shocking jokes were just her wacky sense of humor. He decided to turn the tables.

"Sweetheart, when we make love tonight will you let me tie you up and blindfold you?" he asked.

"On our first date, you go straight to bondage. Okay, but our safe word is 'Red'… no, 'Blue,' to match your eyes."

"Blue is fine—ropes or handcuffs?"

"Handcuffs? What did I miss?" Kelsi asked as she and Dodi pulled their chairs out from the table.

"Bad joke, Miss Manning," Eli said.

"Now that everyone is caught up, can we proceed?" Dodi said, looking at Kelsi to explain the procedure since she had read all the documents. She was there just in case Kelsi promised the law firm would go to Cuba with the couple.

"Your great-grandfathers had to escape Cuba as Castro took over. As you may know, they had very successful businesses, homes, and land. Here are the deeds to the property left for the Cuban government to take over. It is unlikely reparations will ever be made since Cuba has demands of their own. Nevertheless, here are the deeds."

Gina and Eli looked at deeds that were dated before 1958–some dating back into the 40s. Maybe someday they could buy these houses back, but it was highly unlikely because communist countries tend to have the government hold on to private property.

"Next, Carmine Spada and Bernie Swartz wanted to give you some money to help you. You two are the last survivors—I know your mothers are still alive, but Bernie and Carmine only wanted blood kin to get this." She carefully placed five envelopes in front of both Eli and Gina. "They didn't know how many survivors would be left when the flag at the embassy went back up but never thought it would just be two people," Kelsi explained.

Eli opened one of the big manila envelopes and saw it contained two bundles of one hundred dollar bills—each marked ten thousand dollars.

"How much is here?" Eli asked.

"Ten thousand each—twenty thousand in an envelope—one hundred thousand total. Here's a duffel bag," Kelsi said reaching for a couple of nondescript navy blue duffel bags next to her chair. She gave each one a bag. "You also have receipts in there for the bank. They have to report anything over ten thousand. Patriot Act, I believe.

"As I told you before, the trust fund will be paid out when all travel restrictions are lifted. However, the payments that were going to our firm will now be divided and sent to each of you twice a year as directed by the trust. But we have one more thing to discuss with you. It's a mystery to us, as we were not allowed to open the envelope. Only you can open it, and in private. We will leave you to discover what's in it. I can only say it has been a mystery to this firm for thirty-odd years. Here is the envelope." Kelsi slid the faded manila envelope towards them, and both of the ladies from the law firm got up and went over to an office several feet away.

"Damn, Gina—it's Christmas! You open it."

Gina's beautiful long fingers shook as she held the old envelope. Her white French nails contrasted with the old paper. She lifted one corner of the flap and found that the adhesive was still strongly attached, so she slid her long manicured fingernails under the edge and ripped it open. The first item was a letter written with a ball point pen. Gina read it out loud.

The following information may get you arrested or killed but we wanted you to know about it. We had fears for many years that rebels would take over the country and take our property away from us. Well, that all happened on January 1, 1959. We left Cuba from the beach home on the Isle of Pines by boat and plane that day, very early in the morning while it was still dark. We did leave something behind because we couldn't take it all into the country. Our earnings from all of our enterprises on the island of Cuba were put back in a vault. We did hide enough on the boat and plane to live comfortably the rest of our lives. It was nothing compared to what we left behind. Carmine's house on the Isle of Pines near the Colony Hotel on Roja Beach had a detached boathouse and was built into a rock face. When the boathouse was constructed, the big bank vault went in first and all the concrete was poured around it. A ladder went down from the living quarters of the boathouse to the vault. We used a plastic ladder and hatch cover so the Cubans couldn't use metal detectors on it. Before we left, we sealed off the hatch covers with cement, came back and filled in any cracks, polished it, painted it gray, and put a huge area rug over it. There is a button just below the surface dead center of the hatch. Enclosed are drawings, measurements, lists of people who we let stay in the house after we left, and the combinations for the various safes in the vault. If you can use the trust funds to buy back the property, it would be your best alternative; otherwise, you will need to be creative. Best of luck.

Love, Carmine and Bernie

Note: We left $25 million in US fifties and hundreds. Also, there are over 10,000 one troy ounce gold coins.

Chapter Seven

Plans, Spits, and Starts

Gina and Eli stared at the last part of the letter and then looked up at each other smiling. Eli was the first to speak.

"Holy Mother of God!"

"This is batshit crazy!" Gina said and reached over and kissed Eli.

"You're batshit crazy!

"I know it and find it a source of pride," Gina said.

"What's next?"

"Why don't we go to hotel, have sex, and then open a couple of bank accounts and safety deposit boxes?"

"Dear, you are always the practical one. It's the very trait I've always liked about you."

Both waved Kelsi and Dodi back into the room.

"Thank you for all your help on this issue. I'm sorry I can't tell you what was in the envelope. Maybe someday. Once full travel to Cuba takes place, I guess the trust company will use you as intermediaries for the trust funds," Eli said and slid an envelope over to Kelsi marked attorney's bonus. It had been placed in with other envelopes that were marked for survivors. Kelsi took it and smiled, but had no idea how much of the bonus she could keep, if any since, she was just an intern.

Gina and Eli stood and shook their hands then walked towards the elevator carrying the duffel bags. Suddenly Eli had a question of Dodi since she was the real lawyer.

"Dodi, doesn't this money qualify as an inheritance since we're both relatives of the deceased great-grandfathers? And, as an inheritance, it should be tax-free up to like $1 million each? Also, doesn't the state of Florida give inheritance credit against federal estate tax credit?"

"You need to knock the rust off your Google button, Eli. You can receive up to five million and change without tax. If your tax man gives you grief, we'll provide the paperwork needed to resolve it. The Florida sponge tax or inheritance tax went away in 2006. It's all your money and tax-free. However, if there is a ton of money in Cuba hidden away, then you better see us before you drag a fortune home to find out US tax was never paid on it. Contact us, and we might be able to help. I'll have Kelsi research it. Maybe she will learn something that will help her in law school. Good luck to you guys and stay out of trouble if you go to Cuba."

They stopped to wait on the elevator and Kelsi walked over to ask if she could ride down with them. Once the door closed, Kelsi asked, "Do either of you speak Spanish?"

"No, I don't," Eli said.

"Some–a little," Gina said.

"Just a thought—Josh Vargas, my boyfriend, does and is familiar with Cuban law. If you go within the next couple of weeks, we'll be out of our summer session and could possibly go with you," Kelsi said.

"We haven't had time to discuss where we are going to dinner, but give us a number to call," Eli said and then felt a card being pressed in his hand.

"Call me," Kelsi said as she held the elevator open for Eli and Gina's exit and then stepped back in to go up and fight with Dodi for a share of her bonus.

The elevator doors were closing when Kelsi yelled, "Pubbelly! Eat at Pubbelly–Sunset Harbor—you'll love it!" and the doors closed.

Gina's car was parked in the visitors' section of the law firm's lot. Her mom had helped her pick out the 2011 Chevy Trailblazer and had co-signed for the five-year loan. Her mom had plenty of money, but Gina wanted to establish her own credit history. There was no real need for a 4-wheel drive SUV in Miami, no mountains to climb, no deep snow to plow through, and no mud unless you went off road which she rarely did. It was red and Gina did look good driving it. She felt bigger, stronger, and more powerful being above a lot of other cars—except for all the other SUVs which were everywhere. Miami was ready for a great snow storm or a mountain should one appear.

Eli loaded the small piece of luggage which had been left for him at the reception desk at the law firm into Gina's SUV and asked if she wanted him to drive. She waved him off.

"Would it make sense for us to open accounts at Chase Bank since they manage our trust money?" Gina asked.

"Where's the Chase branch that manages the trust?" Eli asked.

Gina was quiet a moment as she turned pages in the document folder she held in her lap. "It's the one here in Miami Beach on Alton Road," Gina said.

"I thought we were having sex at a hotel before opening the bank accounts. Are we just blowing that off?" Eli asked, chuckling. He was well aware she just said things for their shock value.

"Forgot. Can I have a rain check?" Gina asked sheepishly.

"You do realize I'm going to keep up with the number of times I'm rejected. It really hurts, you know."

After some paperwork, they both opened accounts of $8,000 apiece and rented large safety deposit boxes. ATM cards were issued immediately with their pictures on them. Checks were ordered. Both grabbed a thousand dollars in hundreds and put them in their wallets. Neither of them had ever had that much money in cash in their lives. It was empowering.

"I really do need to get a hotel. Can you tell me where they keep the Motel 6?" Eli asked as they sat in Gina's car at the bank's parking lot.

"You, my friend, are staying with me. You're like family—only we aren't related," Gina said.

"So, if we had kids they wouldn't be afflicted," Eli said.

"If they inherit your brain, then it's possible," Gina said.

"Please call first. I don't want your mother to freak out. What's her name?"

"Cherie Spada. What your mom's name?"

"Hana Swartz," Eli said. "We've both heard the names before. It's just been a while."

"I want to meet her. Where do you guys live?" Gina asked.

"Newport Beach, California."

"Hotsie-totsie! Are you next door to John Wayne?" Gina asked.

"He's dead, you know."

"Forgot, but I think he used to live there."

"He did and his old yacht *The Wild Goose* is still there," Eli said.

Gina cranked up the Chevy and drove in heavy traffic until they turned on Biscayne Bay Circle and pulled in front of a beautiful Spanish colonial home. She stopped and pulled her cell phone from her purse side pocket.

"Hey, Mom, can Eli Swartz stay over with us? On the back porch? Isn't that rude? Okay, but I need to tell you we've talked about sleeping together, and I don't know how noisy he is.

"Well, she hung up on me. Can you imagine?"

"Jesus H. Christ! I'm afraid to come in. Does your mother know about your brain being fucked up?"

Cherie didn't wait for them to open their doors completely before she was pulling Eli out of the car and hugging him.

"My God, you are a handsome brute! I see why Gina wants to sleep with you. Don't pay any attention to her. She tries to shock people till they fall apart. She and her dad used to play that game so she could ward off any boys who came around. She scared most of them away. Come into the house, my dear," Cherie said.

"Mrs. Spada, you have a beautiful home," Eli said as he entered the house. "I know I was here for Uncle Carmine's funeral, but I don't remember much. I was only three at the time. I got the notice of your husband, David's death but couldn't make it to the funeral. I'm sorry for your loss."

"Thank you, Eli. And call me Cherie. Let's sit on the patio and have a drink. Do you like margaritas?"

"Yes, love them. Did I hear that someone attacked him at his club?" Eli was curious about what had happened to Gina's father.

"My dad was breaking up a fight," Gina said. "The men were drunk, and one of them stabbed him. He died on the way to the hospital. I used to work at the Caribe Americana on occasions but not after he was killed. Mom sold the place, and I'm glad she did."

"I sent your mom a card when your dad died, Eli," Cherie said. "I always liked Marty and Uncle Moe. It seems as though you and Gina are the end of the blood relatives."

"She appreciated it. She goes out now and then with friends and even dates occasionally, but so far, nothing serious. And yeah, it's hard to believe we're the tail end of the gene pool," Eli said.

"Okay, kids. Tell me about the mysterious meeting with the attorneys. Are you rich?"

"Not yet, Mom, but we're off to a good start. We both got fifty thousand as an inheritance, but it sounded more like expense money."

"Expenses for what?"

"Well, Cherie, it seems that Carmine and Bernie hid a fortune on the Isle of Pines. It might still be there. I haven't had time to discuss it with Gina, but I'm guessing she might like to go look for it with me."

"I'll only go so I can sleep with him, Mom. I have no interest in the money," Gina said with a straight face. Cherie and Eli burst out laughing

"Do you guys want to tell me how much is there?"

"In the millions—so much we'd need a boat to carry it back," Eli said, glancing obviously at the big cabin cruiser docked behind the house.

"Oh, I see what you have in mind. I don't think you can just pull into a Cuban dock in an American boat and hop off, grab your loot, and head back home. I see problems, but I'm just a fussy old mother."

"You're absolutely right, Mrs. Spada, and we have spent very little time doing research on what's available, what's legal, and who might help us. A couple of the law students at the firm agreed to go with us since one is fluent in Spanish. Gina and I need to divide up some research and get on it. We might do a short cruise before school starts back and do the real work when travel opens up more."

Gina moved her chair closer to Eli and ran her hands through his hair in an attempt to make him squirm. Then she whispered in his ear loud enough for her mother to hear, "Eli baby, if we book a cruise, please get a cabin that has a double bed."

Eli turned red and Cherie laughed. "Gina, leave him alone and quit teasing him. He isn't yet used to your craziness."

"Mother, he looks like someone I would like to sleep with. He looks delicious. Of course, I would have to like him first and I kinda do. Then we would have to get along as friends. After that, he would have to be a great kisser, and so far it was just a little peck when we met. When we fall in love with each other—which we will, of course—the next step will be to see whether he wants kids and how many. Money, religion, hair style, choice of clothing, and food preferences don't really matter much. However, trust is way up there, and so is sense of humor—can't live without that. Got all that, Eli?"

"I was feverishly taking notes. You know, I have some prerequisites as well, and they are simple: one is that the girl has a beautiful face and body—haven't seen you naked yet but my initial observation suggests you are spectacular. And that's pretty much it. Some say I'm shallow, but I think they're jealous of my Spartan philosophy."

Both Gina and Cherie laughed out loud.

"Oh, Eli, we are getting soooo much closer to sleeping together," Gina said.

"Gina dear, as they say in Texas, 'you're all hat and no cattle,'" Eli said.

"Why don't we break out laptops and check out trips to Cuba, regulations, and sleeping arrangements?" Gina said.

"I have an idea. Gina, you check the regulations, Eli can check the cruises, and I'll check out what's available on the Isle of Pines," Cherie said.

"Great! I want to make dinner reservations first. Cherie, would you please join us? I'm rich, so I'll pay," Eli said and googled the "Pubbelly." He got an 8:00 reservation and felt lucky to get it.

In a few minutes, Cherie broke through the sounds of the dull clicking of keyboards.

"What?

Fidel changed the name! It's now the Isle of Youth!"

Chapter Eight

A First Plan

Pubbelly Boys turned out to be very good, although not as expensive as Eli hoped since he had a shitpot of money to spend. He and Gina had the steelhead trout, and Cherie had the spiny lobster. While they didn't know their importance, they did see the James Beard awards on the wall.

"Let's get coffee at Starbucks and make some plans, now that we're loaded with information," Eli suggested after he paid for the meal with a couple of hundred dollar bills.

"Why don't you drop me off at the house, and you kids go do your thing. I don't stay up late. You'll be in the guest room even though Gina will tell you she will sleep naked with you in her room—she lies. I know my daughter. But, just for the record, Eli, I'm rooting for you to win her over."

"Mother! You ruin all my fun."

After taking Cherie home, the couple drove to Panther Coffee which Gina said "…is soooo much cooler than Starbucks, dude!"

They sat facing each other, nursing a couple of lattes sporting a surface design of a heart or maybe a triangle. It went away quickly anyway.

"I don't mean to be rude, Gina, but would you let me google some cruises to Cuba on my iPad?"

"What, you choose doing that over having sex with me?"

"Your sex is fantasy sex. If it were real sex, and you really had your heart in it, I'd put my iPad in a wood chipper."

"Such drama. Can I stay in your room tonight? It has two beds."

"You can sleep naked with me if you want. You know married

couples sleep naked together and seldom have sex. Since you have no intention of having sex until you're in love with someone, it would be fun for you."

"Naked with you—it's on!" Gina said more loudly than she realized. Several people looked toward their table and smiled. "Whoops! My loud mouth."

Eli looked at her and laughed. She truly was a lot of fun to be around, and the emotions in her beautiful face danced around in several forms, one more lovely than the next.

"Check this out: a cruise in a motorsailer—goes around the island—has a People to People program. Shit almighty! It's almost eight thousand dollars each. Too much, even if we can afford it."

"What about Kelsi and her boyfriend? You know, if they go with us, we'll have to pay their way. Unless they're rich, they have no income as law students. We need Josh, especially if we get out in the country where no one speaks English. If Josh is good looking we could switch out at night," Gina said and laughed at her continuing fantasies.

Eli ignored her by shaking his head to remove the thoughts she tried to place there.

"Ok, this one is better. Small cruise ship, the Caribbean Star, which leaves out of Montego Bay for seven nights. It stays in Havana two days and gives us time to sneak over to the Isle of Pines or Youth or whatever they call it today. It leaves in three days. Call Kelsi and see if they can go then. The fare is only about two thousand each."

"Whoa! You are a Driver-Driver aren't you? A Type A—leader of the pack. It's so damn sexy. I think I have a hair appointment on that date, however," Gina said.

"Change it, please. Should I call or you?"

"All right already. Give me the number," Gina said.

Gina dialed the number, not knowing any of the particulars. "Kelsi, this is Gina from the Cuban thingy. Look, we found a seven-day cruise to Cuba and would like you guys to go with us. It leaves in three days, and we'll pay your way. Okay. Call me back after you two talk it over."

"Ask if he's Cuban," Eli said. "The information on the cruise said Cuban citizens couldn't go."

"Oh, by the way, is Josh Cuban?"

"No. Puerto Rican," Kelsi said.

"Is he cute?" Gina could not help herself.

"Of course!" Kelsi said, laughing.

"Call us back soon, and thanks!"

"I can't believe you asked her that! Most people won't understand your warped sense of humor."

"Dear, you are so innocent and shy. In time, you'll feel comfortable with me. You need to come out of your shell. Be a wild child like me."

"Give me a break. Oh, we have a phone call." Gina answered the call from Kelsi.

"Yes, Kelsi, what's the word?"

Kelsi told her they were game but needed more information on the cruise. She then gave Gina their full names and dates of birth and told her their email address was on her card.

"Great! Here's the name of the cruise line. Check it out. We'll touch base tomorrow with all the particulars, but we'll go ahead and reserve the rooms. Hey, it'll be fun. Bye!"

"Okay, let me see what I need to do to reserve the cabins. Now that I have money in my account, I can use my new bank card to pay for it. You may need to pay one of the fares since the total might go over the eight thousand I have in the bank," Eli said.

"I'll pay half. We'll do fifty-fifty on everything, but only if you promise to make love to me every night on the cruise."

"You won't do that, but we will sleep together every night. You okay with that?"

"Looking sooo forward to it."

"You're scared, and you know it. It might help if you practice sleeping with me at your house. Just so you get used to it. It will be frightening at first, but when you learn I'm not a rapist, you shouldn't shake so much at night."

"I don't shake, and I'm not scared of you. You are using reverse psychology on me—to get me to sleep with you. What a scoundrel! No one can be trusted these days."

"I'm calling the cruise agent now. These people are up at all hours," Eli said.

Eli called the "Best Cruises Ever" toll-free line. They answered on the second ring.

"Hello, this is Molly Ruben, welcome to Best Cruises Ever. How can I help you tonight?"

"I'm Eli Swartz, and I want to book two cabins on the Caribbean Star for the cruise that goes to Cuba in three days," Eli said.

"Let me pull that cruise up."

Eli could hear Molly pounding on a computer keyboard. "Ahhh, there it is. Let's see what's left. Yes, I have some cabins. It's August—hurricane season--and they aren't full yet. In fact, you're eligible for last minute booking rates. Seventy percent off on balcony rates with a double bed. Uhhh—that will be only thirteen hundred dollars each, with a cabin credit of two hundred dollars. How's that sound, Mr. Swartz?"

All Eli could think about were the words "hurricane season."

"Are there any upgrades available?" Someone told Eli to always ask about upgrades; he thought maybe it was his dad.

"Well, we can possibly do that if rooms are open." More clicking of her computer keys. "Yes—yes, I have two mini-suites available. My notes say if they aren't sold by today, I can upgrade some people. Lucky you. Since the sailing date is so soon, I will need full payment. The price I quoted you included tax, port fees, and your tourist cards in Cuba. You'll have to attend People to People tours, and that's included as well. You can sign up for other excursions on board. I'll just need your credit card information and wrap this up for you. I'll shoot you an email for all the other information I need, such as passport copies, etc."

Eli dug for his new bank card. Just as he produced it, Gina had her card next to his hand.

"Molly, we're going to split the cost for both rooms on two cards. Here is the first set of numbers."

Eli gave her all the information on both cards and his email address for all the information that would come in the next few hours.

Next, he called about airline reservations to Jamaica for the day of the cruise.

"The moment of truth is coming, Gina."

"What?"

"It's time to go to your house."

"So—big friggin' deal."

Eli got up and took the notes he had taken on the cruise and flights written on a paper napkin and jammed them in his pocket. They walked to Gina's SUV. Eli opened her door for her and kissed her gently on the lips and let it linger a bit, then kissed her again. Her smile extended all the way up to the edge of her eyes.

Gina reached over and squeezed Eli's hand periodically during the drive home.

"Nervous, aren't you?" Eli said.

"Not a bit, but you should be. A good-looking sexpot like me snuggled up to you. Gotta have butterflies in your stomach."

"It would be an honor to be next to you at night, but if you're not comfortable, you're welcome to bunk in my room, and we can talk all night—you know—like a slumber party."

"Eli, you've never been to a slumber party, so I'll have to explain how they work. First of all—can you giggle? If you can't, then you'll never get invited."

"I know you talk about boys. Instead, you can talk to a boy. Avoid all the speculation."

Gina pulled in the carport and clicked the door lock after they were out. There were a few lights on in the house, but Cherie wasn't up when they entered the house. They went into the kitchen. A bottle of Cabernet Sauvignon was open and two glasses were left for them. It was a Silver Oak which Eli and Gina knew was a special occasion wine, much too expensive for everyday use. Next to the glasses was a note. It read, "Eli, I am so glad you are here. Make yourself at home. Gina, quit teasing him."

"I love your mom. She looks just like you, so I know what you'll look like when you get older, and it's called 'Still Hot.'"

They took their drinks on the patio which looked out over the marina and beyond to an ocean where the lights of a few boats could be seen in the distance. They talked and looked at each other. There was always eye contact. They liked the way each other looked and they probed and punched verbally, trying to find the absolute center of each other. In about an hour it was time for bed. A nervous time for both.

Gina took Eli's hand and led him to the guest room. They hadn't really kissed yet, and it was time. Gina led him by the hand all the way to his bed. Taking both his hands, she pulled him close. Eli responded by reaching up and holding her face in his hands and kissing her long and deep. When they released, Gina came in and bit his bottom lip gently, pulling on it a little, and then kissed him again. Eli sat on the edge of the bed and Gina sat down beside him. Moving slowly he laid Gina on the bed and then moved in next to her. Lying side by side, he kissed her and pulled her closer to him.

"Wow, you do feel great! All woman—all beautiful woman."

He felt her shaking. He didn't want her to be uncomfortable, so he sat up on the bed and then slid her legs off the bed.

Eli took a deep breath. "Gina, I would be a crazy person if I didn't want you, but I want it to be that passionate time when we can't stand not having each other anymore, then dive on top of each other and never come up— that type of moment. What do you want?"

"You—when the time is right. Can I have the other bed tonight? In three days we'll be sleeping in the same bed for a week—unless Kelsi lets me stay with Josh."

"Of course. But leave your mother a note that you're in the other bed in the guest room so she doesn't freak out."

"I'll be back after I get my PJs on and brush my teeth."

Gina came back to the room and climbed in the opposite bed. She had put on conservative pajamas that had legs and a top. Not anything that was revealing or sexy. She turned off the lights, leaving a couple of small wall receptacle night lights emitting weak illumination.

Gina talked for quite a while across the room. She was excited, nervous, and about to embark on a great adventure. Before they went to sleep, Eli asked her if she would get in bed with him for a minute and kiss him good night. She moved across the room and raised the cover on his bed. He was as he had advertised, completely naked, but she couldn't get a good view since the room was dark. Once she pulled next to him, her shaking became more pronounced. Eli put his arms around her and hugged her until she was perfectly still. Only then did he kiss her. Gina arms were around him and she could feel his cool skin. It was thrilling for her; she had never been in the bed of a naked man. She was a virgin and had stayed that way by scaring off guys with her intimidating language. Eli moved her hands down his back to his buttocks. He kissed her again. "Maybe you should get back in the other bed so your mother will find you there in the morning." She made a whining sound and moved to the other bed.

"Eli."

"Yes."

"Guess who else will be naked on the cruise?"

"The Captain?"

"Good night, asshole."

Chapter Nine

The Cruise

The four tired passengers pulled their luggage through customs in Montego Bay with the energy of starving zombies. It had been a redeye flight from Miami, and no one had slept much the night before. Gina and Eli had been together in bed all night for the first time. She chose a teddy outfit but wasn't sure where to put her arms and legs and what or what not to touch. Eli wanted to touch everything but didn't. The arrangement was like overly polite passengers in a crowded vehicle going nowhere.

Gina told her mother before they left for the airport, "I wish we would get to the point where hands, feet, and legs find a happy home." It was a strange conversation to have with her mother…but not really. Since her dad had died, her mother had become her best friend. She would go over everything that happened on dates and in her life in general. Sex and when to have it was a constant topic.

Cherie laughed and said, "It will happen. Put your head on his chest for a while, then move it before his arm falls asleep. Make sure you take condoms in case you do have sex. I've put some in your suitcase. I know you started birth control pills this week, but I saw your prescription and they take at least two days to be effective, so use the condoms for a week or so."

"Mom, you're entirely too calm about all this. For me, this is all moving so quickly. One day he isn't in my life and then suddenly he sort of—is my life," Gina said. "We hardly know each other, and then we are going on this adventure. It's exciting and a little scary—not the adventure part—the Eli part."

"The best part of life is love, my dear. I wish I was your age going on a great adventure with such a good looking guy. We know his whole family, and he's obviously crazy about you. It doesn't mean it'll work out for both of you, but don't you be the one to mess it up. Work on it. Forgive and forgive again. Sex is just sex. Kinda like blowing your nose, but a hell of a lot more fun. But, love…ahhh, love is a huge shower of feelings that gives sex a purpose and lets you be happy even when that same person blows their nose or farts right next to you," Cherie said, clasping her hands together over her chest.

"Mother, none of that makes any goddamn sense. What's with this nose-blowing and farting?"

Eli came out of the bedroom carrying his small piece of luggage. "You guys ready to go?"

Cherie drove them to the airport and told Eli to take care of her little girl. Eli kissed her on the cheek and told her not to worry. "She is the most important person in my life now. I'll try not to screw it up."

Kelsi and Josh had packed at the last minute and got to bed late. Both looked like they were going on vacation. Kelsi had on shorts and a halter top which accented her shapely body, large bust, and well-tanned legs. She wasn't tall, only five-foot-four inches, but filled out the frame in coke bottle fashion. Her face was attractive, more cute than pretty, and her dyed blond hair topped the whole package perfectly. She also had big, emerald-green eyes that captivated anyone talking to her face-to-face.

Josh was tall, maybe an inch shorter than Eli, and very brown. He was Spanish with deep-brown eyes and facial features like a Latino rock star. He was muscular and thick. It was easy to see how he could entrance a jury—the women anyway—when arguing a case in court. Today he was wearing khaki shorts, sandals, a T-shirt that said *Los Umbrellos* and pictured a Latino dude with two hot blond girls draped all over him. He had gold-tinted sunglasses and ear buds that seemed permanently attached to his ears.

They had all met the night before to get acquainted and have a few drinks, which escalated to a lot of drinks. It was fun, but they were all paying for it today.

After Jamaican customs, they took a van-type cab a short distance to the cruise terminal. As they moved through the line at the huge terminal, they received the ship credit cards, had their picture taken with some old luggage covered with travel stickers to be offered to them later (as color photos) at ridiculous prices, and had their bags tagged and sent to their room. They all were hungry and in desperate need of a drink to soothe the pain of the night before. Once on board, they quickly found the decks that had food. They set up a planning session for after dinner in the lounge next to the ship's small casino. As soon as they had eaten, everyone headed to the cabins for a nap.

Eli and Gina found their luggage just outside their cabin. Both pulled them in and eyed the bed. It was three hours until their seating time for dinner. Both stripped down to underwear mode. Eli stopped for a moment to look at Gina's incredible body. Her stomach was flat and sank in on both sides as it dipped below her lavender panties. Her breasts were pushed out nicely with a matching bra. She looked at Eli in his underwear and ran her hands through his chest hair before they both got under the covers. Gina gave Eli a soft kiss and put her head on his chest and arm for a while, then moved it away before his arm fell asleep. He whispered in her ear that he liked having her head on his chest. Both were sleeping soundly when the lifeboat drill alarm sounded.

"Don't they know we were drunk last night?" Gina whined.

"We got almost an hour's sleep. We should be grateful for that," Eli said.

Gina put her shorts back on but commented that long pants or dresses were required for dinner.

"I didn't bring a dress. Can I borrow one of yours?" Eli asked.

"I hope you brought some pants?"

"Only one pair, since I just came here for that meeting at the law firm. Maybe I'll buy some on the ship. Will you go with me to pick out some stuff?"

"Well, that should be fun. I get to dress my boyfriend—like when Ken was one of my Barbie dolls."

"Maybe I'll pick them out."

"Let me help. Please?"

They followed the arrows to the muster station. Kelsi and Josh were already there. Everybody helped each other adjust the life vests. They lined up and listened as names were called and instructions given—especially about fires. They found out that Josh and Kelsi didn't get much of a nap either.

Afterward, Gina wanted to explore the ship, so they did and found where to sign up for excursions. Back in their room, they found the list of speakers who were going to be delivering seminars about Cuba. The one for tonight was on flora and fauna of Cuba—they decided to blow it off in lieu of the meeting after dinner.

Gina unpacked first and got first pick of upper drawers and shelves. She had more clothes—maybe five times more clothes than Eli. He agreed to shop, maybe after the planning session.

Next was their first shower in the room. "Gina, please take yours first. I'll take mine when you've finished drying your hair and stuff. This is Tuesday. On Thursday, it's shower together night. Captain's orders—water conservation, he said. Can you handle it by then?"

"Do I have to 'handle it' then?"

"Yep."

"I look forward to 'handling it,'" Gina said. She got ready for her shower while Eli sat on the small sofa watching TV.

He watched her from the side as she undressed and wrapped a towel around her waist. She removed her top as she entered the bathroom and shut the door. After she turned on the shower, Eli came to the door and yelled, "I have to pee really bad! Can I come in?"

"You're lying. If you really have to, come on in, but I would think you could wait until Thursday to see all of me."

"I'm just kidding. I wanted to hear you freak out."

The shower turned off and Gina stepped out of the tiny bathroom where she had more room.

"Would you dry my back?"

"Yes, dear." Eli stood up and took the extra towel she was holding. She had one on her waist and one on her head. "Are there any bath towels left for me?"

"One…I made sure you had one."

Eli dried her back and turned her around where she was hiding her naked breasts in her hands. He kissed her causing her to move her hands from her breasts and around his neck. He pulled her close to him and reached under the towels covering her rear and squeezed her butt cheeks. It wasn't the first time he touched her there, but before it was while she was sleeping with him, and she did have a few pieces of lingerie on. She moved closer to him and could feel that he was aroused.

"I think you need a cold shower. Maybe you're not going to wait until we can't stand it anymore?" Gina said.

"I'll try, but Thursday can't come quick enough for me. That might be my deadline. Will you be ready then?"

"I'll check my passion gauge and see what it's set on that day."

"I get to read the gauge. Now, I'm taking my shower."

Gina was at the mirror in front of the dresser fixing her face and combing her hair when she saw Eli undress and walk into the bathroom. She got a glimpse of his erection as he flashed by. It was large, and she had so many fantasies about it. She had felt it against her several times the nights she was in bed with him. She almost reached out once and grabbed it to put in her. It would happen soon. She was ready.

When Eli stepped out of the shower, Gina was there with one of her towels to help dry him off. She had laid his clothes, including socks and underwear, on the bed.

"Well, you'll either make some guy a great wife someday…or maybe a personal valet."

"Which one pays the most?"

"Wives are expensive, I hear," Eli said.

"Think you'll sign one up someday?"

"Just so happens I have one in training now. Slow learner, though."

Gina sat on the sofa and watched him dress. It was not the first time she had seen him naked. She had pulled the covers off him at her house a few times just to irritate him. This time though was slow and educational.

"Looks like the shower got rid of your woody," Gina said.

"Maybe I soaped it and took matters in hand."

"In the future, your 'wife in training' should be required to do that."

"Don't tell me you're going to instruct me on how to train my wife?"

"Anyway, I can be helpful."

Eli stood in his underwear and stared at his clothing options for dinner and looked up at Gina.

"Sweetie, let's go shopping. I know how girls love to shop, so come on."

Gina was already dressed in a basic black short dress with heels. Her lovely long legs were displayed in all their glory. Her mother was beautiful, and her grandmother, Charo, had been a gorgeous runway model. Gina had inherited the genes from both and was stunning. Eli paused after dressing and looked her up and down.

"My trainee does know how to show off her assets. She'll get several points for wardrobe design and selection." He kissed her, and both smiled and locked eyes.

Gina selected matching polo shirts and slacks, plus a blue seersucker sports coat. They also purchased a few accessories, such as belts and socks, along with shorts and a swim suit. Since most were brand names like Ralph Lauren, the bill was over $1,000. Gina found some shorts and an evening dress to add to the tab. They went back to the room with their loot and tried on the new clothes. Eli put on a white polo shirt, navy slacks, and his new jacket.

"Looking hot, baby!" Gina said.

"Look at my shoes." Eli held up his foot to show off an old pair of black Vans sneakers and no socks. "Maybe I can find a shoe store in Cuba."

"Don't worry about it. You look cool—like you just stepped off your yacht—all preppy and shit."

Gina called Kelsi and asked if they were ready for dinner. They were. Kelsi said they didn't have fancy clothes for dinner, but when they met later, both she and Josh were sharply dressed. Kelsi really looked pretty in a simple red cocktail dress that accented her perfectly proportioned figure. Josh had the Latino movie star look with an open, long-sleeve white shirt and light yellow linen slacks. He could have just walked off the set of the old *Miami Vice* TV series set. He also had on Vans, but his were white.

They were in luck at the Aquarius Restaurant and were seated at a table by themselves. Some of the tables held as many as ten people and looked a little cramped. The dinner was good but not outstanding. There wasn't steak, lobster, or even shrimp on the menu, but what they did get was cooked well and tastily seasoned. Dessert was ice cream with chocolate topping. There was something wonderful about ice cream on a ship in the open sea.

They had been underway for a few hours now and would awake tomorrow at Santiago, Cuba. It would require a tour of one of Castro's revolutionary museums. All the group really cared about was getting to Havana and on to the Isle of Youth. Kelsi and Josh didn't know much yet, but they were about to find out what they had gotten into. It was too late now to back out unless they wanted to swim home.

Chapter 10

The Isle of Youth Plan

The four Americans began the planning meeting, all holding drinks in their hands. Somehow, alcohol was going to be the secret to solving their logistical problems.

"Our goal on this mission is to assess the possibilities of either renting or purchasing Bernie Swartz's old home on the Isle of Youth. It was left in the care of the Diaz family on January 1, 1959. Among the documents Bernie and Carmine Spada left were lists of the Diaz and Artiga family members, all the way down to the grandkids. Those relatives will be where we start our questioning on the island. To back up some, we'll spend one night off the ship at the Colony Hotel near the old Swartz home. From there, we will explore. I believe you guys said you were divers the other day, so we might use diving as a ruse to go ashore near the house, if we can rent a boat and dive gear. Everyone have their cert cards?" They all nodded.

"We can assume there is something of value hidden on that property, or we wouldn't risk our asses going there. If we recover those valuable items at this point in time and get caught with said items, we'll likely be thrown in jail, shot, and tortured… and not necessarily in that order," Josh said. "The Cuban government will claim it all for themselves. They're funny that way."

"This trip is not about recovering anything. Don't ask what's there because I'm not going to say. This is a recon-only trip. Once unlimited travel is available, we can come over on Gina's boat and recover it. What we want to know is how we can take control of the house. If it's abandoned, maybe we can offer to restore it. Cuban law, I believe, now allows Cuban citizens to own their own homes, but the investment from foreigners is very limited, even though some things are in the works. Josh, you are our expert here," Eli said.

Josh took a swig of his Dos Equis beer. He looked at the beer and said, "I don't always drink beer, but when I do, I always have two whores at my side." He laughed at his rendition and version of the "Most Interesting Man in the World" advertisement for Dos Equis beer.

"Hey, we're not whores—just your bitches, dude," Gina said and nodded at Kelsi who was smiling.

"The current law makes no concession for American investors. Other countries can invest after a lengthy approval process. An example would be the Melina Hotels, which have a couple of properties in the country. The Cuban government will always own 51 percent of the business. Many things are in the works with the Obama administration. If they are put in place, it will be difficult for a Republican administration to unglue them, but not impossible. Right now, you can't even mail a letter to Cuba, but that might change in the next six months. If you agreed to help repair the house, the money would need to go through an intermediary in another country. You still can't spend US dollars in Cuba. However, I feel sure it's done since billions of dollars are sent, mostly by Western Union, from the states to Cuba every year. There is a law that allows money to be sent to relatives and also a lesser amount to non-relatives. It is with that money, the people have started nearly five hundred thousand jobs," Josh said.

"So, if we had a relative on the Isle of Youth, we could send them money for either rent or repair work on the house. I don't know we could trust anyone to do that," Gina said.

"You guys don't even know if the house is still there. Been some hurricanes through the years. Big one there in the 1990s," Kelsi said.

"Ahhhh, don't say that! It's gotta be there, or part of it anyway. If it's been renovated, it means a government official lives there. If it's been blown down, then the rubble should still be there. If we agree to repair it or rent it, we'll need a good story, other than something valuable is buried there," Eli said.

"Uhhh—haven't you guys ever heard of Google Earth?" Kelsi said, pulling her iPad from her purse. She and Josh had paid the outrageous internet fees on the ship since the fare was paid for them. With everyone else looking over her shoulder, she typed in Isle of Youth, then pinpointed the Colony Hotel. She found it.

"Ok, just scroll above it until you find a large two-story house and an airstrip right above it," Eli said.

"Well, what do you know? It's still there. And from what I can see, there are cars parked there. Let me zoom in. They look like military trucks. There's another smaller building above it on the water," Kelsi said.

"The boat-house. Is there a boat docked there?" Gina asked. "My great grandfather used to keep his boat there."

"Doesn't look like it," Kelsi said.

"How old are these scans?" asked Eli.

"The law office uses them from time to time and that comes up a lot. Google won't tell you when they are going to take whole-earth satellite pictures. Some are aerial photos, especially the ones where you can see your car parked in your driveway. If there isn't much detail, then it could have been done as far back as 2010 when Google Earth started. Usually, a new scan is done every three years. The hotel has fairly good detail, so the house was probably done at the same time. Maybe give or take three to six years," Kelsi said.

"Real good chance it's still standing and used as a military outpost," Eli said.

"Why would they need a military presence in the middle of nowhere?" Josh asked.

"More likely to be a recreational facility for them," Eli speculated.

"Even more likely for the big muckety-mucks," Gina said.

"If that's the case, then nobody lives there full time except maybe for a caretaker," Eli said.

"How do we get there from Havana?" Kelsi asked.

Eli said, "We'll look around a little in Havana. Maybe hire one of the old '56 Chevy convertibles. Then in the late afternoon, we'll take a flight to Nueva Gerona. Once there, we have a car reserved with Cubacar and we'll drive about fifty miles to Colony Hotel. It was a

Hilton when Batista owned it, and he had just got the casino going when it was shut down by Fidel. On the way, we'll stop and ask about relatives on the list we have. Before we check in at the hotel, we'll drive to the Swartz place and see if we can get in or at least see what's there. The next day our flight leaves at 6:30 p.m. and will have us back by 7:05 p.m. The boat leaves at 9 p.m. We have reserved tickets both ways."

"Okay. Will the Cubans let us on the flights if we're Americans?" Gina asked.

"Cuba doesn't care if Americans are here—America cares that we are here. It's US law we're breaking if we are 'vacationing' instead of 'People-to-Peopling.' Unless the CIA is watching, we'll be fine," Josh said.

"If everyone is fine with the plan then let's see what our schedule is for tomorrow and just roll with it," Eli said.

"Hold it! Does anyone's phone work?" Gina asked.

"We bought the phone package too," Kelsi said.

"Here is the phone number for the Colony Hotel from our reservations. I'm going to call and ask the front desk about the big house down the road from them—who lives there—who owns it. You have a problem with that?" Gina asked.

Kelsi dialed the number, gave the cell phone to Gina, and she asked for the front desk. Afterward, she asked for the manager, and he came on the line.

"Alphonse Martinez, como estas."

"English please."

"Yes, how may I help you?"

"My name is Gina Spada, and I will be staying at the Colony in a few days. I have some questions for you."

"Certainly, if I can help, I will."

"Some of our relatives, the Swartzes, owned the large, colonial-style house on the beach not far from you many years ago. Can you tell me who owns it now?"

"Raul Castro did own it for many years, or I guess the government actually owned it. It was used for a retreat for his generals. He hasn't been there in a couple years. Now a couple people from nearby look after it a few days a week. Nobody lives there, but the Cuban Navy patrols the area sometimes."

"Do you know the caretakers' names?" Gina asked.

"Yes, their last name is Artigas."

"Are they relatives of Brian and Alian Artigas?"

"I believe they are, but you will need to ask them. I'll make sure they are available when you are here for your visit. You're with Eli Swartz?"

"Yes, and thanks for the information. We look forward to our stay," Gina said, clicking off the phone.

"Wow! Wow! Did he tell you that Raul Castro owns the house?" Eli asked

"Yes! But actually, it all reverted to the Cuban government once they went communist."

"Jesus, how'll we ever get near the place?" Josh asked.

"Hopefully the Artigases will invite us," Eli said. "We are going to turn in for the night. Let's meet for breakfast up on deck ten. They make omelets up there."

Everyone said goodnight and Eli and Gina went to their cabin. Kelsi and Josh went to the floor show. There was a Cuban dance theme, but the dancers were Russian.

***

Alphonse Martinez rang Hector Zappa in his room as soon as he got off the phone from Gina.

"Hector, someone called about the old Swartz home."

"Who was it, and what did they want?" Hector asked.

"Gina Spada. And Eli Swartz is with her. She wanted to know who owned it. She even asked about the Artigas family. They'll be here in three days. What are you going to do?"

"Maybe I'll keep an eye on them. Thanks for the call."

Hector Zappa made some notes and then opened a beer. He asked the puta occupying his bed if she wanted one. She declined, but did ask for her pay because she had to leave. He handed her twenty

CUCs, and she dressed and left without saying a word. He lived at the hotel for long periods of time. As a member of Cuba's Secret Police, or Seguridad Del Estado (SDE), his job was to look around for things that were non-allowed, which could be just about anything. He wasn't particularly bright, well-dressed, or physically built. What he was good at was being ruthless. Hector had killed twenty men while he held this position, and that was the very reason he was posted at the end of the earth on the Isle of Youth. His superiors were not happy with his quick trigger and mean disposition. He would stay close to the people who wanted to go house hunting.

In a room not far from Hector was Rick Montes, a slight grey-haired man ten years older than Hector, who had told the Colony Hotel that he was a writer and just wanted a place to drop out and work on his novel. They knew almost immediately he was CIA, but played along with his writer disguise. Hector would even have coffee with him and try to get him to admit it. He never would. But he had secretly used CIA service technicians to put in the hotel's wireless network and bug every room in the place including the front desk. After major electrical problems (which were faked by the CIA) in the Swartz house, those same great technicians bugged every room in the place. The US government listened to every high-level planning meeting there while Raul used the facility. Things were quiet right now for the two spies, but very soon both would be busy.

Chapter Eleven

The Isle of Youth Fever

San Juan Hill and a Cuban folk dance demonstration were first on the list of Santiago tour stops. Later it was Batista's former military barracks, peppered with bullet holes from an ill-fated attack by Fidel's rebel forces in 1954. Fidel got his ass whipped and was sent to the big round prison on the Isle of Pines. For some odd reason, Batista bowed to pressure from the populace and let Fidel and his brother Raul out early. From there, Fidel went to Mexico and recruited troops. After he came back, he attacked again at a different place and, as before, was soundly defeated. While negotiating for a cease-fire, his men ran off in the mountains and escaped. Fidel was one lucky guy or more likely, he was fighting against a bunch of frightened and poorly led Batista troops. Fidel did win some battles. Just a few days before the cease-fire, he soundly defeated a 500 man battalion and captured over 200 men and a great deal of weapons. Towards the end of 1958 other rebel movements such as the 13 March group and the rebels led by Che Guevara chipped away at Batista's unmotivated troops. Fidel scored victories at Guisa and several other small towns. Once Batista fled to the Dominican Republic on January 1, 1959, there was no more resistance. Fidel won.

After touring the museum at the Batista Barracks, Josh shook his head and told Eli, "How could a few guerrilla fighters defeat almost 40,000 regular army troops? I just don't get it," Josh said, still shaking his head.

"I would say the Batista troops were green, untested, not motivated, nor willing to die, and saddled with poor leadership. Batista consistently interfered with the orders from the generals. Also, the US placed an arms embargo against Batista in about 1958, which actually helped Fidel," Eli said.

When the tour was completed, they went back to the ship and dressed for dinner. After the evening meal, Kelsi and Josh tried to convince Gina and Eli to go to the floor show with them. The four had drinks for a while but soon split up for other parts of the ship. Kelsi told them they were like newlyweds and couldn't get enough sex.

Finally, back in their cabin, Eli and Gina lay on the bed looking at each other.

"Did you enjoy last night?" Eli asked.

"Yes, but I'll enjoy tonight even more," Gina said.

"It's always fun sleeping with you. I hope my sleeping habits aren't too weird."

"Eli, if sleeping wrapped around me like you are afraid I'm going get loose or escape is weird, then I can get used to being enveloped, as long as you let me do that to you, too."

"Deal!"

It was only about nine in the evening when they returned to their cabin, but they wanted to get in bed early. Gina began to undress Eli, who felt a little uncomfortable since that hadn't happened many times in his life. After Gina took off his shirt, she stopped and started to unbutton her blouse, but Eli took over, removing it and her bra. They were both breathing heavily now. He kissed her shapely breasts. She moaned softly and started removing his pants, which was easy because he didn't wear a belt.

Eli turned Gina around, unbuttoned her skirt, and let it fall to the floor. Now it was her turn again. She was eager, like a child opening a birthday present, and she quickly slid down his underwear. Eli went from partly erect to fully erect when she used her mouth to give him one of the ultimate pleasures in life. After a few minutes, he finished undressing her and gave her the same oral pleasure while she was standing. Gina got a towel and placed it on the bed, then handed him a condom package.

"I might bleed a little," she panted. "Do you want on top or want me there?"

"You get on top. If it starts to hurt, then back off and take it easy. Take your time. We've got plenty of it. We're at sea tomorrow all day," Eli said.

"Baby, I'm so wet, I think it will be fine." She took his hand and placed it on her heart so he could feel her rapid heartbeat. He repeated the motion with her hand on his chest. They smiled and kissed passionately.

Gina climbed on top of Eli and looked in his blue eyes and laughed. "I can't believe we're doing the deed." She slid him into her and felt no pain at first. As she took all of him, there was a momentary twinge of pain.

"Ouch! But…sweetheart, it's a good ouch."

"Feels wonderful to me. Move it in and out a few times to test for pain."

"Best test I ever took!" Gina said

Gina moved her hips in a rhythm that gradually became harder and faster. Eli could see the enjoyment in her face. She slowed briefly and kissed Eli.

"Eli, I am crazy about you, and I want to have sex every day."

"Of all of your ideas—that is the best one so far."

They tried to have orgasms at the same time but the timing was off a little--something they swore they'd work on. They lay next to each other afterward and talked. Gina traced the lines of his face and mouth with her fingers and locked on his eyes, as though she wanted inside his brain as much as she wanted him inside her body. If there ever was a point of no return for their feelings for each other, it had just happened.

The next morning, both were sore from the numerous times they had made love. Neither complained.

Josh and Kelsi arrived first for the omelet line and picked a table next to the indoor pool. Someone had placed a huge blue tarp over the pool in an attempt to stop the water which was splashing over the sides from the movement of the ship. The tarp had only a minor effect on the thousands of gallons in the pool. The couple quickly moved to a table far from the wild water show. They had been in place about twenty minutes when Eli and Gina stepped gingerly over the wet deck and got in the custom egg line. Behind them were two very muscular Cuban men wearing dress shirts and slacks with polished black shoes. Both had sunglasses on and looked like they shopped at the same store for clothes. They appeared official in some capacity.

"Kelsi, see those two Cuban men? They got on the boat in Santiago. I remembered they looked alike and had very little luggage. What's their occupation, if you were going to guess?"

"Police detectives, undercover something, Cuban mafia…no— they are boat marshals. You know, like sky marshals, only on a boat. People try to hijack boats all the time. Are we going close to Somalia on this trip?"

Kelsi finally realized Josh was messing with her.

"Well, when he jams a gun in your ribs, you won't make fun of me then," Kelsi said.

"What's this about a gun in your ribs, Kelsi?" Eli asked as he set his tray on the table, followed by Gina.

"Okay, Josh thinks I'm nuts but I guessed the occupation of those two Cuban dudes that were in line next to you."

"I guess Cuban Secret police. Gina, you guess."

"They have the cop look all right," Gina said. "I say they're hitmen."

As the group continued speculating, the two objects of their theories received their omelets and walked away from the cooking line and appeared to be looking for a table. The table where the foursome was sitting had six chairs. It was crowded in the area since nobody wanted to get splashed near the pool. To everyone's astonishment, the two men walked directly toward their table and asked if they could share the table. Once they were seated, everyone introduced themselves.

The new arrivals introduced themselves as Luis Cimarro and Julio Vázquez.

"We've tried to guess your occupation as you stood in line. So, tell us if we got close: are you government hit men?" Gina said and watched as they laughed.

"Try again," Luis said.

It was Kelsi's turn. "Secret police out to arrest Americans who fail to show up for the Cuban history seminars on board?"

"Getting closer; try again," Julio said.

"Mormon missionaries?" Josh asked, causing the entire table to crack up.

"Way off base," Julio said in perfect English.

"May I approach it differently?" Eli said. "You are very well educated since you are Cuban but have very little of a Spanish accent. You may have been sent to school in another country—possibly the US or Great Britain. You're dressed much too formally for an average Cuban, so you're conforming to the way the government thinks you should dress to represent them. You show no individualism or creativity in choice of clothes, which again goes back to being officials of some kind. I am going to guess you're here to talk about the history of the military in Cuba. Furthermore, each of you flew MIG23 fighters—maybe MIG29s on occasion. Both are now flight instructors at the La Coloma Airport and teachers of military history at Havana University for the Cuban military," Eli said, rather smugly.

"Wow! We have a winner!" said Luis.

"I read the bios on the lecture series for both of you in the ship newsletter," Eli laughed. "They even had your pictures with the article."

"That's cheating," Julio said.

"Julio and Luis, please tell me the likely outcome of a dogfight between an F-16 and an MIG29, given the same amount of training for each pilot?" Eli asked. An engineering student and an amateur pilot, he loved fighter planes.

"Toss up—MIG is faster and more maneuverable, but the F-16 has better toys. The F-16 will fire first from a longer distance. The US and Russia have newer jets, but their new advanced designs are based on who has the stealthiest jet," Luis said.

"You guys have several MIG 29s in your inventory. You got them from countries that couldn't afford to keep them. I have heard your pilots fight over the chance to fly them," Julio said.

Everyone finished breakfast and talked about jets and war. Josh asked how Fidel won the revolution with so few men. He never really got a satisfying answer to his question. He would keep asking Cubans the same question throughout his stay. He was beginning to believe that Fidel Castro never defeated Batista; instead, Batista's army folded because they lost faith in his regime.

The six people agreed to get together for cards and drinks after the two Cubans' lecture. The group enjoyed the lecture and even asked some questions afterward. Julio and Luis were leaving the ship the next day and were off to Havana University. They knew the other four would be on tours but suggested they come by the university if they had time. The card game was fun and they exchanged emails, even though the Cubans didn't have Wi-Fi service very often.

"It will get better. I understand talks are underway to bring US contractors over to open more phone and internet service. It's time we joined the rest of the world," Julio said.

None of the four Americans said a word about where they were going after the tours ended the next day in Havana.

Chapter Twelve

On the Island

The four Americans had breakfast with their new Cuban friends before their excursions took them in different directions in Havana. Eli questioned them endlessly about fighter jets, while Josh wanted more specifics on Fidel and Che's miraculous victories over far superior forces. Even the Bay of Pigs should have been more successful, but it fell quickly to Fidel Castro's revolutionary forces. Nothing was solved, but Josh started doing his own research and each time he did, he found there were several other individuals whom the people of Cuba looked up to who were trying to garner support for overthrowing Batista.

Luis and Julio told the group that if they got a chance to stop by the college, they should check their teaching schedules at the information desk in the administration building. Kelsi was the only one with a card, and they took it so they would at least have an email and phone number. Phones and credit cards didn't appear to work in Cuba. Retrieving their small duffel bags stored under the breakfast table, both Cubans shook hands with the guys, hugged the girls, and walked down to a lower level to leave the ship.

"Did Julio tell you he has 21 cousins in Miami?" asked Gina, to no one in particular.

"Luis has 10 cousins in several different states," Kelsi said.

"You know it seems that as you get to know Cubans it is clear they have this strange relationship with their country. They know it has lots of issues, and they want to have pride in it but realize the rest of the world is so far ahead of them. The government has drilled the idea in their heads that all their problems are because of the US trade embargo. Sure it affects them, but being a fucking communist country is their real problem. Private enterprise will naturally morph from any other form of government in time. Hard-working and clever business owners and professionals rise to the top unless the government stops them, and uneducated and unmotivated laborers will stay on the bottom…unless, however, they work for General Motors and have a really good union contract," Josh said. Everyone laughed at the GM comment.

They left the ship and walked by a series of tables selling Cuban novelties. A few things caught their eyes for later on. First was a small white building about the size of a snow cone stand where you could exchange money. Eli and Gina exchanged $500 each, while Kelsi and Josh exchanged about $200 apiece of Convertible Cuban Pesos or CUCs. All had to pay a 10 percent penalty as punishment for being an American—mainly because Cuba was pissed at the US over the embargo, of course.

With a pocket full of CUCs they found shiny new buses with the same numbers as those buses in Santiago. They didn't just look like the same buses; they were the same. They had been driven all night, over 500 miles to be in Havana for tours there. Apparently, there was a shortage of the nice buses in Cuba. Some said they were made in China. If things worked out for Cuba, they had better call China and tell them to send a boatload of them.

"Did you think it was weird that they took our temperature with those remote sensors before we left the boat?" Gina said.

"If we had a fever, do you think they would have taken us in a back room and beaten us with a rubber hose until the temperature dropped to normal?" Eli said.

"Of course!" Josh said.

The tour took them to another revolutionary square, past a ballpark, and by another revolutionary museum which featured a boat with huge plate glass windows on display. The Americans on board mainly just watched the old US cars go by out the windows of the bus. Many of them were convertibles—many had been transformed from hardtops, and most had been painted with bright colors of house paint. They must know the Americans love these old cars as much as they do.

After the buses parked near the ship terminal, everyone followed the tour guide as he started a walking tour of old Havana, which commenced directly across the street. The first building encountered was a small church built in the 1500s. Next was a cobblestone square which featured a large cathedral. Outstanding old colonial architecture was everywhere. It seemed that everything was a movie set. Kelsi suddenly found a menu stuffed next to her face by a young Cuban wearing a sport coat and tie.

"Look! Lobster for 12 CUCs! We can't go wrong here," Kelsi said.

"Sweetness!" Josh said.

All four left the tour and fell under the spell of delicious seafood. The lunch featured huge spiny lobsters and plates of mystery vegetables and fruit. They were now on their own as the tour had moved on.

"After we eat, let's rent a couple of the old cars and tour the city—maybe stop by the university and say hi to Luis and Julio. They're the only friends we have in all of Cuba," Gina said.

"I'm up for that. While we are goofing off this afternoon, we need to check out taxis and ask how long it takes to get to the airport. Everyone still have their tourist cards on them?" Eli asked. The group nodded in the affirmative.

Eli and Gina hired a 1955 Chevy convertible for 30 CUCs, while Josh and Kelsi scored a 1956 model for the same price. They stopped at the National Hotel, an ice cream parlor, and Havana University. Josh ran into the Administration building and asked in Spanish for a list of classes for Luis and Julio. He was directed to a building across from the Administration building. They asked the drivers to wait and then walked towards the building. A student inside led them to the classroom. The student, who was on a bathroom break, went into the classroom and told the instructors that they had visitors. Julio and Luis rushed out and pulled them into the classroom. It was a sloping amphitheater-type room capable of holding maybe 100 students. Only a few had laptops, which looked strange to the Americans. Both instructors had lavalier microphones and there was a portable one for passing around the room. The two Cubans introduced the Americans

and gave their majors in Spanish and asked the class if they had
questions for fellow college students in America.

"Is your college free or do you have to pay? If so how much?" This
question was asked in Spanish so Josh replied in their language. "It is
free for those who get scholarships, but could be up to fifty thousand
dollars a year for those that don't. All of us have partial scholarships,
some Pell grants, and student loans," Josh said. He could see a few
Cuban students repeating the $50,000 amount.

An English-speaking girl asked Gina what she planned to do with
a Political Science degree. She replied, "It's a good prerequisite for law
school. If I follow what Kelsi and Josh did, then I'd have three years
of law school beyond an undergraduate degree. I'm the youngest of
the group at 19. If I go to law school, I'll be 25 when I get my law
degree." Her answer seemed to satisfy the girl. Gina wanted to say that
she would have a real job when it was over, compared to a $22 monthly
government paycheck in Cuba.

The students asked Eli about his engineering studies, how many
years he would be required to study, and his likely beginning salary.
He answered, explaining graduate school in short sentences as Josh
translated. When he said the starting salary would be $120,000 to
$150,000 with the companies where he had already interviewed, an
audible gasp went through the room as it was translated. "We import
many engineers from India and China since we have a shortage of
individuals with those skills," Eli said.

"I didn't know you would make that much. I like you even more
now," Gina said and Josh translated it for a big laugh from the Cubans.

One stern looking student in the front row asked about the
embargo. "Why do you insist on keeping the embargo in force against
us?" Josh took this and fired off in Spanish.

"It may have outlived its usefulness, and many say it cost us about
three billion dollars in lost trading opportunities. Much more than it
cost your economy. Many US citizens who are of Cuban ancestry will
not let the rest of America forget the human rights violations that have
occurred in Cuba. And the minute I say that, you're going to bring

up the race issues we have had in America. It's true, we've had issues. Today it is more with Muslims. When a country accepts every race and religion and stirs them into a melting pot there are going to be issues. They will never go away. When Fidel took over, most of the whites left for the US as they were then a minority in Cuba—still are. If the whites were a majority here, who knows if there would be issues? I believe Obama will chip away at the embargo. Some say that the US trades with China and Vietnam, and they are communist countries. I say they are more socialist/capitalist entities. Cuba is slowly moving in that direction now that taxes from free enterprise will grow the government coffers. My answer to you is 'fuck the stupid embargo!' Quit letting your government tell you everything would be fine if it wasn't for that awful embargo. Grow your economy like I know you can among the countries you can trade with until the US and countries all over the world are begging to do business with you. China did it. Vietnam did it. And yes, Russia did it. And none of those places have the absolute beauty and charm of your country, coupled with the genuine warmth of your people."

It was quiet for a minute and then there was a standing ovation. Josh was indeed the king of bullshit; he stacked it like a cord of firewood. Josh was the attorney you desperately needed when someone found out you had been screwing your 16-year-old babysitter. The three other Americans clapped but had no idea what he said since none of his speech was in English.

Luis and Julio dismissed the class and invited the Americans for coffee at the student lounge. As they picked up their coffee and sat with Luis and Julio, students would come by and speak to the four guests. Most of the questions and statements were directed at Josh since the communication was easier. The girls, however, were asked about fashions on campuses in the US and said they could only speak for Florida, so some awkwardly asked Eli about California school dress. He answered as best he could. Then came swarms of questions on the best rock, rap, hip-hop, and popular singers and groups. They generally seemed to love everything American except their government. The two Cuban teachers thanked the group for coming by and helping with the class. They all agreed to stay in touch.

The cars were waiting for them, and they agreed to pay for another hour if they could take them to the airport. The drivers reluctantly agreed, reminding everyone that they were not supposed to be in competition with taxis.

It took about thirty minutes to get to the José Martí International Airport. Then the two convertibles, both drivers with large tips in hand, headed back to the city. The group had asked to be dropped off at Terminal 3 because it was for international flights and had the most restaurants and shops. They looked around a while, had dinner, and then stopped at a bar for drinks. They began their long walk to Terminal 1 where their flight to the Isle of Youth was waiting. Each carried small backpacks containing basic toilet gear, a few clean clothes, iPads, and chargers for the flight. It was quite a contrast at the small domestic flight terminal where the only amenities were dirty bathrooms. Everyone checked in at the counter and was given plastic boarding passes. There were no seat assignments.

The security line was short, and the scanning machine was broken, so the uniformed ladies took a quick look in the backpacks and checked their passports and tourist cards. No problems. Each one was asked their reason for going to the Isle of Youth and for any hotel reservations. They all said, "scuba diving at the Colony Hotel." As Eli and Josh left the security line, they couldn't help themselves and took a quick peek at the young security women's legs. Both ladies wore mini-skirts as a part of their uniform.

"God, do I like a woman in a uniform," Josh said and immediately received a punch on his arm from Kelsi. Gina just rolled her eyes in the direction of Eli.

The wait wasn't long because the Cuban flight was actually on time. The line snaked out on the hot tarmac and up a portable ladder into a Russian Antonov-38, a relic of an airplane which held 27 passengers in the relative comfort of a carnival ride. Two propellers blew black smoke out their asses while passengers were greeted with an interior so Spartan it could have been used as a small prison in the sky. It flew.

No flight attendants, no cute announcements over the intercom, and no refreshments during the flight. Even given the deplorable condition of the airplane equipment, they were told they were lucky to get tickets since one month is the normal wait time.

The little plane went up and was no sooner at its apex than it started down again. The entire ordeal took about forty minutes. Out the windows stained by bad breath, snot, and grease, the passengers could see the strangely round Modelo Prison with its guard tower in the center and the rooms in a circle. It was much like an Embassy Suites Hotel—without the plants, without a stream running through the lobby, and without anything nice. A prison with a guard tower inside, it resembled a lighthouse without the charm. Fidel and Raul Castro called it home from 1954 to 1955. A little room in there was fixed up just as it was when they were guests. The prison was just a curious tourist stop now. The Americans didn't think they had time to visit it, but judging by the looks of the other occupants of the flight, many could have been escapees from the old prison.

The group found the Cubacar rental agency as soon as they walked into the small terminal building. Josh had called several times with Kelsi's phone to verify the reservation. He said the agent kept saying, "Are you sure you are coming?"

Every time Josh called he said, "Any car but a Lada." He was always assured it wouldn't be the Russian pile of junk. The agent looked at them and said, "I have a green Lada or a black Lada."

Josh had to be restrained from choking the rental agent's throat. From across the room, Gina and Kelsi yelled they had found another car. Standing under a Transtur rental booth sign, they were both smiling. They had found a Honda Pilot for only twice the fare of the Lada. They took it and asked the lady if they knew either the Diaz or Artiga families. She said she knew dozens of them. Eli asked where the oldest ones lived. The Transtur agent spoke good English and drew a map on the back of the rental agreement.

Paperwork completed, Eli said he would drive first. They headed toward their first stop in the town of La Demajagua about nine miles away. Everyone was excited. Finally, they were on the Isle of Youth, and they had time to explore—a couple of hours before sunset today and all day tomorrow. Eli carefully pulled out on the main road and saw there was very little traffic. He didn't see a black 1953 Chevy pull out some distance behind him. The car would stay back almost out of sight. But it would be there. Eli never noticed.

Chapter Thirteen

A Link with the Past

The only two-story house near the road in the village of La Demajagua was a few steps away from where they parked the car. The road was a series of gullies and potholes. Trash lay in ditches partly filled with stagnant water, and sick-looking dogs stood their ground and barked. A little boy answered the door and said something in Spanish. Josh answered him and asked who lived there. He said his granny, Wendy. Josh asked if he could speak to her. The kid went away. It seemed like a long time before anyone came to the door. Moving slowly, a gray-headed woman in her late sixties appeared.

Recognizing they were Americans, she spoke in English, "May I help you?"

"Are you the former Wendy Diaz?" Gina asked.

"Yes. And who are you?"

"I am Gina Spada and this man is Eli Swartz. My grandparents knew you."

"Blessed Mary—Mother of God! Come in this house." She crossed herself as though a miracle had occurred on her front porch.

Chairs started shifting into the living room as kids brought them in from the dining room. Wendy sat down and looked at Gina. "You, girl—I can see a little of Roman and Carmine in you. My, are you pretty!"

Up and down she surveyed Eli like a human MRI machine. "Some—maybe a little of Bernie and Moe. But, what's with this blond hair and blue eyes?"

"My dad, Marty, who is now deceased, married a Swedish woman."

"Gina, what is your dad's name?" Wendy asked.

"His name was David, but he also is dead. I'm afraid that Eli and I are the last of the Spada and Swartz blood lines. Both our mothers are still alive, however."

"Are you two single? Are you in school? Where do you live?"

"We are currently going together—Gina and me. I go to college in California, and she goes to Florida State. So, we live at opposite ends of the country now. We haven't discussed what we'll do in the fall," Eli said and gave Gina a quizzical look. She shrugged her shoulders as though she didn't know either—something they had forgotten to discuss.

"What about your twin sister Clara?" Eli asked. He had researched all the records Carmine and Bernie left with all the documents and deeds.

"She passed. Got breast cancer about ten years ago. It had already spread when they found it. Rosa, Alberto, and all their kids are gone. Her grandsons, Alian and Brian Artigas, went off to Angola with the Cuban military and got themselves killed. Fidel is to blame for that!" Wendy said.

"What about the Artigases, who are taking care of the beach house?" Eli asked.

"Mary and Pete. They're cousins of Alian and Brian. They know quite a bit of the family history. Rosa and Alberto took care of the house for a long time—lived there even when Fidel and Raul held meetings. The Cuban military brought girls there in secret. It was so far out of the way, they began to use it even less. In the last ten years, you can count on your hand how many people used it. When something needs repairing, the Artigases either do it or hire someone else to do it and send the bill to the government. Sometimes they pay but lately, they delay it or deny the claim. Our government is dead broke," Wendy said.

"Do you think they would sell it?" Eli asked.

"Not to you. Maybe to someone on the island or on the mainland. They won't let Americans buy property."

"If I bought it for you, could you rent it back to me?" Eli asked.

"Americans can rent places, but the Cuban government would have to approve any private business. They might let someone buy it, but they'd never believe I came up with that much money. Maybe someone in Havana or Santiago."

"We'll stop by before we check into the hotel just to look at it," Eli said.

"If you're thinking about digging around there looking for money, forget it. Government troops looked everywhere for money. Rosa barely got the money that Bernie hid for her from under the boards in her bedroom before they busted in. They used metal detectors and special radar. They didn't find anything."

"Well, Wendy, we have to leave as we don't have much daylight left. It's great to see you. We'll stop by tomorrow on our way out." Eli and Gina hugged her and stuck a 50 CUC note in her hand and told her to buy something for her birthday. It was just an excuse to give her some money. From the looks of the inside of her house, she needed it.

Eli pointed the car toward the road that led to the Colony Hotel. Gina said sadly, "So many people have died. These were my people and your people, Eli, and the people who took care of them at the beach-house. I have seen pictures of all those people, the house, and the ocean all my life. Old pictures, mostly black and white but some faded color ones as well. They always looked like they were having fun."

"Gina, I saw those pictures as well. My dad, grandfather, and great-grandfather wore those pictures thin looking at them."

"You know there were movies. Old super-eight black and white—color—yeah, some of those were color. We need to put those on DVD disks. I bet you have some too, Eli."

"Mother does, I think," Eli said. "Why don't we put them together and preserve them?"

"Okay with me."

They drove toward the ocean on a road that had not been repaired since the revolution. If they averaged 30 or 40 miles an hour they were lucky. Anything faster was painful. The sun had changed its hue to orange, setting rapidly in the west, causing an explosion of pinks, reds, and purple colors above it. Darkness followed as long shadows stretched across the road. At the Y in the road was a colorful sign pointing to the hotel on the left and a blank board in the direction of the beach house. It was a couple of miles on a very narrow road to the house. Tall, stacked stone walls had been built on the ocean side to keep the surf and winds from destroying the road.

"Anybody have flashlights?" Eli asked.

A total of three small lights emerged, as they all frantically searched their backpacks.

"I see it," said Eli. A large yellow object could be seen on the left at a distance. As they approached closer they could see a second building maybe 100 yards beyond the main building.

"The boathouse!" yelled Gina."

Kelsi and Josh didn't understand her enthusiasm for a boathouse. Gina calmed down after Eli threw her a stern glance.

"We'll start there and work our way back to the main house," Eli said.

The car passed slowly by the main house. It was obvious repairs were needed as some windows were boarded up, paint was fading, and the grounds were overgrown with weeds. The majestic house was there, however, as evidenced by the smiles on Eli's and Gina's faces. Although it was covered by high weeds, Eli found the driveway that led to the boathouse. Everyone got out and rushed to the glass doors and low windows to peer through with flashlights.

"Wait. Let me try something," Eli said. He fumbled in his pocket and pulled out an ancient key chain. He put the key in the door and held his breath. The door opened.

***

The black car had followed the group the entire trip to the Y. Now it slowed to make the left turn when a white Jeep pulled across the road and blocked it. Hector jumped out of the car and pulled a 9mm Beretta pistol on the other driver. As he reached the window of the Jeep, he found a .45 automatic pointed at his head. Rick Montes smiled and spoke, "Mr. Zappa, those kids will be back here at the hotel in a few minutes. You got no reason to tail them all over this island."

"You don't tell me how to do my job, Rick," Hector said.

"You have a history of doing your job a little too well. Twenty kills. No wonder you're here at the end of the earth."

"Stay out of my way, Rick."

Hector backed his car up and drove to the hotel. Rick headed in that direction but pulled over and stopped on the side of the road. He was concerned, with good reason.

***

Eli and Gina poked around in the boathouse, which appeared to have been neglected for many years. Broken furniture was overturned, dust and rodent droppings were everywhere, and a pool table stood in the middle of the room with its green felt ripped bare. The big rug was there, threadbare, torn in places, but still there. Eli and Gina looked at it but didn't attempt to turn it over to see what was there.

"Gina, you guys go to the big house and I'll lock up here," Eli said as he took his time leaving the boathouse. Once everyone had left, he rushed over and raised the rug and estimated the location of the hatch cover. Shining his light, he could only see concrete with spots of gray paint left under the rug. He rushed some flash pictures with his iPhone, put the rug back in place, and locked the door after him. As he walked to the big house, his eye caught a light out to sea. It appeared to be getting closer.

"Can't see much but appears there's furniture in the living room," Kelsi said.

It was dark now, and Eli could see through the house to the light on the boat moving in towards the house. Suddenly, rotating red flashing lights came on and they could hear a loudspeaker in the distance. It didn't take long for everyone to race to the car and start back towards the hotel.

"What was that?" Josh yelled.

A yellow-orange flame rotated from the bow of a coastal attack vessel. There was no sound at first; then there was deep thump of a .50 caliber deck gun followed by impact noises behind the car. It came again and closer this time. Eli was speeding towards the part of the road protected by the stacked rock wall. At one point, about 800 yards ahead, the wall was taller than the car.

"Turn your lights off, Eli!" Josh yelled.

Eli did and stayed off the brakes, so there wouldn't be a target. Several times the attack boat sent rounds along the road. When the big protective wall came up on his right, Eli eased the car to a stop by gearing it down, never touching the brakes. After twenty minutes the patrol boat gave up and headed out to sea.

Once Rick saw their headlights at a distance, he drove to the hotel. He had heard the machine gun fire and worried they had been hit. He parked his car and stood by it with an open trunk so he could overhear the group. However, the four Americans were silent. It was the first time any of them had been fired upon. The big .50 caliber had made a strong impression. They saw it hit trees, cutting them in half. They watched as huge rocks along the wall exploded into tiny pieces of gravel and dust. They were very lucky to be alive. The subdued group checked in and after a somber dinner agreed to meet for breakfast at 7 a.m.

In their respective rooms, later in the night, Gina and Kelsi broke down and cried from the experience. Hopefully, if the housekeepers took them on a tour tomorrow, they would be recognized as friendly forces. They would take Mary and Pete Artigas's car, which was explained to be the same Jeep station wagon Bernie left 57 years ago. Eli said he wished they could borrow a tank.

Chapter Fourteen

Spooks: Foreign and Domestic

Breakfast found everyone in a better mood, especially when they were told the Artigas couple would be there at 10 a.m. to give a tour of the house. Gina and Kelsi were excited to slip into swimsuits that allowed for maximum sun exposure as soon as breakfast was finished. The two men followed them to the beach, helped them settle in some beach chairs, and headed for the dive shop.

"What dives you have going out today?" Eli asked of a young dive master with a gold ring in his ear and tattoos that spread from his torso up to his neck. He was Cuban, muscular, with sun-streaked long hair.

"Going to the Colony wall and the Roja caves. Both are advanced dives. What are your dive levels?"

"Master diver with PADI," Josh said.

"SSI Advanced," Eli said.

"What about those hot girls you led to the beach?" The dive master looked towards the girls wearing tiny bikinis. Clearly, he wanted them on the boat.

"Gina just has a basic open water cert," Eli said.

"Kelsi is working on her master's cert, but she hasn't had enough dives."

"We can take two dive masters. One can go shallow with the girls, and you guys can do the deep dive," he said and stuck out his hand, introducing himself as Dian Rodriguez.

There was no way Dian would leave two gorgeous girls stuck on a beach when he could be staring at their pretty asses as they swam in front of them.

"Oh, my God! We can't do a deep dive since we're flying out at around 6:30. If we dive, we'll have to stay above one atmosphere and that's still a risk. I think the plane only gets up to about 10 or 12 thousand feet. It might be OK, but I don't think we should risk it," Josh said.

"The tables have some flexibility, but I don't think it's worth the risk for us or the girls getting decompression sickness. We need to come back when we can spend the night after the dive," Eli said.

"Hey, it's up to you guys but that commuter plane doesn't get high enough to trigger DCS in my opinion. But I'm not flying—it'll be you guys," Dian said.

"I think maybe we'll snorkel if the girls want to. Can we rent a boat for that, or is it required for us to have a guide?" Eli asked.

"I'll rent you a Zodiak for 50 CUCs and provide your personal equipment. Sorry, you can't dive because it's a beautiful and untouched reef."

"So we've heard," said Josh.

Josh and Eli walked to where the girls were soaking up the sun and asked if they were up for snorkeling later on. They relayed the dive situation to the girls who said it was no big deal. Nothing much bothered them at this point.

"Girls, you need to know a meteor is headed from outer space for this very beach," Eli said.

"When it gets closer, let us know. We'll be right here," Kelsi said.

Knowing where the girls were going to be for the next couple of hours, the guys beat a trail towards an outdoor bar where they ordered a couple of beers. They were handed Cuban Buccaneers. They took an open table that had a huge red umbrella shade with Cuba scrawled on it in giant letters. They had only taken a couple of sips of the beer, enough to remark that it was very good when a man came over and sat at their table.

"May I join you two Americans?" Rick Morales asked.

"Certainly. You sound like an American," Eli said.

"That I am. Park City, Utah."

"Great ski town," Eli said.

"Yes…Yes, it is. You guys were lucky last night. I saw what happened, and it's a wonder the deck gun didn't take your car apart. I've no idea why they guard the old Swartz house so closely, but they certainly do. You'd think something was buried there. Oh, by the way, I'm Rick Morales, and which of you is Eli Swartz?"

Eli meekly raised his hand.

He turned toward Josh and asked, "So then you must be Josh Vargas?"

Josh nodded.

"Want to tell me why you and two beautiful girls are here?"

"My great-grandfather owned that house. I have the deed—even the keys to the place. I'd like to figure out a way to take back what belongs to my family," Eli said.

"Right! Now tell me why you're really here."

"House is worth a lot, and I want to get it back and the property around it, including the airstrip. Is that too hard to believe?" Eli said. He was beginning to get frustrated by the stranger's questions.

"Then, let me tell you the real reason you're here. Your great-grandfather, Bernie Swartz, was a low-level mobster who, along with his partner Carmine Spada, whose great-granddaughter is tanning her beautiful body right over there, made a fortune in Havana with a small but very profitable casino and night club. Cuban tax records show he paid some taxes but probably brought in 30 to 40 million dollars during a 15 to 20 year period. They owned five of the best whorehouses in the country. Also, they had the best call girl operation in the world. Gorgeous girls that would travel anywhere. They never spent much, except for that house, which Bernie built with local labor. However, on the boathouse, he used contractors from the states. Wonder why? The whole Cuban army searched that place with ground-penetrating radar, sonar, and metal detectors. They found nothing. Believe me; they still think it's there. You think it's there too, or you wouldn't be poking around," Rick said.

"Rick, what do you do, and who do you work for? Why this fascination with an old house? Carmine and Bernie's estate was settled last week and divided between Gina and me. We were handed a deed for a house that was stolen by the Cuban government and would love to have back what rightfully belongs to me. As far as the money goes, both brought a fortune home and lived off it for years. Most of the residual is in a trust fund for us. It may very well be the fortune you speak of, but the trust company won't tell us the total. We don't really need this hidden treasure that I assume you're looking for as well since you seem to be obsessed with it," Eli said.

"If someone in America finds that money, which I believe is on the grounds, under the house, or sunk in the ocean offshore, then there will be a tax adjustment when it comes to the US. I intend to see that happens," Rick said. "Hey, I'm on your side. Cuba would just blow it on some giveaway program."

A man walked up to the table and gave Rick the finger. "And I intend to see that the entire amount stays in Cuba, and the fucking thieving Americans are placed in a Cuban prison," Hector said and then introduced himself.

"Jesus H. Christ, we're popular with everyone," Eli said.

"Well, well. I see now. We have competing agencies after something no one actually knows exist. Can America and Cuba afford to have two very skilled operatives playing spy versus spy at the end of the world? What in the fuck did you guys do to be placed here?" Josh asked. He didn't say that his dad had worked for the CIA in both Puerto Rica and Cuba for many years. He still did embassy work in South America in some kind of diplomatic "attaché" work. Josh was sure he knew what that meant. Josh's mother lived with him, but both were ready to come home to Miami. Josh had a sister in college at the University of Florida, and the family kept a home near Gainesville, although it wasn't occupied very often. He didn't fear either of these men.

"Thanks for all the information. If you don't mind, my friend and I have a beer to finish," Eli said.

"Aren't you supposed to be on some People to People program?" asked Hector.

"Don't tell me, in addition to being a spook, you're also tourist police?" Josh said.

"Cuba doesn't give a shit how often the Americans come over, or what they do when they're here as long as they bring money. The American operative may want to slap our hands, however."

"I don't give a shit either. Have a nice day. The Artigases are here. Have fun on your tour. If you find a stack of money, please let me know," Rick said.

"Just for your information, Rick, the taxes paid to Cuba are direct tax credits against any US taxes due for foreign earnings. Most of the time it was on par with the US tax, which means no tax was due. Since you guys have all the old tax records, you're aware that they were audited twice by the IRS. But, I'm sure a slick CIA guy like you already knew that," Eli said.

"Well, Josh, if there's no money there, you didn't need to do that research. Dig a little deeper. For five years, the US tax bracket for high income was 90 percent—much higher than Cuba's 35 percent. You owe me the difference," Rick said.

"No problem. If we find any money we'll just bring home the 35 percent kind," Josh said and laughed. The two intruders got up and walked in opposite directions.

Eli and Josh went into the lobby to meet the caretakers of the house. The young couple introduced themselves as Mary and Pete Artigas. They were an attractive couple in their mid-thirties. Pete knew the history of the house from stories from his relatives who had been caretakers as well. They were excited to meet relatives of the owners. They had questions, though.

"Why do you come to see this house?" asked Pete.

"I have the deed for the house and property from Bernie Swartz, my great-grandfather. We would like to own it again, and we intend to petition the Cuban government for the ability to buy it back or rent it. I need to see its condition and see if it's worth the fight that is ahead," Eli said. He piled the bullshit higher each time he talked about the house.

Pete and Mary didn't respond to his explanation.

"We'll get the girls and then we'll be ready to go with you. Is there room for all of us or should we bring our car?" Eli asked.

"All can go in the Jeep station wagon," Mary said. She and Pete got the wagon and pulled it up in front of the hotel.

Gina and Eli had seen pictures of this vehicle their entire lives.

"This will be like being in the same covered wagon your relatives had used to go out west," Gina said.

The wagon had a row of extra seats in the rear, so everyone fit. The wagon had carried their great-grandparents, grandparents, and the Artigas and Diaz families for almost 60 years. On the way, the Artigases mentioned that some of the rock wall had been damaged and trees had been chopped and split in half.

"Those damned Cuban Navy gunboats will shoot at anything," Mary said.

The four Americans didn't say a word. In a few minutes, Pete stopped the Jeep in front of the faded yellow house.

"Ready to go in?" Pete asked and walked to the front door to unlock it. Everyone stood and stared at the house. They would go in but wanted to just look at it first. It was a legend. A legend needed to be taken in for a while.

Chapter Fifteen

The Beach House

Eli was the last to enter. The front porch was now bare. No longer were four wooden rocking chairs placed in a row. It had once been a place of solitude while the back patio was always noisy with kids playing all the way down to the beach, in swing sets, in the sand with toys, and back and forth to get glasses of lemonade. He had never been there but had seen so many pictures taken during the years… and, of course, the movies. The movies had no sound, but he knew the sounds kids made. Finally, he left the front porch and entered the house.

"Very little remodeling has been done. Some new appliances were installed—not top of the line since those are hard to get here—trade embargo is to blame," Pete said, smiling.

One room, once a large den or family room, had been converted to a conference room and furnished with a long, fake mahogany table. Several ashtrays were on the table, which suggested it wasn't a non-smoking building. The table had several cuts in it where soldiers had stuck their knives.

The house had been swept and no trash was visible because of Mary and Pete's care. Gina and Eli checked pictures, bookcases, desk drawers, and shelves for any record of their relatives but found nothing. They took pictures with their iPhones of paintings and furniture, hoping to find matches in the old pictures and movies. It appeared anything of value had been purged, including silver and china. Most had been replaced with cheap plastic plates, cups, and glasses. The silverware was Cuban military issue as were the cooking utensils. Everything was junk. Plaster, wallpaper, drapes, shutters, carpet, and floor tiles had deteriorated or been damaged.

Eli looked at Gina, who was about to cry. "Sweetie, it will have to be gutted and totally redone," Eli said. She nodded and wiped her eyes.

Josh and Kelsi had gone upstairs. They called for the others to come up. When Eli and Gina arrived at the top of the stairs, they found bedrooms with linens and pillows on beds and furniture intact with rugs on the floor. The bathroom downstairs was a horror story, yet the upstairs baths were clean and stocked with towels.

"It makes sense," said Kelsi. This is where they take the girls."

As they had done downstairs, Gina and Eli took pictures to record everything in the rooms. When they opened drawers in the bedside tables, they found condoms and sex toys.

Done with the upstairs, the group went back down and through the outside doors to see what was left of the patio. One outdoor table with two chairs was there; trash, broken lawn mowers, and old furniture lay rotting all the way down to the beach.

"This side of the house has taken a beating. Windows are broken, ceiling tile is missing, and there are cracks in the stucco. At least someone has boarded up the windows," Josh said.

"We did that," Pete said. "We would have done more but didn't have any funding since they only pay us $23 a month."

"Jesus! Jesus! What a fucking mess!" Eli said. "Let's look in the boathouse."

Eli said nothing to Pete and Mary about having keys to the front door. They let Pete open it and take them on a tour. Eli stayed outside for a few minutes, but this time it wasn't to look at a legend—this time it was all about the rocks. Suddenly he knew why no one had discovered the hidden vault. He looked down and realized he was standing on solid rock. He walked on the right side of the boathouse and saw solid limestone and granite. Beyond that, and protruding from the ocean side of the structure was rock—lots of rock. Anyone looking at the boathouse, especially if they were an engineer or architect, would easily see why the concrete piers were anchored against the huge rock face. The foundation and the concrete floor were two feet thick and poured directly on top of the rock outcropping. Nobody would suspect that the solid rock had been drilled and dynamited to hold a chamber with a huge safe. If concrete walls were present or any excess structure built near or attached to the boathouse, it would have caused suspicion. The design of the boathouse was pure genius. The concrete flooring may have only been two feet thick, but the rock chamber below that was another ten feet deep.

Eli walked in and smiled at Gina without saying a word. The furniture in this structure had also been turned to junk. As they exited to the boat ramp, it was through doors covered by plywood, since the original glass was missing. Most likely, it had been blown out during storms. The dock was down a series of concrete stairs leading to a concrete docking platform where automobile tires were attached to the walls with rusty steel cables. The dock was designed to accommodate large boats at different tide levels. It was actually a large chute between two long rock outcropping. The outside points on the rocks had warning lights, but everyone felt sure they hadn't worked in years. Since new nylon ropes were tied to cleats along the dock, it was apparent boats had been docking there recently.

"That coastal patrol boat could fit in here, don't you think, Josh?" Eli asked. Before he could answer, Pete spoke up. "All kinds of government boats tie up here. In that shed at the end of the dock, they store diesel and gasoline." He pointed to a green metal building that had a flammable skull and cross bones sign painted in red on the door. "It's a Cuban Navy filling station. Those guys are not nice. They stop drug smugglers all the time, steal their cargo, steal their boats and money, execute the crew members, and push them overboard. Occasionally a body will wash ashore. The navy ties a rope on it and pull it out where the sharks can feed on it. The Cuban patrol boat crews are nothing but independent pirates."

"Yuck!" Kelsi said.

"The drug business is fraught with difficulties, so I hear," Josh said laughing.

Standing on the dock, Eli looked up at the structure that fit so perfectly onto a solid ocean rock face. It was a beautifully designed seaside dwelling, much like the design Frank Lloyd Wright created at Falling Rock. The huge two-foot thick concrete floor extended from the rear of the structure at least ten feet and served as a shelter from the elements. Eli wondered if Frank Lloyd Wright had designed it or could have had one of his students do it.

The house was built in the forties by a Havana firm after the war. The boathouse was constructed in the early fifties with the main purpose of concealing a vault or hidden room in solid rock. Only once had any hint of the architect been mentioned. Bernie had written in a note to Carmine that he had decided to go with a young, talented but unknown architect from Arkansas who had studied under Frank Lloyd Wright in Arizona. He paid the architect a bonus for destroying his copies of the plan but then became concerned when the gifted young man emerged as a celebrated architect a few years later. The drawing, however, never surfaced again.

The group walked the grounds and looked over the airstrip, or former airstrip since now it had small trees growing out of the gravel. The complete estate needed so much work to keep it from reaching the point of no return. It was almost there.

Electricity had been tied into the Colony Hotel line before Bernie had to escape. It was not functioning now because the breaker box was locked. Fans or air conditioners were a must in the stifling heat before anyone could stay in the house, yet another item that would cost a renovator a lot of money.

They had seen enough. Everyone loaded in the Jeep and headed for the hotel. Mostly everyone was quiet. Eli asked Mary and Pete if they could have lunch with the entire group so they could discuss repairs. They agreed. On the way to the hotel, the patrol boat moved in closer to shore. They could see the navy officers looking at them through binoculars. A chilling and evil feeling came over the group every time they saw the patrol boat.

During lunch, Pete and Mary took notes regarding repairs that needed to be made to stop further damage to the house from the elements. Eli gave them 500 CUCs to begin repairs to the tile roof and some windows. Gina gave them money for their labor. There was a huge risk that their efforts would never be enjoyed by the Spadas or the Swartzes, but they had to stop the bleeding or there wouldn't be a house left. They exchanged personal information, and Pete and Mary drove away in the Jeep.

Eli and Josh went by the front desk and asked for a late checkout so they could go snorkeling. Given a 3 p.m. checkout, they rented a Zodiac and collected masks, snorkels, and fins. Hector and Rick sat at different tables and watched the Americans' little adventure very closely. The rubber boat started on the first pull of the starter handle, and they pointed it toward a coral head a few hundred yards away. Josh leaned over and stuck his head and mask in the water.

"Wow! It looks great down there."

All were decent free divers and would meet up at the base of the coral heads and poke around looking for lobsters and eels. They were having a good time and failed to notice the patrol boat moving in near their position. The group all dove down at once to see a moray eel in a small cave opening as the creature opened and closed his toothy mouth. When they returned to the surface the naval patrol boat was anchored next to the little Zodiac. A man with an automatic rifle was motioning them to climb aboard. Gina could feel the warm pee in her swimsuit.

Chapter Sixteen

A Navy Gone Astray

A ladder was swung over the side of the navy vessel which appeared to be about 75 feet long armed with twin deck-mounted .50 caliber machine guns. Its complement of deck guns included one 30 millimeter cannon as did most patrol boats, but this gun was covered with a tarp and didn't appear to be functional. The Americans saw missile attachments and launching platforms but no missiles were visible. This was an old boat made in Russia. At one time it was a Komar-class attack boat, but now, much like the old American cars, it was a pieced-together relic of the Cold War. For all practical purposes, it was a Cuban pirate ship.

The girls were separated from Eli and Pete and man-handled by the crew. The looks in the eyes of the crew combined with their jeering smiles transmitted their intent. The girls screamed as they were being dragged to an inside cabin.

"Stop! Stop! You can't do that! We're Americans here on vacation. We know people in your military!" Josh yelled in Spanish.

Curiously, the men stopped where they stood with the girls. "I am Captain Ivan Polzin. I wonder why you think I care if you know military in Cuba." He spoke English but left out words occasionally.

"You may have been operating outside the laws of Cuba. If your command knew about it, you would be finished."

"You shithead American fucker! Who you going to tell? In few minutes, you will be dead, and your ladies will be too. After we fuck their brains out, of course," Ivan said menacingly.

The two men holding Gina and Kelsi began to rip off their bikinis. They spoke to their captain in Spanish and asked if he wanted the pussy first. The girls screamed and the men slapped them across their faces. Gina and Kelsi had blood running out the edges of their mouths.

"You see, my men are most generous. Tell me again about your friends in the Cuban military."

Josh blurted out Julio and Luis's names in a hopeless intent to bluff these renegade sailors.

The entire crew went quiet. The pistol that Ivan pointed at Josh and Eli moved down to his side. The two men holding the girls released their grip and immediately the two nude ladies grabbed their torn swimsuits and ran to Eli and Josh. They struggled to find enough material to tie together something resembling a swimsuit.

The Americans looked shocked. Just who were their new friends in Havana?

"Both of these men have been given the 'Hero of the Republic of Cuba' medals. Only a handful of Cubans have ever received it," the captain said. "They are finest MIG pilots in the world—better than all the Russian pilots. How would you know such people?"

"We assisted them in teaching a class at the University in Havana," Eli said.

"So you not good friends? They would not know you dead for quite a while, no?"

"Let's put it this way, Captain Ivan: once they find we are dead at your hands, your reign as The Pirate of the Caribbean will end," Eli said.

Captain Polzin laughed it off and decided he just didn't care and began to raise his pistol.

He brought the pistol up until it was aimed at Eli's heart, while two sailors trained automatic weapons at all the captives.

A shot from outside the boat dropped Ivan to the deck where he lay motionless. Two more shots caught the two sailors in their foreheads. Over the side of the boat, the Americans spotted Hector in a Zodiac. Josh and Eli helped him aboard. Another deckhand rushed out of the main cabins shooting wildly with an AK-47. Hector was hit but returned fire, killing the shooter. Another sailor came around the bulkhead and opened up on Hector. A shot from the Secret Police's 9mm hit him directly in the chest and penetrated his heart.

At the stern of the ship two more sailors had heard the commotion and ran to assist. They started firing wildly before they could pick out targets. One yelled for everyone to surrender, and waved the gun erratically as he fired mainly in the air. For some reason, he briefly looked towards shore and the hotel with people playing in the sand. There were three thuds, two in his chest and one next to his nose, generating a small pink mist behind him. The sound of that shot was heard a microsecond later.

The second man and the last of the sailors started firing towards the direction of the shooter from the shore. Bullets ripped through the wood on the stock of his AK47, throwing splinters into his face and temporarily blinding him. A microsecond later a thud was heard as a round drilled into his heart. All the rogue sailors were now dead.

They would later learn that the shot had come from Rick's rifle as he lay prone on top of the dive shack. Hector was mortally wounded but managed to tell Josh he had been investigating the patrol boat for a year, waiting to take them down. A file on the entire crew was in his room to be given to his superior officer. Josh told him he would make sure the officer got it. Hector died before they could get him to shore.

The dive master and his assistant made sure the patrol boat was secured to a buoy. The bodies were left in place for the investigation. A team of investigators from the SDE, the Cuban Secret Police, had been contacted by the hotel manager and would be on site in a few hours.

Rick met the Americans as they motored in on the Zodiac. "Get packed and head out of here. If they need to interview you, they can do it on your cruise ship," Rick said.

They did as they were told and thanked Rick for saving their lives.

"Hector was the hero here," Rick said. "Granted, he was an asshole, but he saved you from that Russian captain who should have been stopped many years ago. You kids get back on your boat and lay low a while. You said something that made them hesitate from shooting you. What was it?"

"We told him about our military contacts in Havana," Eli said.

"Who?" Rick asked.

Eli said, "Two military pilots named Julio and Luis. They teach at Havana University."

"They are probably the best-liked individuals in all of Cuba. You couldn't have made up better friends."

"They aren't made up, Rick. We helped them at a class in Havana. Met them on our ship," Eli said but wasn't sure that Rick believed him.

Pete and Mary were at Wendy's place when the four travelers stopped to see them before they left the island. They told the story of being on the ship and the shootout to a shocked audience. "Maybe now the house could get fixed up without the patrol boat messing the house up with their whores," Pete said.

"We'll try harder to find a way to buy the house or rent it since there is a good chance no one will be using it. We still need a Cuban to inquire about buying it, so we can at least rent it from the new owners. We'll work on it. Meanwhile, I'll continue to send money for repairs to you, Pete. You can email me pictures from your phone at the internet office in town," Rick said.

They told Wendy goodbye and pressed a hundred CUCs in her hand. She tried to hand it back but no one would let her.

They were early for their flight and tried to settle down, read books, and play solitaire on their iPads and iPhones. Gina hugged Eli often and Kelsi clung to Josh. The sickening feeling of almost getting raped and executed was something they had never experienced before and didn't want to ever happen again. While they were waiting, Rick Morales arrived in his car. After picking up what they assumed to be his ticket, he walked over to the Americans.

"You probably won't see me again. I will be off to another assignment somewhere, maybe South America, Central America, or hopefully Tahiti."

"Say hi to my dad if you're in South America. I think he works at an embassy somewhere down there," Josh said.

"I'll be on the lookout for him. Look, boys, if you are questioned on the boat, you don't know where those shots came from that took out those chaps about to blast holes in you. Could have come from anywhere. Hotel security, I'd say. If they ask, you met me and I am a writer. Believe it or not, I'm really writing a book about a love story that took place on the Isle of Pines back in the 40s and 50s. 'Passion under the Cuban Pines' I believe I'll call it. Publisher has approved it but needs editing and some rewrites. Look for it in a year or so."

"Thanks again for your help. I hope we didn't screw up your assignment at the Colony Hotel," Eli said.

He tipped a newly-acquired straw hat in their direction and walked over to a quiet part of the terminal. Even though he was supposed to be on the same flight as the group, they never saw him or spoke to him again. They believed a special plane may have landed for his benefit.

Eli looked at Gina and kissed her lightly on her lips. She was at the window, and he had an aisle seat. Across from him sat a well-dressed Cuban man with a briefcase at his feet. Eli said hello to him and the man politely replied.

"Did you have a good time on your visit to the Isle of Youth?" the man asked.

"We were at the Colony Hotel and were treated well by the staff. It's on a beautiful beach, and the water was crystal clear. We may go back and try the diving next time," Eli said reaching for all the positive things he could say.

"I love to hear that. I'm afraid our government has ignored the island in recent years. We have our work to do there. Please come back when you get a chance." He handed Eli a card with his name, and under it was printed, "Government de Cuba, Tourism, Land, and Investment Property Representative."

"Uhh—I know as an American I can't yet buy property in your country, but in the future would it be possible to go in with other Cubans to—say open a bed and breakfast on the island somewhere?" Eli asked.

"In time, my friend. Today we are talking with an American and a Cuban who want to open a tractor company in Cuba. We will own 51 percent of course, but that doesn't mean we will take that percentage of the profit. Keep my card and call me or email me when you have ideas. It will take a long time, and although Cuba will make you jump through hoops of fire—stick with your idea. Things will change. We have watched China and Russia and want to avoid some of their mistakes, such as the criminal element that flourished during their transformation to a capitalist country."

Eli thanked him and turned and smiled at Gina. She looked

changed. At times she had a far-off stare. They had faced death. Two spies from two different counties joined together to save their lives. No one would believe their story, even if they were allowed to tell it.

As their flight touched down in Havana, two men were waiting for them. It was Luis and Julio, and they didn't look happy.

Chapter Seventeen

With Cuban Friends

None of the Americans said anything as Luis and Julio ushered them into a small room near the security office at the airport. There was a table with an ashtray that looked as though it hadn't been emptied since the airport first opened. The four were seated across the table from the two Cubans, whom they now admired more than ever because of the revelations of the Russian Captain Ivan and Rick Morales. For a minute no one said anything, and the Americans weren't going to speak first.

"First, Luis and I are pleased that our new friends from America are still alive," Julio said. "It appears you came close to being shot on the patrol boat. Hector Zappa performed a heroic act saving you on the boat and gave his life in the effort. We in Cuba had known about Ivan Polzin and his pirate crew for a long time. We had been asked to fly cover for the planned operation to take him down. We had no idea you were going to the Isle of Youth. If we had, we would have specifically warned you about this man and his patrol boat. He was running drugs with other dealers, including ones that were smuggling drugs to Florida. The US DEA had a bead on him and were waiting for the next time he entered their waters. Why didn't you tell us you were going over there?"

Eli spoke first. "Probably because it would have opened up a line of questioning from our new-found Cuban friends that may not have been comfortable for us. Gina and I had great-grandparents that owned property in Cuba—casinos, whorehouses, and real estate that was quite valuable at the time. The most intriguing of all the assets is a beach house on the Isle of Youth. Supposedly they hid money there, but

I understand Cuban officials used radar and metal detectors over every inch of the grounds and found nothing, so maybe it was just a rumor. Or maybe somebody else has already recovered it. We had to see the place to know if it was still standing. It was the topic of conversation between our two families for 57 years. They shared movies, snapshots, and tall tales all of those years. So it was an obsession—still is. We stopped by when we first got to the area of the Colony Hotel, but it was late so we looked with flashlights. The lights must have alerted the patrol boat, and they opened up on us with machine guns. Scared the shit out of us, and had it not been for the rock wall, we probably wouldn't be here talking to you. The next day we went snorkeling and were kidnapped by that asshole and his crew of misfits. I think you know the rest," Eli said.

"Do you know why they contacted us?"

"As they were about to shoot us, we said we knew people in the military. We were just buying time before we died. Everything came to a standstill when they heard your names. They couldn't believe we knew you because you were famous. Hero of the Republic of Cuba Medal and all. Then we told him we went to your class and assisted. He wasn't too impressed and again positioned his weapon to shoot us when Hector showed up. Knowing you guys actually saved our lives," Josh said.

"We shared this with the hotel manager who contacted your people about the shooting," Eli said. "Sorry you had to get involved."

"Someone other than Hector helped you. The hotel manager said shots were fired from shore to take out the last of Ivan's men. What do you know about this?" Luis asked.

"Yes, it's true someone else took out a couple of crew members who were about to shoot us with automatic weapons. We don't know who did it, though. Maybe the hotel manager knows, but someone took out these killers from a long range," said Josh. He was the best liar in the group, thanks to his ongoing training as a lawyer.

"My government says there was an American agent at the hotel?"

"I think Rick Morales was the only American besides us who was there, and he's a writer. He had some books published and one in the works," Eli said. "Because he was living in the hotel, the manager may have assumed he was some sort of secret agent. I don't think so."

"Well, he's gone now. Private plane picked him up on the Isle of Youth."

"Really? He was at the airport the same time we were, and we expected him to be on our flight," Eli said.

"We're going to give you a ride to your cruise ship. Government agents will interview you on the boat when you get to your next stop. Just tell them what you told us." The two Cubans got up from the table and pointed to the door. Gina picked up the ashtray and dumped it in a nearby wastebasket. Luis looked at her like she was crazy. "It was making me sick," she said. He laughed at the absurdity of it all.

"Julio, even though we fucked up, we really had a good time in your class. We're sorry to have dragged you into this mess. Knowing you saved our lives, though, that's a good thing—huh?" Gina said.

"We're still friends. We don't want our friends killed in Cuba. Can you imagine the bad press we would have gotten all over the world if Ivan had killed you?" Luis said.

Gina slapped Luis on the shoulder. "All we mean to you two is 'bad press'?"

He laughed and stuttered, "Well, no, but—."

"Don't worry. We won't tell the US government about this unless they lock us in a room and beat us," Eli said.

"Waterboard me, and I'll tell everything I know," Kelsi said.

The Cubans laughed and couldn't believe the Americans' good spirits after what had happened. "Please don't hold a bad image of Cuba when you go back to the US. It's so rare that something like this happens. We'll look forward to your emails and someday Facebook. We are not allowed that yet," Luis said.

"Luis and Julio, I want to purchase, rent, lease, or jointly own in partnership with someone in Cuba our old property on the Isle of Pines—uh, Isle of Youth. Look forward to us asking you to help us with that in the future. The only people using it in the past few years were Ivan and his bandits. So there should be little activity. We're paying a little to have it maintained," Eli said.

"Don't know how much we can help you with it, but we can put you in touch with those who can," Julio said.

"Is this guy legitimate?" Eli asked and handed Julio the card from the Cuban official.

"We don't know him personally, but his office is real. We'll check him out for you," Luis said as they pulled up to the cruise terminal.

"Enjoy the rest of your cruise…and please stay out of trouble," Julio said.

The girls hugged them and kissed their cheeks. Eli and Josh shook their hands.

The ship personnel welcomed them back aboard. "Did you guys have fun today?"

"You just have no idea," Gina said with a smile.

They hadn't had dinner, so they rushed to their cabins and changed for the evening meal. It was late, but they did get seated. They ordered drinks and looked around at the nicely decorated tables and well-dressed passengers. Only a few hours before, grubby crew members were stripping the clothes from Gina and Kelsi and they feared they were about to die an awful death from gunshots. Eli proposed a toast once their drinks were delivered.

"Here is to spies—ours and theirs."

"I never met a spy before," Kelsi said.

"I've met my dad. He always says to quit calling him a spy. He says he is just an analyst. And, you know what, that's probably what he is. I can't picture him being this Jason Bourne dude. No way would he fight someone or even shoot them. When I press him, then I get this explanation that he's an Analytic Methodologist. What the fuck is that?" Josh said.

"Stone-fucking killer!" Eli said. "It's always those quiet family guys—your dad's an awesome dude!"

"Right—you've never met him. He's more likely to be starring in Revenge of the Nerds Five," Josh said.

"Was there a Four?" Kelsi asked. No one knew the answer.

"So where will we go after Havana?" Gina asked.

"It's beach day at Maria la Gordo. If you want, we can book a snorkeling trip for 50 CUCs." Kelsi said. She always knew the schedule and all the options for shore excursions.

A chorus of "Fuck no" and "Are you shitting me?" went quickly around the table.

Everyone would go to the beach, have the beach barbecue, drink some beer, and chill out. It was needed. Gina and Kelsi wanted to shop for new bathing suits after dinner. Kelsi suggested they find one with a built in pistol. They all decided to attend a show in the big theater to get their minds off things. After dinner, Josh and Eli found a bar close to the stage show area while the girls tried to replace a bad memory by shopping.

The two had started on their second drink when a ship's officer walked up to them at the bar.

"Are you Eli Swartz and Josh Vargas?"

"Yes. Who wants to know?"

"The captain would like to see you in his cabin. If you will please follow me."

Josh and Eli knew it had something to do with the patrol boat incident. How many people were going to question them?

The ship's officer walked them past the bridge to a cabin directly behind it. He knocked on the door to summon the captain, who introduced himself as Stavros Katsaros and said he was from Greece.

"I'll make this short. I understand you were on the Isle of Youth today and were taken aboard a Cuban patrol boat and threatened at gunpoint. A Cuban agent came to your rescue and lost his life in the process. Someone from shore killed the last two crew members while the Cuban agent lay dying. They were going to rape the girls, shoot you, and then kill the girls later. Is that about it?"

"Yes, sir," the men said in unison.

"Tomorrow, men from the Cuban Secret Service, Cuban Navy, and Military will question you."

"Sir, may we request that someone from our American Embassy be there to represent our interests?" Josh asked. He knew the new embassy was staffed for cases like this.

"Certainly. They have been notified. You have done nothing wrong except taken a trip that wasn't part of the People to People program you signed up for. Cuba doesn't care and the ship doesn't care. We put together programs that will satisfy The US government's restrictions on travel. You may have stepped out of that protective environment. I would guess that Cuba isn't too happy one of their agents was killed. They'll never acknowledge he was an agent, and I doubt you will ever acknowledge that Rick Morales was CIA."

"Where will the meeting take place?" Eli asked.

"We have a large meeting table next to my cabin. You will be allowed to go ashore after the meeting. The ladies need to be present as well. The meeting will take place at 10:15 a.m. One of my ship's officers will come to your cabin to escort you. Thank you for your cooperation." He stood up and opened the door for them.

Both went back to the bar where they were to meet the girls. They were already there.

"Where did you guys go?"

"Special tour of the captain's cabin. Meeting 10:15 a.m. Be there or be square."

"Holy shit. Here we go again. Are we in trouble?"

"Maybe from the US, unless we can say our trip to the Isle of Youth was People to People-certified," Josh said. "We could say we were doing an article about the hotel there, maybe researching for a book we're writing. Does anyone in our group do any writing?"

"I do." The entire group turned and looked at Gina.

"You never told me you were a writer," said Eli.

"Uhh—you had your mind on other things. So you never asked."

"Care to tell us what you are writing?" Eli asked.

"*The History of the Spada Family*. It's on my laptop, so I can bring it to the meeting if you like."

"We like!" Josh said.

"Why don't we take in the show and get this shit off our minds?" Kelsi said.

They all agreed and found great seats not far from the stage. It was a show of Cuban dance performed by Russian dancers. Earlier that day, they had seen a Cuban patrol boat performed by a Russian captain. How ironic.

Chapter Eighteen

A Cruise Inquisition

They ate breakfast the next day with the attitude of "what can they do to us?" They had a right to be on the Isle of Youth, except they weren't with the package tour. They had checked the education purposes box under "the self-declaration of the twelve reasons to be in Cuba." Gina had checked two boxes. She had also checked research and made a note about family history. She didn't tell anyone because it didn't seem to matter. The ship had that record and would probably give it to the investigators. They hoped the information about the research found its way to the Cuban and American authorities.

They had gone through the omelet line again, which seemed shorter as most people were rushing to catch the tender that took them to the beach.

"Take your time, folks. We don't have to be there for another hour," Eli said.

"When we do go in there, does anyone have an objection if I represent the group? I am pretty good in a courtroom," Josh said.

"I don't mind if you do, Josh, but will this be like a trial?" Eli asked.

"I'm going to say more like a deposition. Less fun than a trial, because it'll appear that no one's on your side. We'll need to try to take charge and throw them off their line of questioning," Josh said.

"Having been the only one who has seen you in action in trial mode, I can speak to your skills. I can also speak to your skill at being an asshole and pissing off everyone in the courtroom. You win—you always win, but you leave a trail of carnage behind you. So I suggest you tone it down here," Kelsi said.

"I appreciate your concerns, dear, but a deposition doesn't really lend itself to needing my asshole skills."

"Josh, you've always been nice to me," Gina said.

"Of course, and I always will be, unless I find you are opposing counsel."

While everyone else played with their iPhones, iPads, and Kindles, Josh reviewed the rules and regulations for traveling to Cuba and the penalties for not following them from every source he could find. He then got up and walked to an empty section of the sundeck and faced the water. He began talking to the water. A few people noticed and looked amused. Kelsi explained that trial lawyers are like actors. They rehearse not only what they want to say, but how they want to say it.

"I was opposing counsel on a murder case where we had the man holding the weapon that killed a man a few feet from his truck; he confessed, and it was slam shut—air tight. Josh came in and had the entire case thrown out on several technicalities. I had worked so hard on the case—never got to present it. He's amazing," Kelsi said.

"Well, hell, this might be fun!" Eli said.

"Hope he doesn't piss off everyone, and we get thrown overboard!" Gina said.

It was finally time for them to face the tribunal. They marched into the conference room and found eight individuals waiting on them. They looked like high school principals who were trying to find out who flushed a cherry bomb down the boys' toilet.

They introduced themselves with long titles like "Deputy Secretary of Tourist Affairs," and other strange positions in the military and government. The three from the US embassy looked the unhappiest of them all. Two of the eight were translators, and they looked both puzzled and frightened.

Josh introduced his friends. As soon as he did, he looked over the group and spoke to them without smiling.

"Why are we here?"

He quickly found out who professed to be their leader.

"Young man, we are here to investigate the shooting that occurred on our Cuban Patrol Boat yesterday on the Isle of Youth," said a Cuban military official with several medals pinned to his chest. He spoke decent English, but it wasn't his first language.

"I'm sorry. Don't you mean we need to address the kidnapping of four American visitors and the threatening of their lives by a Cuban Naval vessel? Also, don't you mean to address the attempted rape and sexual assault of these two American women? I hope that is what we are here for. If not, you are wasting our valuable time."

Shock was the common expression on every face. Next to speak was some assistant diplomatic aide from the newly reinstalled US Embassy.

"Josh, you need to . . ." He was cut off immediately.

"You may address me as Mr. Vargas. I am not your friend, and we are not on a first name basis and probably won't get there today. Again, I demand to know what this meeting is about."

"Mr. Vargas, this meeting is to discuss the events that occurred yesterday, to determine for our records a proper and detailed account." Now the leader of the pack had emerged and most likely their legal counsel. Josh now knew the throat to cut.

"What is your name and position with this group?" Josh asked.

"I am Homer Vasquez, Cuban Adjutant General's office. My job is to look for breaches in military law," Homer said.

"Mr. Vasquez, care to explain to me why a military attorney needs to pass judgment on the actions of this group of civilians?"

"It is not to pass judgment on this group but to find what would provoke a 20-year naval officer to be suspected of unusual activity aboard his vessel."

"It is my understanding that your agent Hector Zappa had a lengthy file compiled for quite some time on Mr. Ivan Polzin. I also realize you are not able to discuss the file or whether Hector Zappa was an agent for Cuba. It will suffice to say that by whatever means you uncovered your information, you knew about Mr. Polzin's drug smuggling, his murders, and other crimes not sanctioned by the Cuban Navy."

"I'm not at liberty to discuss any of those items."

"Then are we done here?"

"No! We are not done. George Montgomery from the US embassy," a second man introduced himself. "Mr. Vargas, you and your group had no permission to be on the Isle of Youth. You had specific instructions to stay with your People to People group, and you disobeyed explicit instructions and violated the Cuban Assets Control Regulations and may be subject to a fine for your actions."

Now here was another throat to cut. Probably legal counsel from the state department out to make brownie points with the Cubans.

"Let's see, Mr. Montgomery, if I have this straight. You are representing me as that little spot of land in Cuba which is American soil. A place where I can come for help if I get in trouble in Cuba. It appears that you are trying to impress your new Cuban friends, but you do not impress me. The sanctity of the CACR has not been breached and you should know it. We filled out the required form and self-declared the reasons for our visit; we attended the lectures, and tours required under the People to People program. One member of our group, however, chose to do research for a book she is writing on Carmine Spada and his partner Bernie Swartz. Here is her manuscript on her computer. If you look closely, she is 33,435 words in on the book." Josh slid the Toshiba laptop over to Mr. Montgomery so he could see the word count at the lower left part of the screen. It also noted her being on page 135.

"She wanted to visit relatives of the caretakers of the Spada family and visit the home place on the island. It wasn't something we were going to let her do alone. We were there for her safety. We were fortunate to visit Wendy Artigas who knew both Eli's and Gina's great-grandparents and grandparents. The current caretakers, Mary and Pete Artigas, also knew some of the family events that took place. This visit complied with CACR for both People to People and for the section that allows for research for literary interest. Also, as you are aware, there are no restrictions on trips to the Isle of Pines. The Colony Hotel is a haven for scuba divers all over the world. I am sure that our Embassy does not want to put a bad name on one of the few successful businesses on that island."

"Mr. Vargas, after you were taken on board the naval vessel, and there was a weapon aimed at you, Mr. Zappa felt there was a risk of you being harmed and came to your aid. After he was mortally wounded, more of the crew emerged and began firing their weapons; then, shots from shore struck them and they were killed. Please tell me what you know about the person who fired those shots," Montgomery asked.

"I don't know and neither do my friends."

"What do you know about Mr. Rick Morales?"

"He was an American writer."

"Is that all you know?"

"Yes, and I am asking that this meeting be concluded as we have a beach to lie on. If there is nothing else, we would like to go," Josh said and stood up.

The Cuban lawyer began to speak to the others around him in Spanish and assumed Josh didn't know the language.

"We will get nowhere with this asshole. Let him fuck up, and we'll jail his American ass."

"This asshole hasn't fucked up yet, so keep your fucking jail for somebody that deserves your company," Josh said in rapid Spanish.

The man looked shocked and ducked his head and left. As others stood up to leave the conference room, Josh pulled George Montgomery aside.

"Mr. Montgomery, your Embassy has several purposes. None of them includes harassing American citizens with violations of laws you don't understand. My father works for the state department and my complaint on your actions will be made through him. I suggest you look for other employment before the United States requires you to seek it. Have a nice day."

The group went to their cabins and changed into swimsuits, gathered their towels, and caught the next tender going to the beach. The group of investigators must have taken an earlier ride because none of the group ever saw them again. As they walked to the end of the long pier they came upon a covered bar with a few items for sale. To the left of the bar was a stand for internet cards. The cost was two CUCs for one hour on the internet. Josh bought one and walked to the internet center at the end of the cabanas on the beach. He wrote the formal complaint in his head on the way. Once he was there, he got online and finished the composition that was about to end the career of a very bad attorney. Josh sent the information to his dad's email address with an explanation. The thing that upset Josh the most was that Montgomery practically asked Josh to give up Rick Morales, his own CIA agent. This was unforgivable.

Now he would have a beer or two with his friends.

Chapter Nineteen

New Plans

Their time on the beach was relaxing, the food was good, and the beer was cheap. They all went back to ship to rest a while before dinner. Gina and Eli took a shower together, then made love. Most of the positions had been tried, repeated, and modified. Gina liked being on top as that was her first position with Eli. Eli liked being on top with Gina's legs under him. They liked all the positions but found themselves going to their favorites quickly and often. Gina's birth control pills were fully active so they were now enjoying the freedom of unprotected sex and the natural sensations were wonderful. The entire love making pushed the events of the past day way back in their minds. They lay next to each other and traced the outline of each other's faces with their fingers. Eventually, one would gently bite a finger and the other would say, "Oh, I wish I had washed that finger." It was the quiet, gentle time after passionate love making. It wouldn't last long since other thoughts about the future crept up.

"Sweetheart, I know this isn't a great time to bring it up, but what are we going to do about school this next semester?" Eli said.

"I don't think I can be away from you very long. If I transfer to a school in California, the out of state tuition will be outrageous. If you go to a school in Florida, they may not have a college that is a peer to Cal Poly," Gina said.

"How about your mother, and how about my mother? Both of them have their only child living in their state. Just a few hours away from each of us. Will they freak if we change schools?" said Eli.

"Probably, but there's the bonus of running naked through the house with their boyfriends," Gina said.

"You have a valid point."

"With the money, we received from the inheritance, we could take turns flying out to visit. If we did that, would we feel comfortable sleeping with each other at our own houses?" Gina asked.

"Your house seems to be fine. Your mother is cool with it. I need to spend some time with my mother to get us cleared for intimate contact. I have had girls overnight there before, but I didn't sleep with them at my house," Eli said.

"Okay. If we were together once a month for a weekend, then we could split holidays between the two families and take turns with them during spring break and summers. It won't be too horrible. If you don't have labs on Saturday, and if we were to arrange our classes where we have Fridays off, it will give us more time to be together. We might be able to fly out on a Thursday night. Have you already set your classes for the fall semester?" Gina asked.

"I know what classes I need but haven't set them yet. I'll be a senior this year, so I have first choice of classes. I may do graduate school someplace else. Even though most people don't know it, Cal Poly isn't ranked very high in the engineering world. Stanford, Berkeley, and MIT are top dogs, and I hope to get a full ride at one of them next year," Eli said.

"Is it settled? We will stay at our schools and meet up once a month until next summer when we will spend every day and night together," Gina said.

"Yes, unless we're miserable; then we fly every weekend," Eli said.

Later, Gina and Eli met Josh and Kelsi for dinner. Tomorrow they would visit Cienfuegos, Cuba, and the next day they would be back in Jamaica to catch a flight back to Miami. At dinner, they decided on research assignments.

"Josh, you and Kelsi are our legal team and life-long friends now, we hope. Could you two find out what hoops we need to jump through to jointly own Cuban real estate? Gina and I will concentrate on the beach house, and if they are willing to sell it to anyone. If someone from Cuba bought it, maybe it could be rented back to us on a lease purchase basis until these regulations are relaxed," Eli said.

"Be glad to help, but law school doesn't leave much free time. Most of my downtime is consumed by Kelsi's enormous sexual appetite."

"I feel your pain, Josh. I'm thinking about renting a bottle of oxygen so I can make it through the night with Gina."

"Both of you guys are full of shit," Kelsi said.

"So, are both of you game for another shot at recovering the money next summer? All expenses paid and a large bonus if we get it back into the US," Eli said.

"What's our share of this elusive pile of dough?" Josh asked.

Gina looked at Eli. This wasn't anything they had discussed at length. They got up from their unfinished omelets and walked to the rail and faced the ocean.

"I want to declare this money as an inheritance split between us, and I want it reported as foreign income where taxes were paid. Carmine and Bernie included all those tax returns, so I feel we would only have to pay the difference between foreign tax and the prevailing US tax at the time. If they had hidden it on US soil, then there would be accumulated penalties, but the money was left on foreign soil. I'm not sure of any of this crap. We'll pay a tax attorney to sort that out before we move it home. But back to Josh and Kelsi. What do you think? A million to split between them?"

"Eli, what if we only clear a million after taxes? Is that a possibility? If it is, then maybe we should use a percentage and a minimum amount. Remember, they almost got killed on the last trip."

"Okay, how's this, Gina? One million or five percent of the total, whichever is less. In no case would it be less than a hundred thousand each if the value of the entire amount is reduced by taxes or penalties. As a bonus, you will divide ten percent of the gold coins found at the site that do not have a numismatic value above fifty percent of the face value. Since you're basically a pre-law student, we'll let you draft this document and present it to us for approval," Eli said.

"Holy shit, are you an engineering student or another damn attorney?"

"I took a course in engineering patents for inventions," Eli said. "You do realize law school might be in your future?"

"I'll be a nice lawyer—the very first one," Gina said.

"Ha! Let's present this to the two almost-lawyers at the table."

Eli went over the details and they approved. The first thing they said was, "What gold?" almost in unison. Eli explained that Bernie was a collector. His collection wouldn't be a part of the ten percent, but all other gold coins would be. Eli said that if there were as many as they thought, then weight would be a problem.

"Wow! Wow! This time next year, Kelsi and I could be millionaires! What a way to start off our law careers! We'll be able to buy a huge shingle to hang up. Of course, our first visit to the Isle of Death was a tad dangerous, and I can guess when we actually pull out the money how many people will be gunning for us. My guess is—we'll earn our money."

The next day a tour bus took them around the city of Cienfuegos. Every time they stepped off the bus, they noticed two men in suits about 100 yards from them. They just stood there staring at them. As the group explored the La Union Hotel and came out on another street, they were there watching from a distance. How they got themselves in place so quickly was amazing, but the Americans ignored them. The next day the two mystery men observed from a distance as the group left the ship in Jamaica. They stayed with the group until they boarded a flight back to the states. However, at one point Josh pretended to go to the restroom and circled behind the two men, tapped one of them on the shoulder, then took a picture of them close up. He then ran to where everyone was boarding the flight. He would send those pictures to his dad to see if they were known spies. Later, the picture would be sent to Julio and Luis to see if they knew why they were assigned to the Americans.

As soon as they landed in Miami, they split up and planned for a dinner out later in the week. Cherie was there to pick up Gina and Eli.

"Mother, did you get to run naked in the house with your boyfriend?" Gina asked.

"Of course. We made love on the dining room table too," Cherie said without cracking a smile.

"Ugh—I'll never eat in there again," Gina said.

"I guess you're now bored with 'fooling around' after the cruise. Did you guys have a good time?" Cherie asked.

"Mrs. Spada, it was an adventure. Hopefully, we will go back next summer and recover the assets which we hope are still there. About the 'fooling around,' I'm bored with it, but your daughter has this unearthly insatiable desire that I'm not sure I will be able to keep up with."

"I trust you will try. Gina, dear, please work with him so he doesn't leave you for one of those girls that just lies there during sex." An older lady standing next to them at the baggage carousel overheard the conversation, frowned, and stepped out of earshot. Cherie looked at Eli and Gina and laughed. Eli thought Gina's mother was the coolest person on earth.

"Mother, I am going to California in a few days to visit Eli's mom. Do you want to go with us?" Gina said.

"No, you should go first. I'll go out and visit Hanna later. Your dad's funeral was the last time I visited with her. I did call her this week and described in detail how intimate her son had been with my daughter. It's been a few years since I've seen her. But, I'll tell you one thing, she is drop-dead gorgeous," Cherie said.

"Thank you Cherie, but so are you. Well, I'll say this, the Swartzes and the Spadas knew how to pick their women, and I trust you were kidding about telling on me to my mom," Eli said.

"Of course, Eli. I didn't say that, but I told her the relationship looked pretty intense. She also knows you two shared a cabin for a week. I'm sure she has figured it out, but you can be the one to go into the intimate details with her."

"Never! She can just use her imagination," Eli said.

"I wonder if that statement about the Swartzes picking their women passes the test of time," Gina said as they loaded the luggage into Cherie's Escalade.

"No doubt in my mind," Eli said.

They decided to go out for dinner at a seafood place, but once they were there Eli ordered a small steak. "I haven't had good beef in a week."

As they were leaving the restaurant, Gina called Josh and Kelsi.

"You guys home?" Gina asked.

"Yes, relaxing and having a glass of wine. Why?"

"We're buzzing by…want you to meet my mom. That okay?"

"Sure, but the place is a mess."

"We're not coming in. Just come out when we honk."

In a few minutes, Cherie pulled up at their student apartment complex and lay gently on the horn. They were outside in seconds, carrying their wine. Everyone stepped out of the car and greeted each other as though they had been apart for months.

"Mom, I want you to meet Josh and Kelsi. Josh, Kelsi, this is my mom, Cherie Spada. You will be seeing a lot of them now as we are just about brothers and sisters after this trip."

Josh and Kelsi greeted Cherie and said they would all go out for dinner in a couple of days. Cherie said it was nice to meet them. Afterward, she headed her SUV towards home.

"Mom, I wanted you to meet them so that you had faces to put with the stories about the trip," Gina said.

"So how are you kids going to see each other when both of you are on the other side of the world?" Cherie asked.

"There'll be no transferring of schools for now. We'll fly out to see each other once a month. Maybe switch out and share Thanksgiving and Christmas with you and Hanna. Maybe you can fly out with us once year and Hanna can fly here. We never want to leave you guys out of anything. Josh will be looking for another engineering school after this year, and we might coordinate schools then. When the baby comes, we want you close by." Gina couldn't help laughing when Cherie nearly wrecked the car.

"Just kidding, Mom. Wanted to see if you were listening. You know, Eli, we haven't discussed that much. Does the subject make you nervous?"

"It would be inconvenient right now, but I want kids and more than one. Gina, you have a number in mind?"

"More than one—two or three. You know a big family might

be fun. Mom couldn't have more kids after me because she had a hysterectomy, and as I remember your dad had some health problems," Gina said. "While we're healthy, let's crank out a bunch of kids."

"Cool! Pick out a target date to start. Either after grad school or when we get the loot."

"You kids have no idea how much I'm enjoying this conversation!" Cherie said.

Chapter Twenty

Back in School

During the months following the two couples' return from Cuba, Gina and Eli continued to build their relationship even though from the day they met, it was as though they were already married. Their attraction to each other had been instantaneous when they first met at the bank and grew from then on. Seldom did they argue except to amuse each other, and if and when they got married, they both agreed absolutely nothing would change. They immediately bonded as though a bucket of super glue was poured over them. The idea of visiting once a month worked well, but a few times it was twice a month. At spring break, Eli asked, "Gina, would you like to go to Cancun?"

"I want a bed, Eli. No alarm clock. No long plane rides. No books. Lots of sex. Lots of lying by the pool. Can you fix that up for me?"

"Palm Springs okay?"

"Book it!"

He did, and it was perfect. She flew into Los Angeles, met Eli, and camped by the pool at the Marriott in Palm Desert for a week. While they were there, they made plans for the summer. They booked direct flights to Havana for June 15 and asked Josh and Kelsi to do the same. They would meet with Julio and Luis on the 16th and hopefully finalize the beach house partnership.

Kelsi and Josh had now lived together for over two years and were best friends first and passionate lovers second. The issue with this couple was the huge divide between Josh's courtroom skills and Kelsi's lack of the same. However, Kelsi was the worker: she would wear a keyboard out researching what Josh needed for a trial, and he would put together his script and acting job. Kelsi's scores on tests in law school usually bettered Josh because of how hard she studied.

"Josh, I would let you do the case study on your upcoming assignment, but you always get bored and start watching porn. And as you know, that leads to other distractions. So I'm going to do it for you," Kelsi said.

"Distractions be much fun."

As a team, they were unstoppable. But this was college, mock trials, and the University of Miami School of Law, not Harvard. Yet, many thought Josh could hold his own with them. Very few trial lawyers come out of law school ready for a heavyweight bout. He was one of the rare litigators. A natural.

The beach house was not forgotten during this time. Josh and Kelsi researched ways to own the property in partnership with Cuban citizens. What would happen with the money and how much tax would be owed on it? After analyzing all of Carmine and Bernie's old tax forms, Kelsi found that Bernie did file for both of them in the US and Cuba. He had to file in America in order to get the foreign tax credit paid in Cuba applied against the US taxes. He did it every year, and he was shrewd about it. First, all of their businesses were incorporated as normal "C" corporations, which enjoyed a 50 percentage tax bracket compared to a 90-plus maximum percentage for individuals.

After all of the write-offs, Bernie rarely paid over 10 to 20 percent tax and kept his and Carmine's salary low enough that the taxes were low there too. It didn't matter that Bernie may have "cooked" the books because rarely did anyone request to look at them. When there was an audit, and it appeared he had three, adjustments were made, and life went on.

"Josh, this guy Bernie was a tax genius. He used all the tricks to show very little taxable income at all their businesses. I would venture to guess the whorehouses were mostly cash and mostly underreported. The expenses at their casino, the Caribe Shores, practically ate up all their profits. How these guys survived three IRS audits beats me. However, in each case the IRS guy came to Havana," Kelsi said.

"Let me guess. Free whores, booze, and maybe a few lucky spins at the roulette wheel," Josh said. "Remember, these guys were low-level mobsters and they knew all the tricks. Once the IRS agent accepted any of these favors—they had his ass forever."

Josh and Kelsi believed the money was clean—even though everybody knew it really wasn't. It wasn't so much that it was clean, but it had been cleansed by virtue of inspections, audits, and tax returns that were accepted. No way to go back and check it now. The IRS would have the same old tax records that Eli and Gina held. And they definitely would receive it as an inheritance. They had the document where Carmine and Bernie had left it to the survivors of the families. Most likely, $5 million apiece could flow into their bank accounts tax-free. The rest was a big question mark on the estate tax issue, and they still didn't tell Kelsi and Josh the full amount. Kelsi had seen all the money they grossed from going over the old returns she worked on. She knew it was a lot of money. All of the information on the vault, combination to the safes, and location markers had never left their safe deposit boxes in Florida. They didn't take any of that information with them while they were in Cuba.

The two lookouts had appeared a couple of times in Florida and once in California. Josh's dad ran their pictures through the CIA files and found nothing. When he ran them through Interpol, he got hits on both. They were low-level thugs working for a firm called "Found Assets Inc." out of Moscow, Russia. The firm had a reputation of stealing treasure away from salvage operations as they awaited approval from the court system of whatever country claimed it was theirs. The Russian firm was hard to pin down to a physical address. Somehow the rumor of a fortune hidden in Cuba had drifted over to Cuba's old buddies. Mr. Vargas said they were armed and dangerous. While treasure ships' discoveries are awaiting approvals, these guys sweep in and remove everything they can in the dark of night, melt it down, and sell it for scrap gold and silver. Fuck a bunch of court decisions concerning the proper ownership of the wreck. If you steal it—it's yours.

Progress had been made on the rental-purchase plan for the property on the Isle of Youth. Because the friendship with Luis and Julio had continued, they agreed to see if they could purchase the property using loans from Gina and Eli. Restrictions between Cuba and the United States had eased somewhat, but it was painfully slow. The government offered the house and land to the two Cuban heroes for $150,000 to be used as a small hotel. During the past several months, Mary and Pete had done a remarkable job fixing all the windows and roofing tiles. They hired someone to pick up all the junk strewn from the back patio to the beach. One of the hardest jobs was restoring the airfield to good order. The trees that popped up had to be cut, and then someone had to grind the stumps below the surface. New gravel was laid, and binding oil was sprayed on it. Eli and Gina wanted a functional airstrip for Luis and Julio to land a small aircraft.

Since they had extra privileges, small planes were available to the military pilots for their private use. In May of 2016, Julio and Luis flew over in a Cessna 172, which had been in their inventory of planes for many years. Once on the airfield, Pete and Mary picked them up in the Jeep and gave them a tour. The house looked much better than when the four Americans were there. Besides the new windows and tile, Pete had painted inside and out. Gina and Eli had been steadily sending money for repairs. The two Cuban visitors loved the place and saw plenty of potential for a small hotel or bed and breakfast. They would make an offer to the government.

"Julio, I think a hundred and fifty thousand is too much because of all the money we, that is Eli and Gina, will have to put in to convert this to a hotel or bed and breakfast. Uhhh--how much cash do you think they have to put in because we got nothing? It's also so damn remote as well." Luis rubbed his temples while he thought about numbers—numbers as they related to money that seemed so unobtainable to him. He knew the number but wanted to hear it from his partner.

"You know they told us they had sixty thousand dollars to spend on the house, Luis," Julio said.

"Okay, we'll offer sixty thousand. You are sure they have that much in cash?" Luis asked?"

"Yes—yes. For God sake," Julio said, exasperated.

"Truthfully, the main reason they want it is to look for the hidden money. If they find it, we're all rich. We get forty dollars a month as jet pilots and twenty-two bonus dollars as teachers at the university. It's laughable, and we're double-dipping in the system. I'll help them to dig for the money," Luis said.

The two Cubans looked around, took pictures, and left to visit the Colony Hotel before taking off at the airstrip near the house. They would make the offer in a few days. They would not lie to the government about the funds. It was being loaned by Americans for part ownership. The Cuban government would have 51 percent and the other 49 percent would be split between Luis and Julio and Eli and Gina. In a separate private document drafted by Josh Vargas, they gave $250,000 each to Julio and Luis if cash were hidden on the property with a value of at least $3 million US dollars. The default amount of $50,000 would be paid to the two Cubans if only a million was found. Eli and Gina believed either all of the amount would be found, or nothing at all because someone else had found it and left an empty vault.

Eli had emailed the pictures of the two men who had either followed or shadowed them and also sent information on their identities. The group was hopeful that their Cuban friends might afford them protection against these strange intruders. Julio and Luis were allowed personal firearms since they were military and easily qualified for permits. Cuban citizens could buy certain guns if they passed the registration process, and on approval, each gun would have a personal identifying mark.

The Americans hoped the two Cubans would have their guns in the summer when they came to visit the beach house, just in case those guys came around. The Isle of Youth was like the wild west of Cuba where most people had guns. Mary and Pete had a shotgun which probably wasn't registered, and the manager of the Colony was holding a pistol by his side when all the shooting took place last August. Josh had mentioned he saw him stick it back in his pocket after they came to shore in the Zodiac. The four Americans wondered what Rick did with his rifle. It was probably hidden near the dive shack. Maybe they would look for it when they got to the island. It wouldn't be long before they were back in Cuba, and this time they hoped it wouldn't be a dry run.

Chapter Twenty-one

Return to Cuba

Eli was on the same flight as the other three Americans, even though he had flown in from California to Miami the same day. Now there were several flights into Havana and more cruise ships waited their turn to dock each day. Cuba was exploding.

They met Julio and Luis at a small café named Rancho Luna in Havana for dinner. It featured small wrought iron tables and chairs in an outdoor patio setting next to a graphic arts studio in the middle of a cobblestone street. A table for eight was created since the Cubans had invited their girlfriends. Julio's was Russian and Luis's was from Spain, and both were late for the party. The servers were bilingual, so communication was easy.

Everyone had experienced a good school year, the four Americans with new knowledge seeded in their brains, and Julio and Luis who had spread those seeds in Cuba and possibly outside the classroom. They all shared the highlights of the last year and agreed that finals were a bitch, but somehow they survived them. The Americans expressed their amazement at the progress in Cuba, and the Cubans explained that the raise in their government salaries had not yet caught up with all the excitement. As everyone chatted away, Josh noticed two men watching them. They stood at opposite ends of the street where the café was located, like human bookends, with their arms crossed as though they didn't care if they glaringly stood out in the crowd of tourists. Both were tall, thick, and had short military looking haircuts. Their looks and manners suggested they were Eastern European—maybe Russian. There were plenty of them still in Cuba. Josh pointed them out to Julio.

"Luis, we have visitors—Russian goons," Julio said.

"Let me make a call," Luis said and pulled his cell phone from his pocket. In rapid Spanish, he gave the descriptions of the two men and their location. "In a few minutes, they will be in custody, but I doubt they will talk. They never do."

Almost at the instant Luis clicked off his cell phone, two tall young ladies, one blonde, and one dark haired Latino, walked up to the table. They were jaw-dropping beautiful. Possibly fashion models, and no one would have been surprised if they said they were Miss Russia and Miss Cuba. Julio introduced the straw-haired girl in her early twenties as Svetlana Barkov. She was wearing a striking, red, low-cut sleeveless top and a white miniskirt. Her body was tan, and she stood regally on multi-strapped stacked heel sandals, which accented her exquisitely sculpted, shapely legs.

Eli and Josh looked at her legs longer than they should have. Their girlfriends jabbed them in their ribs.

Luis introduced Cande Rivero to the group. She was gorgeous enough without seeing her eyes--her eyes were unbelievable. Deep emerald green, they peered out from a face of soft, perfect features. Her lips were large and sexy. Eli and Josh could barely speak. Finally, they were able to stammer out their names. "I have heard all about you guys from these two Cuban playboys. I can go with you to Isle of Youth?" Svetlana asked in heavily accented English.

"Me too. Por favor!" Cande said, her eyes looking even greener, if that were possible.

"Later about that," Julio said, and he and Luis pulled chairs from the table for them.

Once they were seated with menus in their hands, movement in the street caught Luis's attention. The entire table watched as four uniformed soldiers attempted to take one of the huge men into custody. The man broke away and threw two of them to the ground as if they were small sacks of potatoes. The first volts of electricity from a high-powered Taser made him pause. A second powerful shock dropped him to the bricks on the street as it was applied to his lower back. Even though he fought the effects, it did no good, and he found himself cuffed and overpowered.

At the other end of the street, five men faced an even larger and stronger man. He still stood unmoving with his arms crossed as they approached. He was at least six-foot-six and had arms the size of his attackers' legs. Two of the soldiers shot Tasers from a short distance. Fifty thousand volts shot from each device, but voltage wasn't what would bring him down. A million volts without any amperage won't disable anyone. Add .0036 amps between two metal prongs fired and stuck into flesh and most people drop like a rock—many die. This guy had double the effect and was not yet subdued. He kicked one of the military men in the head and slugged another. They were trying to recover when the Taser finally had the desired effect. All was normal in the street again.

"My dear Julio, vot vuz dat about?" Svetlana asked reverting back to bad English.

"Some of your Russian friends were stalking us, Lana," Julio said using his nickname for her.

"Did they tink you ver gay?" Lana asked.

"No, they think we're after something they want. They can't have it. What you just saw might let you know the dangers of going with us to the Isle of Youth. Over there, I don't have friends to protect you like I do here," Julio said.

"I think those guys that tailed us will be back—if not them, their replacements," Josh said.

"I agree," Julio said.

"Me too, but I hope they're smaller versions. Those guys were monsters," Eli said.

They ordered dinner. Lobster was the favorite since they were local, fresh, and cheap compared to the states.

Julio had news on the loans. It was what they wanted to hear. Their offer of $60,000 had been accepted—and there was even better news. Initially, Julio and Luis had been turned down several times on the counter-offer. The official in charge of real-estate transactions told them it was potentially a million dollar property, and the $150,000 price was a gift—an offer because they were war heroes.

Luis hated to do it but made the call to the highest office in Cuba for assistance. The follow-up call from Raul Castro was picked up and answered in an irritated voice by the loan official. In Spanish, he received a long, seemingly endless tirade regarding his probable illegitimate birth and very shaky future as part of the Cuban government and the human race. The color drained from his face. His breathing elevated to short and rapid gasps followed by his undigested lunch being deposited inside a metal waste basket. He finally regained his voice and dropped the price to $50,000. The entire table cracked up laughing. Eli and Gina beamed. They had brought a blank cashier's check for the full amount. Now they would go to a bank and open an account, have a check made for $50,000, and take $10,000 in cash for expenses. They had an appointment to close on the property the next day at 1:00 p.m., so there was time to get all that done.

Julio Vázquez and Luis Cimarro had fame, respect, and quite a bit of power in their native country. What they lacked was money. Their greatest source of income was speaking engagements on cruise ships. They received $500 each week a cruise ship hired them for seminars. They saw these opportunities dwindling as the People to People requirement became less rigid. American tourists could now create their own People to People tours without the need for the structure a cruise ship gave them. A wide open tourism announcement would surely place the last nail into the seminar coffin. The hunt for the money at the beach house on the Isle of Youth meant a different kind of freedom for them. They could travel, purchase a car, open a business, and most of all, get married and have kids. They were as excited about the beach house purchase as the Americans if that could be possible.

Luis's phone sounded off to the tune of Cuban salsa. "Hola. Si—Si—Gracias," Luis said at the end of the long call. It was apparent a lot of information had been given to him.

"Our two spies were from Russia, as we had guessed. Interpol wants them for many crimes, including murder. However, it is unlikely Cuba will give them up. Instead, the extradition process will begin with Russia since numerous charges are pending there. It may take a while. The close relationship we once held is not as strong since they quit the trade arrangement with us. Here's a problem: they have attorneys who are asking for bail. It will be a few days, but it is likely Russia has high powered attorneys who could make it happen since the stalking incident is a minor offense here. They agreed to call me if they are granted bail."

"I wonder how many of these goons are waiting on us on the Isle of Youth," Eli said.

Their food arrived and the group talked about going scuba diving while they were there at the Colony Hotel. Each couple had a room there since electricity had not been restored at the beach house. Josh had called several times to get it turned on but couldn't find the person who actually pulled the switch. Hands would most likely need to be greased.

"I have obtained passes for all of us for the Tropicana tonight if you want to go," Julio said and explained it was one of the perks given to the military.

"May I speak for our group? Hell yes, and thank you very much!" Eli said.

"We have a couple of loaner cars and will pick you up at your hotel. I believe you are at the National Hotel—right?" Luis asked.

"Right. They have a great salsa band playing there this afternoon if you want to bring the girls by to dance and have drinks," Gina said.

"I would. How about you, Cande?" said Lana.

"Love it, if the boys are up to it," Cande said.

"I see an afternoon of drinking and sweating in my future," Julio said.

It was a memorable day and night. The trip to the hotel became an afternoon of lots of drinks and dancing. Cande and Luis were the best dancers, with Josh and Kelsi coming in a close second. Everyone tried various dance steps, and it seemed easier the more they drank. The Cubans and their dates left around five as they had dinner plans elsewhere but said they would be back at eight to take them to the Tropicana.

They arrived at the nightclub in time to be seated close to the main stage and in view of all the other stages that would suddenly appear out of nowhere. The outdoor seating was part of a six-acre area unlike any place in the world. Rum and cigars were placed on tables with soft drinks as setups. No one could count the number of dancing girls and costume changes, but everyone loved the experience.

Eli invited everyone to the hotel for breakfast, but they had other plans. Later Gina said, "I do believe they want to sleep late with their girlfriends. Do you blame them?"

The next morning after a patio breakfast, the group headed for the bank with the cashier's check in hand. They chose the National Bank of Canada because of their proximity to the US. The transaction went smoothly with the bonus of debit cards issued for Gina and Eli on the spot. A new cashier's check for $50,000 was issued.

Josh had done his best to understand real estate transactions where a property was owned by the Cuban government and then transferred by title to a joint ownership venture between Cubans and Americans. It was really important to get an approval letter from the US State Department to avoid breaking any laws. Also, the Cubans used a term called a usufructuary arrangement, which amounted to a lifetime lease. They had been known to sneak it in on unsuspecting buyers. Josh was on to all their tricks. The laws for real estate in Cuba were extensions and offshoots of *Registro de la Propiedad* from Spanish mortgage laws that had remained basically unchanged since the 1860s. Well, of course, they were changed dramatically when the revolutionary government took ownership of all properties. When a sale was authorized, the rules and regulations were surprisingly market friendly, and if the hoops required by Cuba and America were jumped through, the rest of the process was easy.

Everyone appeared at the Registrar's office in a Soviet-style building across the street from Revolution Square in Havana's office district. Gina noticed there was no sprinkler system, and stains from water leakage around the windows and ceiling tiles seemed to be prominent. She had walked with the fire marshals several times while they inspected her dad's nightclub for automatic sprinklers and fire extinguishers. She doubted the existence of either of them in the entire city of Havana. Communism had no use for such frivolities.

Eli pulled out a chair for Gina. The office was small, so Cande, Lana, and Kelsi waited in a nearby reception area. Julio and Luis handed Josh the paperwork they had accumulated working on the purchase for several months, which included the certificate for the purchase with the price of 50,000 CUCs listed. Gina held two checks, one for the 50,000 CUCs and another for 2,000 CUCs for the 4 percent tax on the transaction. The notary's fee would be 35 CUCs, and they would accept a local check for that amount. The CUC conversion rate was on par with the US now, except for a small conversion rate. There was still talk about a single currency system in Cuba, but nothing happened fast in this country.

If a legal question was asked, Josh was there to answer it. The government official accepted the Cuban and America exceptions for the purchase since the property was going to be a business. It was listed as a hotel. Several US hotels were preparing to break ground with similar deals on a bigger scale. The ownership was 50-50 between the Americans and the two Cubans, but the government of Cuba retained 51 percent ownership. They would receive tax on any income but didn't require any other share of the profits. A certificate was issued by the registrar and copies of the deed would be mailed to each of the owners. Checks were dispersed and the sale was final. Tomorrow they would fly to the Isle of Youth and take possession of a house that had come back home to two families that enjoyed it 57 years ago. Eli and Gina felt somewhat vindicated and extremely happy. Julio and Luis had never owned a house or anything else—not even a car. A dormant spark had ignited in them, and they were hopeful the power and freedom of wealth might be at hand. All of them had the feeling someone would try to take it all from them. Someone called Luis before the real estate closing to inform him that the two Russian had been released from jail.

Chapter Twenty-Two

Back on the Isle of Youth

There was the usual battle at the airport on the Isle of Youth for cars that weren't Ladas. Even with Pete and Mary's Jeep, the group was certain there would be times they would need two cars. Finally, two Hondas were secured and they were off.

Pete and Mary had met them at the airport to discuss the things that needed to be done to the house that week. They had given Luis, Julio and their girlfriends rides to the hotel from the airstrip at the beach house earlier in the day. They had flown over in the same Cessna 172 they had flown in May. This time they had it for a full week. Pete said the girls were at the pool when he left and made a fanning motion on his face that suggested they were hot ladies. Everyone laughed, but Eli and Josh couldn't wait to see for themselves. It was late, so they didn't stop to talk to Rosa but instead drove directly to the Colony hotel and checked in. They caught the other couple as they were going to dinner.

"Julio, did you guys get a dive in this afternoon?" asked Eli.

"Two tank dives, and it was beautiful. Saw turtles and a nurse shark," Luis said.

"For some reason, the dive masters stayed with us girls," Lana said.

"Can't imagine why," Josh said laughing.

"Maybe you had attractive swimsuits," Eli said.

Smiling broadly, Cande remarked, "Just barely."

"The food is supposed to be horrible here," Julio said, "but lunch was okay."

"Maybe the complaints have been addressed," Eli said. "I think it would be hard to get fresh supplies in here. We brought food from town, and you guys did as well, didn't you?"

"We did," Luis said.

After finding a table for eight, they ordered, then had wine and Crystal beer while they waited. Before each group left Nueva Gerona, they stopped at markets and loaded the cars down with vegetables, fruit, and meats. The hotel staff was astonished and slightly embarrassed that guests would bring in food supplies. Alex, the chef, was actually grateful, especially after the group explained they understood it was hard for the staff to take off and get supplies every day. Now there would be no excuse for poor quality food at meals. The group just hoped he knew how to cook. They had read the reviews of the hotel and found the restaurant rated in the awful to terrible range. Each member of the group ordered meals consisting of the produce and meat they delivered. There weren't many other guests, only ten others who were part of a dive group from Germany. The front desk said that some men were coming in from Havana the next day. Luis asked if they had Russian names and the clerk said he couldn't say but smiled and nodded.

Salads were crisp, with tomatoes, avocados, and cut up strawberries. Chicken, fish, and steaks were presented nicely with vegetables cooked to perfection. It seemed the chef could cook if he had the right food in front of him. From that time on, as long as fresh supplies were there, the meals were excellent, and once they began to deteriorate, one couple would head to Nueva Gerona and shop the markets and canvass the docks for fresh catches from the local fishermen. It seemed there wasn't much of a budget at the hotel for fresh food.

After dinner, someone suggested card games and they chose an area near the lobby to play. Eli taught everyone a card game he had learned in California. It was called Clagg and had a history from World War II pilots in England. The name was derived from "Clouds low all aircraft grounded." Eli couldn't explain the need for the second "g," but he did know all the complicated steps, especially when one had to bid before they saw their cards and then look at their cards and bid before they knew the trump card suite. Gina had played it before with Eli and his friends on visits to California, so she played with Julio, Lana, and Josh. Eli played with Kelsi, Cande, and Luis. Eli had brought printed scoring sheets that explained there were 20 hands for each game. They caught on quickly and became very competitive vying for the best score per table for the championship. Much beer and wine was consumed as they played. Lana was clearly the best player. Her bids were conservative and accurate. After she won the championship of the recently named Isle of Youth Clagg Association, she admitted she was a master bridge player. Obviously, she had been born with a deck of cards in her hand. She loved the game and requested to play every night they were there.

Eli and Josh took Luis and Julio aside and asked if they could leave the girls for a few minutes. The girls were happily cutting up in the bar as the men walked out of the hotel lobby to the dive shack. The night was warm, and a bright moon lit up the sand. The sparse low-level hotel landscape lights were a good distance from the scuba shop. Eli led them behind the small dive building, which hid them in darkness and shielded them from the swimming pool. A couple of guests were in the pool talking and making out. There appeared to be no one else on the grounds.

"The individual who saved our lives last August had a rifle," Eli said as he looked towards the roof of the dive shop. "He didn't have it with him when we came to shore, and I believe he fired from the roof of the shop. Don't ask me about him because I can't say anything. One of us can be hoisted to the roof to look around, and the rest of us can dig here in the sand to try to find the weapon. I really think we'll need it. Mary and Pete have a shotgun we can borrow, and I'm guessing Julio and you, Luis, brought your pistols?"

"Yes, we did," Julio said.

"Does anyone doubt they will attack us when they think we have the money in our hands?" Eli said.

"Maybe before then," Luis said.

"Who wants to look on the roof?" Eli asked.

"I will," Luis said.

Eli and Josh locked their hands to make a step for him. Once on the roof, Luis began to explore under the palm fronds where a normal shingled roof lay. The palm leaves were just to give the building a tropical look. He had to raise each one.

Everyone else began to work in the sand at the base of the structure. They quickly discovered that below the sand were concrete blocks about two feet apart that held the footings and crossbeams of the floor of the shop. There was space underneath and something that appeared to be a pile of rags. Julio reached in and felt something hard under the rags. He pulled it out with the rags.

He took it a few steps away where the moonlight would illuminate it, and then unwrapped the object. Josh was familiar with this gun; he had fired it at a range. It was a Remington model 750 semi-automatic rifle with a Redfield 3X9 scope and a synthetic stock chambered for 30.06 rounds. Two clips were found in the rags. One was a standard 5 round clip, and the other was for 10 rounds. Some of the rounds were missing.

Luis spoke from the roof at a level the people in the pool couldn't hear.

"I've found ammunition up here, and I'm tossing it down."

He threw plastic bags containing the bullets and the ground crew caught them.

"I'm not an expert on guns, but we used these in Cuba since there aren't a lot of semi-automatic rifles around that aren't made for the military. It's a damn good gun, but if you leave bullets in those ten-round clips a long time, it weakens the springs and causes them to jam. I say we take at least half of them out—maybe all of them--until we need them," Julio said.

"Great information. I'm a little bit familiar with the gun since my brother has a two-seventy in the older seventy-four hundred model. He loves his, but only uses the five-round clip. He told me that the ten-round clip was iffy unless you got the best after-market available," Josh said.

"We can set up targets on the airstrip and get some practice in since we have plenty of shells. I don't get to shoot much in California.

When my dad lived in Vegas, he would take me to hunt feral pigs on private property because they were considered a nuisance. I used a thirty-thirty Winchester lever action and a nineteen-eleven forty-five ACP pistol. I wanted the handgun in case one of the big males charged us," Eli said.

"We brought our service pistols, Makarov nine-millimeters, with twelve-round clips. They're a bit heavy because they are blow back designs, but they're good and accurate weapons," Julio said.

"Glad you brought them," Eli said. "The Russians make fine weapons."

"Yeah," said Josh.

"One of us needs to put this gun in a car trunk. Josh, our car is the closest. Will you do the honors? The rest of us need to see if the girls have picked up one of the Germans at the bar," Eli said. Josh took the rifle and made sure it was wrapped well with the rags before he carried it to the car.

It was a clear night with a beautiful array of stars blinking in the night sky. Josh just happened to glance out to the waters beyond the beach. Possibly a mile or two from shore was a powerboat. He didn't think it had been there while they were looking for the gun. It was maybe a 40-to-50-foot craft and was sparsely illuminated with only its bow and stern navigation lights on. The cabins and the wheelhouse were dark. It didn't look friendly.

As Josh returned to the bar area, the Germans had moved in for the kill with the four beauties the group left behind. Their hopes were shattered when all four guys found their places next to their girlfriends. The Germans had been diving all over the world, and Cuba was on their bucket list. There were two women and the rest were guys. They were older, in their late 30s and early 40s with plenty of disposable income. Two were doctors, both world-famous surgeons from Berlin, and the others were successful business owners. Julio and Luis wanted to know how they opened their businesses. Clearly, the Cubans wanted to make some money. They were tired of standing in line for food and living off what they could squeeze out of the revolutionary government.

On the way back to their rooms, Josh asked everyone to meet in his room. Once everyone was there, he told them about the boat and brought up the Russians coming tomorrow to the hotel.

"Julio and Luis you are our military minds. How do we fight a war on two fronts with one rifle, two pistols, and maybe a borrowed shotgun, if Pete and Mary loan it to us?"

"One area where Fidel and Che Guevara excelled was fighting superior forces with few weapons and ammunition. He fought a forty thousand-man army with fifteen hundred poorly armed rebels. In the mountains with little food, in miserable conditions, in constant hiding from Batista's soldiers, those two men taught guerrilla warfare until it spilled out the rebels' ears. They knew hit-and-run tactics, they knew ambushing techniques, they knew improvised explosives, booby traps, and they were motivated and willing to die," Julio said with a passion the others hadn't seen in him before. "However, the rebel forces could never have won a direct battle with such overwhelming odds. The minds and souls of the Batista fighters had to be changed. And that, my friend, is what happened. Most of them laid down their arms rather than fight their own countrymen."

"The Cuban military still teach these skills today, even though we have a military that is large and fairly well-armed. Especially pilots who might get shot down and need to survive on their own. I say that tomorrow we send a recon squad into the villages for supplies. Fertilizer for bombs, guns from civilians, knives, electrical fences, cattle prods, nail guns—I think you get the idea. It appears that way too many people know why we are here. We will make a list tonight and one of us should go with the others since we are Cuban and well-known," Luis said.

Eli looked around the room at four really concerned young ladies. "If you girls are nervous about what's about to happen here—you should be. We'll take you to the airport tomorrow for a flight back to Havana if you are not absolutely sure you want to be shot at—maybe killed," Eli said. He looked into each one's eyes and made contact.

"We will stay and help any way we can, including being a part of a firefight. We've also had military experience, myself in Russia and

Cande here in Cuba. She's from Spain but did training here. I was an instructor which allowed me to meet Julio. Luis did some training and quickly picked Cande out of the crowd for more—let's say intense training," Lana said laughing.

"More soldiers than I expected. Why don't Luis and I go for the supplies since I have money to pay for everything and a bank card to get more? Everyone stay away from the beach house until we have a plan and weapons to carry it out. We'll meet for breakfast with a list that will turn us into a new Cuban Revolutionary Army that would make Che proud," Eli said.

Chapter Twenty-Three

Russian Treat

"If you Americans would like us to have our hearts in this dangerous mission you are about to undertake, we'd like to be cut in on whatever's going on here," Cande said. "Our two boyfriends haven't shared much with us," she said as she took a drink of her morning coffee and caught Eli with a large bite of omelet in his mouth, unable to respond.

"Goes for me too," Lana said.

Gina looked at Eli, and he smiled and nodded but couldn't talk around the load of egg he was chewing. "Same cut as Julio and Luis," Gina said.

"Uhhh, how much is that?" Cande said.

"Two hundred and fifty thousand each," Gina said.

"Holy mother of God! What in the shit have we gotten into—hope it doesn't involve drugs," Lana said.

"Their great-grandfather supposedly hid a fortune in the house. Unfortunately, the word is out," said Julio. "Some very bad guys want it too. As soon as the Americans arrived, a lot of people assumed they were finally here to uncover the hidden money. My guess is the Russians checking in at the hotel are a part of "Found Assets, Inc." out of Moscow. The boat must be a different group. Pirates, I would guess," Luis said.

"Is there a military force on the island?" Eli asked.

"There's a small army garrison building, but it's rarely occupied. The navy has a port facility, but it's manned primarily by civilians. Cuba has financial problems, and the military becomes less effective each year," Julio explained. "The Isle has a handful of local police funded by the government and one coastal vessel for this island. Used to be two but thanks to a shootout, one was retired," he said as he cut his eyes toward Josh and Eli. "They fly in people if it's needed. People are fleeing this island almost every night. Frankly, I can't blame them. If they make it to Mexico and then the US border, they have it made."

"I would have it made with a quarter of a million dollars in my purse," Lana said.

"Julio and Luis. You guys are the military experts. How do we apply guerilla methods to our little group here?" Josh asked.

"First, we need to have the momentum coupled with legitimacy. All of them are thieves, but we are protecting an asset that belongs to us. If we use all methods, we can handle ten-to-one odds, but only if we are mobile, vigilant, and constantly wary of everything. Guerilla warfare is a weapon of the weak. We must assume we are weak compared to the forces coming to the hotel and on the boat. We must be mobile, operate in small units, and fight only when it is advantageous to us. We must study the terrain around the house, road, airstrip, and the waters out from the beach house. If the enemy attacks, we retreat. If the enemy retreats, we attack; if the enemy halts, we harass. The sole habitual tactic of a guerilla unit is the ambush. The fight is not an apple that falls when it is ripe; you must make it drop. We need accurate intelligence. Sabotage and raids are keys to success. Now let's talk specifics. I will let Luis take this part," Julio said.

"We will pay to have someone at the hotel let us know when the Russians leave there and if possible, check on their inventory of guns. If fishermen work around here, then a nice sum of money would pay for eyes on the boat. We need to build some explosives from materials we buy in town today. Eli, you're an engineering student: possibly you can wire a circuit switch that will be activated by a cell phone. If not, an explosive set off by a gunshot could work. Maybe tanks of compressed air or some explosive gas. We have cell phones that work in mainline Cuba, but I don't know about towers here. We need more phones to supply our intelligence assets. Maybe we can buy burners in town. Eli and Gina, if you can fire from the line of trees as the Russians go by—then practice with targets on the road.

"We need a way to sabotage the boat that comes around. Maybe a Molotov cocktail if a diver kept it dry in a plastic bag, then lit it and threw it on the boat. We need to rent a couple of tanks and dive equipment for that task. Their car shouldn't be hard to disable if they don't keep sentries around.

"We need guards at all times at or around the beach house in twos night and day. We must ask Pete and Mary where we can buy more guns. They have friends and relatives that have them. All of us need to be armed. Buy them, rent them, or steal them. The hotel manager has a pistol. Offer him a large sum to rent it.

"If it is possible to build or use a bunker, it would get us out of the line of fire. There is a small concrete fuel building on the airstrip. See what it would take to build a firing slot in it or on top. I want to rig an IED for the road leading to the beach house. I bet they rented more than one car. Must take them out, however many they have. We'll go now to the small towns and buy what we can. You guys set up the shooting positions and the bunker. Good luck," Luis said.

Once Luis and Julio walked over to confer with their girlfriends, Josh spoke to the Americans in a serious voice.

"We're four young college students, with two military heroes who were actually jet jockeys, and two beautiful girls who have some military training, but possibly were intensely trained in Julio's and Luis's bedrooms, to make up our little army. There's a good chance we will face experienced Russian thugs with far superior weapons— maybe automatics. If we take all the knowledge Che Guevara passed along, including everything he learned from studying Mao in China, we still will be at a disadvantage unless we attack first. There is one thing that Julio and Luis didn't tell us. Guerilla warfare, many times, means you lose all the battles but win the war because you change the heart of the people. The US won every engagement in Vietnam. But they lost the war because they lost the hearts of the American people. It is clear our little army on the Isle of Youth can't afford to lose many battles…or maybe any," Josh said.

"Eli. You ready for the recon mission?" Luis asked.

"You betcha. Let's rock and roll!"

Eli handed a wad of cash to Gina. She Kelsi and the two girlfriends of the Cubans walked into the lobby and asked to see the manager.

"Alphonse Martinez. How can I be of assistance?"

"You are the manager?" Gina asked.

"Yes."

"We need to meet with you in private…in your office," Kelsi said.

"I doubt that is necessary. We can discuss it here."

"You wish to discuss a gun attack by Russian spies against Julio Vázquez and Luis Cimarro in the lobby where all your guests can hear what they're about to be in for?"

"No. Of course not. Right this way." He led them behind the registration desk, down a hallway, and into a very nicely appointed office with a huge credenza behind a real mahogany desk. He had two chairs at this desk but there were other chairs around a small conference table in the room. Once everyone was seated, Kelsi began to speak.

"As you are aware, Mr. Martinez, I was here last summer and was kidnapped by a renegade Cuban boat captain while we were snorkeling. Thanks to two people at your hotel, we were saved. One gave his life trying to save us. Very soon, some very nasty people will make an attempt again to harm us. We don't want you to suffer bad publicity for your hotel, which isn't at the occupancy rate you desire anyway. We need your help."

"What on earth can I do?"

"First, we are going to ask to borrow your pistol and all the ammunition you have handy."

"Out of the question! I flatly refuse!"

"You are refusing to assist two heroes of the Republic of Cuba in their need to protect themselves from your guests who are known Russian murderers?"

"How do I know they are the ones staying at my hotel?"

"Here are their pictures and names. Yury Bortsov and Iosif Zykin. I asked at the front desk and they are expected in tomorrow with some others."

"Why are you afraid they will attack your group?"

"Our group just purchased the old Swartz beach house. They think money is hidden there, so they will come after us to find it and take it away from us. Julio and Luis are also owners. You will be doing your country a great service by assisting two of your greatest war heroes. Now please let us borrow your pistol, or we'll have Julio and Luis report you to the SDE for failing to help a countryman in need. You know as I do they are all around us. It may have been they stayed at your hotel in the past. Possibly Hector was one."

Alphonse finally got up and opened a locked cabinet that was a part of his credenza and pulled a large revolver off the shelf. With it was a leather holster and a full box of shells.

"Return this as soon as hostilities are over." As he handed the weapon over, Kelsi gave him a US hundred dollar bill.

"One other thing, Mr. Martinez: here is a cell phone number that works here. It is Cande's phone." Cande smiled and gave him a little salute. "Please call me with reports on the Russians. Who they talk to, their movements—you know like you did for Hector."

"Okay. How bad are these Russians?"

"Stone-cold killers. Cuba is in the process of extraditing them back home, but they have good lawyers. May take a while," Kelsi said.

"Mr. Martinez, can you give me some names of local fishermen that live close by?" Gina asked.

"We buy fish from two or three of them." He wrote down the names of the fishermen and the towns they lived in and phone numbers if they had them.

"Thank you, Mr. Martinez. After all of this is over, we will mention your helpfulness to the SDE," Cande said. She was the only female there who spoke with a Spanish accent and maybe gave the whole transaction some credibility.

Eli and Luis had already started the car and were studying a map when Cande and Gina motioned for them to roll down the window.

"We got the pistol, and he agreed to inform for us. Don't trust him, though, so we need to recruit some others. Here are the names of local fishermen and towns where they live, even a couple of phone numbers. Have a great run and we'll see you tonight," Gina said.

They drove away from the hotel and headed for Santa Fe to contact a fisherman listed as living there.

"Hey, the girls did all right, didn't they?" Eli said.

"If those four beauties asked for my pistol, I would have asked if I could shoot myself for them. Old Martinez is probably in the men's room playing with himself," Luis said.

"Luis, I have an idea for IEDs and it's very simple. We get a tank of either compressed air like at the dive shop, or find a welding shop with cylinders of explosive gasses, or get some compressed propane bottles. We place them along the road or in the water in the path of that boat. Once they're close to it—we shoot a hole in it with the rifle with the scope. Wham! Blow them up as they go by in a car or boat."

"Great idea. Probably shouldn't tell the dive shop why we need extra scuba tanks. It could actually work as good as some sophisticated bomb with an arming switch."

"I think a small fertilizer bomb would still be useful if we had a way to detonate it," Eli said. "Or, we could make some TATP if you're brave enough."

"Is that the explosive terrorists call the 'Mother of Satan'?"

"Yes, Acetone and Peroxide. Make it into a crystalline substance and tap on the bowl and blow yourself to kingdom come. Unstable as hell."

"If I shoot into a propane bottle and it blows a car in half and sets everyone on fire, wouldn't that do the job without mixing up the Mother of Satan?" Luis said.

"Just bringing it up. Then could I interest you in a nice nitrogen fertilizer bomb? Rarely do they blow up in your face," Eli said.

"I'll get back to you on that."

Chapter Twenty-Four

The Shark Dog

The powerboat was a work of art. Melville Oliver was glad to have it and told everyone about the deal he got. The boat was close to a million dollars when new, but he picked up the 22-year-old boat for $200,000 and financed most of it. Measuring 63 feet long, sleek, powerful, and meant for long trips, the Blue Water 623 named *Shark Dog* had space to sleep most of the seven people he had on board. It looked like it was moving when it was dead in the water. He wasn't sure he could make the payments on it, but if plans came to fruition, money wouldn't be a problem. Almost a year ago he was present at the hotel when the shooting took place on the Cuban patrol boat. He had learned why the four Americans were on the island and at the same time gleaned enough information to learn they would be back after classes were out the next year. For ten days, he had waited for them. A friend at the Cuban Registrar's Office alerted him the sale had taken place. Melville had heard about this hidden money his entire life. His grandfather had worked at Carmine and Bernie's night club. All of the staff knew Bernie and Carmine quit using the local banks because everyone was paid in cash on a weekly basis. They knew Bernie had an airplane. It didn't take much imagination to decide he was digging a hole somewhere and dumping money in it.

Justin Clay and his girlfriend Sami Brooks were both divers and had been to the area for a couple of years. They had also learned of the fortune hidden around the beach house and struck up a friendship with Melville at the dive shop at the Colony Hotel at the same time of the August shootings. They had planned for a year to come back for the elusive fortune. With them were four divers who had all worked for Blackwater in Iraq. They had been fired by the mercenary forces for excessive aggression while in country. They were all armed with illegal automatic weapons, rebreathers, and enough long knives to carve up a wooly mammoth. Melville and Justin didn't trust any of them but needed the muscle if they were going to be successful. The entire boat and crew had learned that two famous Cubans had bought in on the beach house. The job would be tougher now but not impossible.

***

Eli drove his rented Honda at a speed that allowed for the consistent dodging of huge potholes, which had not been repaired in years. This was a forgotten road on an island given up on by the Cuban government. Luis reached in his camouflage daypack and pulled out a booklet which appeared to have been photocopied and stapled. He read and mumbled. At times, he would make grunting sounds and then say, "Well, that won't work."

Eli couldn't see what he was reading, as keeping the Honda from being torn to pieces by missing pavement had his full attention. Finally, his curiosity got the best of him. "Okay, Luis, what are you so engrossed in?"

"Our idea on the propane bottles doesn't work. They have safety blowout valves even if they're set on fire. They might blow up later when most of the liquid gas has been expelled, but it would take a long time, and they would have to be set on fire somehow. Acetylene might work, but it only becomes highly explosive when it is mixed with oxygen. Aluminum scuba tanks just spew air out and scoot around the ground. Steel tanks do cause a lot of havoc if they are hit with a big bullet—thirty-aught-six may do it. They need to be filled to capacity. We only saw aluminum tanks when we went diving at the hotel."

"What in the hell are you reading?"

"Oh, it's called *The Anarchist Cookbook*. Sort of standard training for the Cuban military." Luis then dug deeper in the backpack and pulled out another homemade book so large he needed both hands to hold it. "This is *Beginner's Guide to Bomb Making* by Adnan Shukai. It's four hundred pages of instructions translated from Arabic and is used by Al-Qaeda wackos as their ultimate proof of a terrorist activity. The US tried to find this Shukai man and found it was just his pseudonym."

"Is there anything we can use in there—that is, that won't blow our fucking heads off when we mix it up?"

"It's not the explosives I'm having trouble with, Eli, it's the detonation process. These mixtures need a secondary explosion to set them off. Even in the case of the dive tank, a shot has to go all the way through the tank just as a car drives by. The timing would be very difficult, and the tank might strike the car or may go streaking toward us."

"Do you think any construction company or mining company on the island has any plain old dynamite?"

"If they did, no way they would sell us any. Most of the mines are shut down along with the marble quarries. If they had construction storage buildings, they may have left some behind. We'll look around. You may have come up with a great idea. They would also have detonators stored with them."

The first town, La Fe, was coming into view, and it was time to question a couple of fishermen, if they could find them. Town was a term that glorified the scant structures that stood in this tiny community.

***

Two ugly green Lada rental cars met and passed on opposite lanes from Eli and Luis as they entered the small village of La Fe. Neither set of occupants paid any attention to the other and really had no reason to. In one Lada were the two Russians, Yury Borthov, and Iosif Zykin. The other held three Ukrainians, Miloslav Sirko, Jaro Shevchenko, and Branka Balanchuk, who were hired by the Russians since they were ex-Spetsnaz for the GRU. This meant they were Special Forces for military intelligence—generally extreme badasses. There was no love lost between the two countries and their people, but the Ukrainians n needed work desperately and had been trained in Russia by Russians before the recent fighting started in the Ukraine. To make the friction more intense, the Russians nicknamed the three in the separate car, Mil, Jarhead, and Brank. Yury and Iosif were huge guys and built like body builders, which of course they were—but they weren't skilled military killers. The Ukrainians were. On the way to checking in at the Colony, Yury received a satellite call from his boss Horst Wolf, a German national, who had moved to Moscow twenty-odd years ago and was now head of his company, Found Assets, Inc.

"Yury? Have you checked in yet?" Horst asked.

"No. We're about fifteen miles out."

"When you get there, stay at the hotel until you hear from me. I understand the Americans have four Cubans with them—two are military heroes, so don't kill them unless you have to. How are you getting along with the Ukrainians?"

"We don't like them, and they don't like us. We are not scared of them."

"You are idiots. Those men will unscrew your heads and shit in them."

"Maybe we take care of ourselves."

"You have a job to do and so do they. See that it is done. I will call you soon."

***

"Cande, please look in that shed next to the boathouse and let me know if there is a sledgehammer in there," Julio said. He was walking in the direction of the small fuel bunker on the airstrip. His plans were to bust out some bricks and make a firing slot in the rear of the small aircraft maintenance building that faced the beach house. Extra fuel in five-gallon cans was stored there since the nearest aviation gas was about forty miles away.

"I've found two. I'll bring you the lightest one." Cande lifted the tool on her shoulder and carried it through the gate of the airstrip, then across the gravel about fifty yards to the little building. Across from the shed, past the airstrip, and near the shore was the old bunkhouse.

It was just a shell now as storms and age had removed most of the roof and all the windows and doors. Locals had stripped the useful lumber many years ago. However, Julio had explored the possibility of using it for a sniper "hide." Everyone had a project. Julio and Cande decided to work together on the airstrip project since they were not a couple and would most likely not be distracted.

Lana and Josh worked on building a couple of shelters to shoot from in the line of woods across from the road. As it turned out, they made three places because of an unexpected discovery of an old bulldozer blade and four car tires and rims barely visible in the vines and overgrowth.

"There's no way we can move that big steel blade, Lana, so why don't we just camouflage it in place and clear a line of sight in front?"

"I agree. Let's divide the tires into two different hides so we can move back and forth."

"You're a genius, girl. If Kelsi ever runs me off, I'll come looking for you."

"You guys are so made for each other. She finishes your sentences, and you have a pillow for her every time she sits down. You're friends first—lovers second. Works every time."

They divided up the tires and rims for the other two bunkers and cleared a shooting lane for them. The steel rims and thick rubber would stop most rounds, except for the armor-piercing variety.

"I'm hoping for small caliber automatic pistols and compact automatic weapons on their part. During the Vietnam War, American military experts went to small caliber weapons such as the AR fifteen, which used a small two-twenty-three round. I heard the theory was the modern soldier could carry twice as many rounds as they did with the old seven-six-two rounds used in the older M fourteen. They failed to tell the fighting men that a blade of grass could deflect the little rounds. They also might need three times as many rounds to bring a Vietcong down while he shot back with an AK forty-seven using the same large point seven-six-two rounds the US had given up on. A blade of grass would not deflect these rounds. However, after the war, many countries did adopt smaller round automatic weapons because of the weight, concealment, and the issue of the number of rounds available. I'd be pleased if they only had pistols, but failing that, maybe they'll just use small bullets."

"Me too, but I don't want any round making a home in my body. I've shot AK forty-sevens and wish I had one here now."

Kelsi and Gina entered the house to work on a defense system and to see if they all could sleep there that night. They were amazed at the work that had been done by Pete and Mary. All the broken windows had been replaced, the cobwebs were gone, it smelled of fresh paint, and everything was spotlessly clean. It still needed new appliances and upgrades in about every area, though. The electricity was on since Josh had finally made contact with the right people. Now that power was restored, the pump for the well worked, so water was on in the house. The refrigerator smelled awful but was cooling again. Ceiling fans were turning, a few lights came on, and the one window air-conditioning unit in the living room was sputtering along, rattling out a little cool air. Upstairs had two units—1950s style which for some reason still worked. The theory was that the Castros had new coolant put in them.

On the second floor was a side balcony with a ladder leading to the roof. Mostly it was a sloping, red ceramic tile roof, but the center was a metal cistern to store rain water or at least to collect it first before it drained to the storage container in the basement. From a distance, it looked much like a captain's walk found on many Victorian homes. It was plugged with debris, so Gina had agreed to work on it and also construct a firing position from there. Since no water was in the cistern, she found an old twin mattress and some pillows. If someone wanted to fire a rifle off the roof, they certainly had an advantage up there. The drain broke free after she pushed a broom handle down it. Now she would check the basement for the holding tank. She didn't expect it to be a pretty sight.

Kelsi looked in each room for barricades against bullets coming through windows. There were sofas and large stuffed chairs, heavy tables and a monstrous curved bar made of some dark wood from four to six inches thick. If it was ironwood it certainly would stop most rounds coming through the front window. A large carved desk was in the next room and showed promise for cover behind it. There were two bedrooms downstairs. One was the master bedroom and the other was for the staff. Mary and Pete stayed there when they were working late and wanted to hide from their kids for a while.

Everyone on the team had worked to get ready for whatever might happen from the Russians and the big powerboat waiting off shore. There was no doubt they both would come in when they thought the money had been uncovered—maybe sooner.

Chapter Twenty-Five

An Arsenal Comes Together

Luis and Eli found the fisherman whom the hotel manager identified as the person fishing in the same waters where the big powerboat had been seen. His name was Pedro, and according to him, there were at least seven men onboard. He guessed the boat was about 60-70 feet long, and he had spotted weapons aboard. Some onboard were white—probably Americans; others were Latino and black. They had not bothered him while he fished.

Luis asked if he took a gun with him fishing, and he said he did. It was a semi-automatic Remington nylon .22 rifle with a huge scope. An excellent small caliber weapon. Josh bought it and 500 rounds of ammunition from him for $300, which was a fortune for Pedro. He suggested if they wanted more guns they could go to a hardware store in Nueva Gerona. It wouldn't look like a hardware store or a store of any kind. Pedro described a metal shed with the words "Viva Cuba" on the door.

"Thank you, Pedro. Would you ask some of your friends if they would sell their guns and ammunition? We'll stop by your house on the way back through to see if we can buy them. See you soon," Luis said in Spanish.

"Be careful, my friend. The persons in the hardware store all carry pistols. They may just rob you and kill you."

"Thanks. We will stay alert," Luis said.

"Let's try this store in Nueva Gerona. Also, I heard from someone that most of the marble mining took place in sight of the town. Maybe they used explosives," Eli said.

"We'll be very careful with this old shed. I will go in the front, and you cover me by coming in the back way if there's an entrance. We will be dealing with criminals who have no honor. Do you know how to use the pistol the ladies bought from the hotel manager?"

"It's just a revolver. It has a safety and a trigger. When I fire, it'll be ready to go again. My dad had one of these but quickly moved up to automatics. I'm not reluctant to use it if you're about to be killed."

"Hope it won't be needed."

It took about 20 minutes to drive there from La Fe and the shed with the Viva Cuba sign wasn't hard to find. Two shabbily dressed middle-aged Cubans stood outside the front door. Eli drove around back and parked. No one was around. Luis walked around to the front and put his pistol in his belt behind him. Eli waited a while before he entered from the rear. The metal door wasn't locked and didn't seem to have a mechanism to secure it. Once inside, Eli saw it had brackets to hold a large plank of wood to block it from the inside. Even though it was just a metal shed, it wasn't as small as he had imagined. Tall shelves held motors, alternators, radiators, and car parts of every description. Lower shelves were crammed full of tools, nails, paint, and a good supply of general hardware merchandise. He didn't see any guns but wouldn't be surprised if a tank was parked in there somewhere. He heard voices from the front and eased down an aisle toward the sounds of Luis talking to three men.

"Where do you come from? Are you police? What do you want here?" These questions were being fired out by a rough-looking, well-built Cuban about six feet tall. He was dressed in desert-type fatigues and flip flops and wore a New York Yankees ball cap turned backward, allowing Eli to read it. His hand was on a pistol that was being pulled from its holster.

"Hands off the pistola!" Eli yelled with enough force to scare two other men standing behind Luis. They now knew they had two armed intruders to deal with. The two unarmed men were staring at Luis's pistol. It had been stuffed in his pants from behind but was now out of his waistband and held firmly in Luis's hand, yet still behind him.

The ball cap guy turned and pulled his gun completely out of his holster but froze when he heard the shot. Eli fired a .357 magnum into the old metal roof, causing dust, rust, and bird shit to rain down on everyone.

"Drop your gun!" yelled Luis in Spanish. Eli added the English version. The ball cap guy obliged quickly and eased it down on the dirt floor of the shed. The other two men disappeared as though they were ghosts who could change to ectoplasm and move through walls. When the smoke, dust, and debris quit falling from the ceiling, the two unarmed men were gone.

"We came here to do business. We have money and wish to buy some supplies," Luis said in his native language. He walked over, picked up the pistol from the ground, and removed the rounds in the man's gun before returning it to him. Luis held his pistol on him while he talked. Eli shut the front door and latched it and then walked to the back and placed the big board in the back door. Satisfied he wasn't dangerous, both men put their guns away.

"What supplies do you need?" the hardware store owner asked.

"Your name?" Luis asked.

"Dian Gonzalez."

"Dian, we have a beach house that some bad guys want for themselves. We expect to be attacked by two separate gangs. We have very few weapons and need to defend ourselves. Maybe you have heard of me? I am Luis Cimarro."

"Of course I have heard of you! You are a famous hero of the republic." Dian was thinking that a complaint from a military hero would land him in a prison where no sunlight filtered in.

"Guns, ammo, explosives, detonators, bulletproof vests, hand grenades, and anything else to help us protect ourselves," Luis said. "Oh, yeah, some burner phones would be nice."

"All of those things are illegal except for the phones, but I guess you know that," Dian said through a crooked smile.

"What these fucking goons are going to do to us ain't legal either," Eli said in English, and it appeared Dian understood.

"I have a shotgun—twelve gauge and some shells—buckshot. I'll let you have it for two-hundred CUCs."

"We'll take it," said Eli.

"What do you have in the way of blasting caps or detonators?" Luis asked.

"Nothing. Some people say some dynamite and caps were left when they abandoned the town quarry. It's fenced off, but there is a shed that has an explosive warning sign on it," Dian said.

"We need bolt cutters, a battery in case we find detonators, and some gas cans," Luis said. "We'll take eight of those vests I see piled by the wall. Give you $50 a piece rent and will return them."

"If you have a jackhammer and a small compressor, I will rent it and return it," Luis said.

"I'll rent them for a hundred dollars each. What you need those for? Doing mining?" Dian asked.

"Something like that," Eli said.

"We would pay a great deal of money for an AK forty-seven, and we'll return it to you after this danger passes. My guess is you have one for your personal protection." Eli held several hundred dollar bills in the air and smiled.

"A thousand dollars and I include five hundred rounds," Dian said.

"Eight hundred dollars and a thousand rounds and an extra clip," Eli said.

"Nine-hundred dollars, a thousand rounds, extra clip and a hundred tracer rounds. You return it to me as soon as your little trouble is over with whatever rounds you have left," Dian said.

"Deal!" Eli said. We'll send the gun back with Pete and Mary Artigas. Do you know them?

"I know who they are, and I have seen their Jeep."

Eli and Luis helped load the tools, ammo, vests, and guns in the car. The AK47 was in excellent shape, the ammo looked clean, the shotgun was well-oiled, and functioned well. The tracer ammo looked old, but Dian assured them they would ignite a can of gasoline if that was what they needed. It wasn't one of the options they talked about, but now it seemed to be the simplest way to blow something up, if you didn't mind being roasted to a crisp.

"Let's go find some dynamite," Eli said.

"You know, Eli, when it gets old, the nitroglycerine will sweat on the outside of the sticks of dynamite. They say you can throw it and it will blow up without lighting the fuse—either when it hits something or blows up in your hand."

"I've studied explosives some in school. The dynamite starts weeping after about a year, and the drippings will seep to the bottom of the box. If we find some, we need something to carry it in or it will blow this rental car to bits."

"Didn't we pass a sawmill on the way into town?" Eli asked.

"Yes. It's on the right side about a mile from here," Luis said.

As they approached the saw mill, it appeared to be abandoned except for some kids playing on the old machinery. They ran off when the car pulled up to a huge pile of sawdust. After filling up a cardboard box Dian had given them for the tools, they placed the box and wood shavings in the trunk.

"Are you ready to break into an old mine?" Eli asked.

"Hey, if we're caught with automatic weapons—lots of other guns without a hint of a permit, and enough ammunition to start a small war, we will be in deep shit. This little intrusion into an old quarry will be a minor infraction compared to all our other crimes. So let's add it to our resume," Luis said.

It was a short drive on a side gravel-and-dirt road to the mine's front gate. Next to the sign displaying the words, Attention! Keep Out! Danger! and in Spanish, ¡Atencion! ¡No entrar! ¡Peligro! was a chain and lock wrapped several times around the entrance gate.

"We want to cut a link that won't be noticed. There's so much chain, we can wrap it back and nobody will know," Luis said.

The big bolt cutters bit through the chain links easily. It was quite a distance to the storage shed, so they drove in and parked behind it. They couldn't be seen from the road since it was much lower ground. The mining shed was never a quality structure. It was some type of prefab metal shed about twenty feet long and ten feet wide with one small window in the front and a larger one in the back. Both looked in but only saw piles of trash, a desk, a chair, and shelves with boxes sitting on them. A good metal roof had kept rains out, but 100-degree

Cuban heat must have baked everything in there. There was a vent cap that moved when the wind blew to let some super-heated air out of the building.

"Let's try the front door," Eli said as he tried the door knob. It was locked.

"Maybe we can bust out a window or kick this metal door in," Luis said as he watched Eli drop to his knees and started a search on the small porch of the shed. There were rocks lying around, some made of material not consistent with the marble being mined there. One large rock on the porch was very light when Eli turned it over. As he fumbled with the bottom side, a part of the rock slid open—there was a key.

"How could they remember all these keys for construction huts? And, it works!" Eli opened the door and entered but let a rush of heated air and musty smells exit first. They kicked trash out of the way and made their way to the shelves. Box by box they carefully explored safety helmets, flashlights, time sheets, portable oxygen tanks, and first aid kits. Nothing even suggesting they blew things up. As they prepared to leave, Eli noticed a small wooden box on the floor opposite the shelves and covered by a rotted blanket. When he moved the blanket he saw the words, "South African Nitrogen Products, Inc. ANFO Blend High Explosive." In addition to the explosives, there was a controller, wireless detonators, and all the equipment needed to set off explosives from a remote position. They took most of the contents of the box including the instructions on how to use the main control center. It was more than they ever expected.

Chapter Twenty-Six

Weapons and It All Begins

Gradually, everyone working at the beach house began to drift indoors. They had found several shooting positions and set them up for action later on. If they had guns to use in the bunkers, it would make more sense. Luis called Cande and told her they had some good success and should be back in an hour. They had one more stop on the way back in and asked for someone to find some 9-volt batteries at the hotel store. He recommended they eat dinner at the hotel even if the Russians were there.

Luis and Eli arrived back in La Fe and quickly located Pedro and five of his friends. They had guns to sell—too many guns. Between them, they had 10 weapons of strange varieties. Another AK47 in bad shape surfaced.

"Mind if I test fire it?" Luis asked and the man nervously said it was okay.

Luis aimed at an empty Crystal beer can in the road which was a safe distance from any houses. He pulled the lever and placed a shell in the chamber from a twenty round clip. He aimed on single fire and it burped to life. Automatic fire worked flawlessly. The gun just looked like it had been to war and lost. They settled for $400 dollars and got ammo in the deal. There were two 8mm Mauser-type bolt-action rifles of WWII era.

"If you want a bolt-action rifle, the Mauser is king of the world," Luis said. "These babies grab the spent round and throw them out. Hard to jam and don't need springs like the other makers"

There was ample ammo, and the test fire went well. Three hundred dollars apiece bought them and a bunch of ammo. Next was a .30 caliber US carbine and plenty of ammo. The man settled at $350 and was thrilled to get it. The rest of the weapons were single-shot 410 and 12 gauge shotguns. Eli didn't want them, nor did he want old .22 caliber single shot rifles. As they were about to leave, an old man said to wait a minute. He went inside Pedro's house and returned with a weapon wrapped in an old quilt.

"What have you got there, old man?" Luis asked.

He carefully unfolded the antique wedding ring quilt, layer by layer, as though a statue of his mother were being unveiled. All of the Cubans at Pedro's house were peering at the presentation as though they had never seen the object. Maybe they never had, because as the last layer of quilt was moved aside, there was an audible gasp from everyone. What lay in the old man's loving arms was a Thompson sub-machine gun in pristine condition. It could have come from the Colt factory yesterday. Eli took it as if he was about to hold a newborn baby and looked at the metal stamping and serial number. Maybe he could research its history later. It did have Colt listed on the main assembly, and .45ACP was stamped along with model 1921A. The wood was beautiful; the quality was outstanding, along with chromed parts on the inside of the weapon. Luis held it carefully and both decided it was genuine.

"Mister, where did you come by this weapon?" Luis asked in Spanish.

"My grandfather worked for the FBI in New York. He took it after a raid on a whiskey operation in the Bronx. The bad guys had several of them so he took one and hid it. It has been in the family for many years," the old man said as Luis translated.

"How much do you want for it?" Eli asked.

"I would like five hundred dollars. I have drums and ammo as well."

"I will give you five hundred in cash and write you a check for a thousand dollars more, as this is a very valuable weapon. Americans can buy these, but only if they were registered before 1986. I'm going to guess you didn't do that." Luis translated all of this to the man, who seemed delighted.

Eli paid for all the weapons and ammo, loaded them in the trunk, and drove towards the hotel. All were loaded except the Tommy gun. Luis held it, examined it, and patted it like it was a small child the entire trip. They both thought it was truly one of the most magnificent pieces of engineering ever created.

"Luis, can you believe collectors pay in the high five figures for these guns?"

"They are works of art in the gun world. Ultimately, they were too expensive to manufacture during the war, so only a limited number ever saw action. Even though they use smaller pistol-sized forty-five ACP ammunition, they were devastating at close range. We are damn lucky to have a hundred-round drum and two big clips, one a 20, and the other a 30 round capacity."

"Of all the stuff we scored, I'm excited we got flak jackets for the girls. We don't need them to get hurt in this operation," Eli said.

"We made out like bandits—which I guess we are now. We wrapped the chain back on the gate at the mine, and only took what we needed out of the explosives box in the shed. Locked the shed back and left the key where we found it. It might be years before they find some explosives missing—if they ever do," Luis said.

"I agree. Now let's get something to eat at the hotel. Maybe we'll have tea with the Russians."

***

The other members of the party were at the restaurant and had ordered for the two gun runners by phone before they arrived. It wasn't crowded, just the big dive group and the Russians who ignored everyone else and stuffed their faces with food. The Ukrainians sat at their own table, oddly separating themselves from the Russians.

Lana observed the situation. "Those soldiers do not like the Russians. I am going to guess the others are from someplace like the Ukraine. I may go by and speak to them to see what they're up to even though I know they'll lie to me."

"Be careful not to piss off those two big ones. I don't have a gun on me," Julio said.

A salad arrived with some of the produce that had been brought in for them by the party of eight. Lana took a few bites of hers, then stood up and headed for the three guys wearing desert fatigues across from the Russians.

"Hello, I'm Svetlana Barkov." She spoke in Russian, and the Ukrainians rose to their feet at the sound and approach of such a beautiful woman. Miloslav, Jaro, and Branka introduced themselves, and Lana knew immediately they were Ukrainian. They knew she was Russian.

"Are you on vacation here?" she asked, knowing the answer would be a rehearsed statement.

"We're scuba divers and heard this is one of the best spots in the world," Branka said, clearly attracted to the pretty Russian.

"Indeed it is. We also plan to dive. Our Cuban and American friends bought a beach house not far from here. We will help them work on it. They are nervous about people coming by to harm them which I know you wouldn't do. They are not so trusting, so please, for your own safety, don't trespass on the property. Your Russian friends will surely tell you to go there, but the results will not be good. I think you have been pushed into working for them. If that is the case, we will pay you more to work for us." She whispered this offer so the Russians couldn't hear at their table.

"It was nice to meet you, and I hope we get to go diving together." Lana hugged each one, catching them off guard and causing a universal blush to come over all three faces. She smelled wonderful to them.

As she walked past the Russians' table, she gave them the finger and smiled. Each responded by sticking his finger through a closed fist and moving it up and down rapidly. They laughed and dove back into their food. Both the Ukrainians and Russians checked out her beautiful legs and ass as she walked away. It was impossible not to, as she wore very tight short shorts, and her long, tanned legs were perfect in every way.

"Well, you got them excited didn't you?" Julio said, with a tinge of jealousy.

"Recruiting, my dear,—recruiting."

"After dinner, why don't we go to the house? We bought a large lock for our front gate and several other items of interest," Eli said.

"I hope you scored some booze for us," Gina said.

"We got beer, tequila, rum, vodka, wine, a few mixers, some food, bottled water, coffee, and breakfast stuff. We stopped at a little grocery store outside of La Fe. Picked up batteries too and a couple cans of gasoline," Luis said.

"I'm going to get orange juice to go here for my screwdrivers," Kelsi said.

After dinner, they drove their two cars to the front of the beach house. Along the way, everyone pointed out the bunkers and how they would be used. When Luis and Eli told everyone about getting two AK47s and a Tommy gun, a feeling of relief came over the group. When they explained they had high-explosive remote control detonators, a hush went over the crowd. Everyone was thinking the same thing: *"We are seriously going to kill some people."*

Once inside, Julio laid out a sheet of paper and drew where he thought the guns should be placed and with whom. He hadn't forgotten about the boat and had a plan there for a floating explosive charge. The explosives wouldn't be aimed at sinking the boat; instead, it would be positioned to take out landing parties in either Zodiacs or other small craft. They took the guns out of the cars and laid them on the table: two pump shotguns, two 8mm Mauser bolt action rifles, a semi-automatic 30.06, two AK47s, a 30 caliber carbine, a semi-automatic .22 with a scope, and a Thompson sub-machine gun. Ten long guns and three pistols. Plenty of ammunition, weapons, and explosives. They were now a little army, but not a well-trained one.

"Tomorrow we will set up a target range near the landing strip. Please don't shoot my airplane," Julio said with a smile. Then he turned serious. "What's likely to happen is that the people who want to take the money will shoot to kill. They are well trained. The Russian goons not so much as the Ukrainians, but both groups are experienced. Lana may be able to turn them later if we have time.

"Just a comment. I know Julio has laid out a series of bunkers and sniper hides. The one on the roof is essential but should be expanded to more than one shooter. The ones in the woods by the bulldozer blade and the old tire rims, in my opinion, should be used as decoys. Make a dummy person—dummy gun—clothes—hat and let them be drawn to it. They might have night vision capacity on their scopes. We have one set of binoculars that has starlight capacity. These men will not come in a car down our road. They will stay in the tree line—move at night and hug the rock wall in front of the house.

"The bunker by the airstrip has a good view of the road on the tree line side. The people on the roof have a good view of the near side of the rock wall. I think the rock wall will be irresistible to the soldiers and the very reason we will set explosives by it every so many feet. They can't observe us placing them. The same with the tree line above the decoys. As they think they are ambushing us, we will set off explosives. We have tracers for gasoline cans and enough firepower to keep them pinned down. Where are we weak? Backside of the house and on both sides. We need shooters there and gas cans close to where they might hide but in line of sight for our rifles. We have paid three people at the hotel to tell us when the Russians move out. They will try to avoid everyone, so we can't count on them.

"We're not ready, but they may be set to do recon on our position. So, I suggest we put people on entrance points while the rest of us are working on laying explosives, making dummies, and covering our weak places. However, if I were them, and wanted to capture this place, I would attack as quickly as possible while we're nowhere close to being ready. We have a few hours of daylight left, and I suggest two or three people on entrance points with automatic weapons. Be careful that they don't get behind you and garrote you. It might deter them if they see how well armed we are.

"Eli and I will start laying out explosives. Cande and Lana can help. We have wireless detonators but we only have three channels, so we must spread them out where several areas are covered with each blast. Gas cans need to be placed along the wall and covered mostly with dirt. Leave a little of the top to be exposed for a tracer strike. We don't have much time. Josh, will you take Kelsi and Gina near the fence by the front gate to the property? Find observation points and stay hidden. Have your phones turned on. Show them how to use the automatics. Julio, why don't you take over the operations with a command post on the top of the house? Take the sniper rifle and the starlight binoculars. It's your call to take out those coming in and to point out targets. All of us placing explosives will have our weapons. Everyone, put on your vests and head out. Most likely what we will see tonight will be recon teams gathering intel." Luis's voice suggested he was in full battle mode.

In the boathouse, storage room sacks of nails were found and placed on the explosives by the wall. The jackhammer and compressor were stored there and covered with a tarp. While Lana, Luis, and Cande were laying charges every twenty feet along the wall and covering them with dirt and nails, Eli headed to the tree line and hid explosives at the rear of each of the improvised bunkers. He took clothes, hats, and some old shoes up and stuffed them with pine needles. He then walked back in the tree line about fifty yards to a spot that looked like it might be a good observation spot and planted two explosive charges in the front and rear of the clearing. He then returned to help the two girls. Julio checked in periodically by calling everyone.

When the charges were all set, Eli and Luis hurried to the airstrip bunker and sent Cande and Lana to the roof observation area. He asked them to keep an eye open for the boat at the rear. No one had seen it lately, but it was somewhere and probably observing.

"Jesus, Eli, do you know what charges go with these Smart Shot detonators?"

"One and two are along the wall. I think number one starts the closest to us because we placed them first. Three is in the woods," Eli said. "Are you sure you can you see those numbers in the dark?"

"Barely, with this baby flashlight." Luis produced a tiny flashlight attached to the end of a keychain.

"Luis, in America we call those nerd lights."

Luis ignored the statement and kept studying the wireless detonator. He turned the base station on, lighting up a green keyboard and a blue screen. It asked for a pin number and he entered it since it was taped to the top of the screen. He plugged the connectors into the base station under their corresponding number. A signal would be sent to receivers placed on each explosive. The signal would then activate a battery which would heat up a wire attached to a PETN initial detonator that would set off the explosive charge—in theory, that's the way it should work. The lights above the three plugged in remotes were red. Both men thought they should be green. Eli took the set of instructions and started studying it.

"It makes sense about the locations, Eli, but if we see someone in the woods, then we have to set those all off at once. We waste explosives that way, but it can't be helped."

In a few minutes, Luis's phone buzzed. He answered, "Yeah. What's up, Julio?"

"Got three men in the woods above the dummies walking towards them, and two headed this way at the far edge of the airstrip behind your bunker. All are armed."

"Holy shit. What now, boss?" Eli asked.

Chapter Twenty-Seven

The Russian Attack

Lana turned to Julio. "Dear, everything depends on those two guys in that bunker. Can we help them?"

"We can call in their shots. There might be enough moonlight for me to take a shot, but it doesn't look good. Get on the phone and call in the three people by the fence. Have them stay on the beach house side of the rock wall. They have to blow the explosives by the dummies right now."

"What is it, Julio?" Luis asked as he nervously grabbed the phone.

"You gotta blow the fucking explosives in the tree line. Now!"

Eli and Luis pressed the button above the number three red light. Nothing happened.

"What the fuck?" Luis said.

"It says here in the instructions there is an activation switch somewhere on the control box," Eli said as he reached for the base station.

"There it is!" Luis and Eli found it at the same time and flicked a red toggle switch on top of the main box. The red lights above where the three wires were plugged into the transmitter apparatuses blinked off and on. One at a time, they slowly turned green. Finally, after what seemed like a lifetime, the light above the number three detonator flashed green. Immediately, Eli pressed the button under it. It dinged and instantly they heard three deafening blasts come from the tree line and a yell from someone.

"One of the three Ukrainians is down—the others are carrying him out through the back of the tree line. Most likely they're going back to the hotel to get medical attention. I'll have Lana call for the

German doctors to go check on them. She can translate for them if needed. I really don't think they'll be back in the fight.

"The other two are closer to you now—about ten paces apart. They appear to have night goggles on—probably have infrared capability. They will make you out unless you hide your body heat behind the brick hut. Do you have any gasoline in there?"

"Yes. Some aviation gas," Luis said.

"Good. Do you see a glass bottle and some rags?"

"Yes—we see what you're getting at. I see a coke bottle and some rags. I'll fill it with gas—put some oily rags in and light it from the back of the hut. You need to tell me when they're close enough," Luis said. "Eli, those night goggles work great in the dark, but give them a flash of bright light and they'll be temporarily blind. We then move out and shoot from both sides of the hut."

"Sounds like a plan," Eli said. "A Molotov cocktail for two deserving Russians."

"Throw it now!" Julio cried.

Eli lit it with a butane lighter he had brought along in case they needed to light fuses on the explosives. Luis stood back from the hut and hurled it over the shed in the general direction of the two men moving towards them. The glass bottle hit the gravel driveway and skidded to a stop without breaking.

"Holy mother of God—nothing's working tonight!" Eli said.

The Russians, not knowing what was thrown at them, instinctively shot at the burning object. One of their bullets struck the coke bottle, freeing the gasoline and igniting it from the attached burning rag. The explosion was not so violent as it was a huge fireball of burning aviation fuel. While the Russians were temporarily without their normal sight, Eli and Luis opened fire on both of them using fully automatic weapons from the front side of the hut. Both hit the ground but only one got up again; he was clearly hit as he was limping badly.

Julio's voice crackled over Luis's phone. "You got one—he's down—not moving—probably dead—looked like a head shot. The other is wounded in the leg and moving towards the old bunk house."

"Shit, Luis, he's going to be hard to dislodge from that place. Can you get a shot off from here?" Eli asked. As he spoke, Luis let go a stream of .30 Caliber rounds from his carbine at the object he saw running away from him. The man went down again but quickly rose up and ran to the bunk house.

"I must have hit his vest. Eli, can we rig up another cocktail?"

Eli ran back into the shed while Luis lay prone on a little bit of high ground above the bunkhouse. There were no more bottles but there was a two-gallon plastic gas can about half full of aviation fuel. It had a plastic cap. Eli removed the cap and stuffed some rags in it. It wouldn't blow up, but they might get lucky and start a fire with the old decaying wood in the structure. As he ran over to where Luis was lying, another idea came to him.

"Luis, how far from the top of the house to the bunkhouse?"

"I don't know—maybe a hundred and fifty, two hundred yards. Why?"

"If we throw this gas can on the roof it might start a fire, but most likely the rag will go out, and we got nothing. If, however, we got someone on the top of the house to fire a tracer round in that gas can, all hell will break loose, and Mister Wounded Russian will leave his new happy home; he can give up or get dead. Whaddya think?" Luis didn't answer but buzzed his friend on the house top.

"We're going to toss a gas can on the roof of the bunkhouse, Julio. Do you think you can hit it with AK rounds?"

"In the daytime, when I could actually see what I'm shooting at—yes—maybe. If you can illuminate it somehow."

"We'll light the rags as best we can. I saw a big spotlight in the hut—I'll go get it."

"Be careful, Eli. Stay low."

As soon as he turned and hunched down to run to the hut, a series of automatic gunfire blasted from one of the windows of the old wooden shack. One struck his vest on his right upper back, knocking him to the ground. Another bullet whizzed by his ear, tearing off a small chunk at the top. The round sounded like the world's fastest and meanest hornet. Luis answered with several rounds aimed at where the muzzle blast was last seen.

"You okay?" Luis asked.

"Fine, my ear is smaller now." He reached up and felt the blood streaming down from his injured ear but decided to bandage it later.

His back was in pain from the round hitting his vest. It would be a bruise for sure.

Inside the hut, there were several large spotlights which may have been used to land a plane at night. He tried one that was heavy and large. A strong bright ray of light flashed on and hurt his eyes it was so strong. In an instant, he was back next to Luis above the bunkhouse.

"Is he ready?"

"Says he is."

Eli moved behind Luis and lit the rags.

"Cover me!"

Luis opened up on full automatic and then put in a fresh clip and started again as Eli swung the gas can through the air and onto the roof. The area where it landed was level so it stayed there. The rags were still burning, but the gas didn't spill enough to cause the fire to spread. Scrambling next to Luis, he turned the spotlight on the gas can. Immediately he drew gunfire from the wounded Russian. Since they were on higher ground, most of the rounds went above them, but the spotlight was now a beacon for target practice for the Russian.

"Wow! Look at that!" Luis said as tracer rounds slapped, sizzled, and thudded on the roof of the bunkhouse. It was a fireworks show and would have been highly entertaining if a man in an old cowboy-type shed wasn't trying to kill them.

"He ain't even close, Luis. Why don't you walk him in like it was artillery rounds," Eli suggested.

For about twenty minutes, while Eli held the spotlight and Luis spotted for Julio, the Russian continued to fire up at the two men occasionally spattering dirt from the rounds in their faces. Julio would give coordinates by saying, "Move up twelve inches and eight inches to the right."

Finally, like someone lighting the torch for the opening of the Olympics, the gas can exploded with a blinding intensity, and the old cowboy bunkhouse started going up in flames.

"There he goes!" yelled Luis as he climbed out the back of the partially collapsed structure. The Russian turned and fired a volley at both men while he took several rounds to his body and head from both the Tommy gun and the Carbine. He collapsed and made no more moves.

It was over for a while, and suddenly a question came to everyone's mind. *What would they do with two dead Russians?*

Chapter Twenty-Eight

Branka to the Hospital

The bodies of the two Russians were recovered and placed in the trunk of one of the rental cars. Everyone except Eli and Gina left to go to the hotel. Lana had called ahead and found out the two German doctors who had been scuba diving at the Colony Hotel were now back in their element and working on Branka. A large piece of wood had blown through his upper right thigh and was still lodged there. The Germans were both outstanding surgeons, and one was a specialist in vascular surgery.

Julio was planning on flying Branka to a hospital in Havana that would have a better operating room. He hoped the two doctors would go with him. Luis and Lana were going to take the bodies to a funeral home on the island.

Gina bandaged Eli's ear and checked the large bruise on his back where the bullet had struck his vest.

"Sweetheart, we're going to take advantage of our down time here. Pick a bedroom," Eli said.

"How about one that has a bed in it and a lock on the door?"

The couple chose one of the upstairs rooms where Mary and Pete had washed all the linens in preparation for the new owners' occupation. The windows looked out over the ocean where the beach and the white tips of waves could be seen in the moonlight. There wasn't a boat visible, nor were there any lights in the distance. A bright, almost-full moon illuminated the beach as noisy waves crashed every few minutes. Occasionally, dark clouds would paint the moon and cause total darkness. The waves were getting stronger suggesting a storm might be brewing.

In the distance, lightning pulsed and flickered beyond the distant horizon. A storm was on the way. Soon, the blood spilled on that night would be washed into the sea. For now, Eli and Gina had catching up to do. The two lovers removed their clothes and stared at each other, feeling lucky to be alive. They watched the approaching storm for a few minutes, then moved to the bed and made love as the sounds of distant thunder vibrated the world around them.

"Eli, I'm so glad you're okay. I realized while I was on the roof how lonely and lost I'd be without you."

"We'll earn that money buried below the boathouse. I hope no one else dies—but if we're attacked by the people on the boat—well, we'll defend ourselves. Hopefully, Lana is recruiting the Ukrainians right now."

Eli placed himself inside her and stopped, enjoyed the feeling, kissed her, and then began slow and deliberated strokes. She smiled and responded to his motion. The thunder was louder, the wind was stronger, and it all added to the pent-up passion. It was a wonderful night to make love.

***

"What do you mean 'hurricane warning'?" Cande asked Julio.

"Martinez just told me that he heard it on TV. Not supposed to be a big one but a hurricane nonetheless."

"Crap! You know that means we can't fly Branka over to Havana or even take him by boat," Cande said.

Julio and Cande were standing in a passageway outside the Ukrainian's room. Luis had gone for coffee for everyone, and Lana was in with the doctors, translating Russian to English and some words in German. Mostly it was English since it was a language the Germans used fairly well. Josh and Kelsi were in the hotel manager's office calling the island's hospital to check the availability of an operating room and to find out if doctors were available. Josh explained to the nurse at Heroes del Baire Hospital in Nueva Gerona the urgency of the situation. She seemed unfazed.

"Sir, this hospital does not perform surgery at night. We were damaged 80 percent by hurricane Gustav in 2008 and haven't repaired everything yet. The American embargo has slowed our repairs."

Josh lit into her in Spanish. "In a short while, Luis Cimarro and Julio Vazquez will bring a wounded man to your hospital. Two German doctors will work to remove a log stuck through his thigh. Please have surgical nurses and an attending physician on hand to help. There's another hurricane brewing, so make sure your new emergency generator is online. Here's a number to call if you or the doctors have a question. Have a hand saw available. Do you understand?"

"Si." She hung up and began to assemble a team that would not embarrass the hospital in front of two war heroes.

Josh walked to Branka's room and let him know he was being taken to the local hospital. The two doctors, Lana, Julio, and Branka went in one car, while the other two Ukrainians, Luis, Cande, and Josh rode in one of the other rental cars which held two dead Russians in the trunk. Kelsi didn't want to go. She was tired and hungry. After she was fed, she would find Eli and Gina and get some sleep.

Several calls to Nueva Gerona by Luis finally found the funeral director. What everyone wanted was to see the dead Russians shipped to Moscow and picked up by Mr. Wolf, no questions asked, but they felt certain it wouldn't happen that way.

The Heroes del Baire Hospital had the capacity at one time for about 300 beds. Since Gustav tore through the island in August of 2008, it had never fully recovered. It was designated as a teaching hospital, so doctors came over from Havana during the week and were then on the first flights out on Friday afternoon. Skeleton crews were there on the weekend. Even though this was the summer, the medical school was still going on, but it was not as well attended as in the fall and spring. Also, this was Tuesday and there was staff around, even though they were mostly at home relaxing. The phone call Josh made changed all that.

Both cars pulled up at the emergency room entrance and found a wheelchair for Branka. He was so sedated that he was barely conscious. He had lost a lot of blood, but when Lana asked for his blood type, he knew it was AB positive. Several in the group were O positive and agreed to be donors since it was universally accepted as donor blood for all types. The attending nurses took care of the blood donations as soon as they could. When they saw Branka's leg with a huge tree limb sticking out from both sides they gasped and staggered backward. It looked impossible to save his leg or maybe even his life as he had been impaled for several hours now.

Josh and Lana stayed to translate to English when needed. The rest of the group had dead bodies to deal with, so they set off to meet with the local funeral director.

The teaching doctors, who included some talented surgeons, were all willing to assist, and the German doctors accepted their offer. Everyone who entered the operating room had to put on scrubs and remove all street clothes. Josh and Lana were translators but still were required to wear scrubs since they would be in the operating room. They were handed their set of green scrubs and told to change in the hallway.

A row of chairs was dimly lit by a few surviving fluorescent bulbs in a ceiling full of burned out bulbs. The floor had been swept but not polished. There were broken windows and a few that were boarded over. The wind from the storm whistled through the broken panes. Far down the hallway, they could see an area roped off with a pile of construction rubble within the warning tape. The hospital didn't smell clean, and even though it was a teaching hospital it was nothing like the pictures of the hospital Fidel and Raul had shown the world. Josh had heard that a few good hospitals were open for foreigners who paid for their services. Any hospital that didn't get these funds were substandard—even filthy, and you were required to bring your own linens and bed clothes, clean your own room, and family or friends brought your food since the hospital food was inedible or non-existent.

The sight of Lana undressing in front of him blurred the picture of hospital horrors and snapped his brain to attention. She stood in front of him wearing only a pink thong. Her tanned and slim body was much like a lingerie model except for her large breasts which actually pointed upward—a phenomenon he had only seen in pictures. He wondered, *are they real?*

"Do we have to take off our underwear as well?"

"Yes, they may hold harmful bacteria." Josh had no idea if underwear needed to be removed, but he did know he wanted to see this beautiful Russian girl naked, and he was so convincing she practically ripped them off. He held her arm as she wiggled into the cotton pants with a drawstring at the waist and helped her with the pullover top. He removed his underwear and began to pull on the hospital scrubs, turning away from Lana somewhat to hide his erection, but she spotted it.

"Hot Russian girls turn you on, Josh?"

"You do have an incredible body, Lana. I'm sorry, but it was a natural response."

"I feel honored you find me so attractive."

"Let's hope it goes down in the operating room."

"If the room is cold like most of them, it should shrink up quickly," she said.

It wasn't cold, though. The OR didn't have air conditioning, only two large fans in two corners of the room. It looked like a movie set for a 1950s movie. A few monitors were new, and the lighting was modern. The German doctors looked over the medical instruments and frowned. Some appeared to be rusty and the selection was sparse. The Germans removed all of them and spread out the equipment they had brought with them, particularly the delicate equipment needed to repair, clamp, and sew blood vessels. A total of three Cuban surgeons assisted. They were smart and well-trained for standard operations such as gallbladders, hernias, and colon resections, but none of them had ever seen anyone repair blood vessels. A few had seen bypass operation, but stents were not done in Cuba unless foreign doctors performed the task in Havana. They desperately wanted to learn everything they could from the Germans; not that they would use it in this hospital, but the better hospitals for foreigners would have the equipment to perform more delicate procedures.

Dr. Fredrick Hinz received his medical degree from Harvard. His residency was completed at the University of San Francisco. He had been recognized as one of the top ten vascular surgeons in the world. He now had his hand wrapped around the large piece of wood running through Branka's leg. The other German doctor had turned towards the ceiling lamp and placed an old-style x-ray against it. They had taken the image when Branka first came into the hospital. The lamps in the x-ray reader on the wall were not working. One of the Cuban doctors said, "It was broken because of the American embargo." Many had learned this excuse almost at birth.

The doctor holding the x-ray was Herman Kunze. He had stayed in Europe for medical school and chose Oxford Medical School. His residency was completed at Vienna General Hospital in Vienna, Austria, which is the largest hospital in Europe. He was also ranked as one of the top ten surgeons in the world. After a few years, the two friends opened their medical practice in Berlin and since then had been asked to lecture and train all over the world. It could very well be that the two best surgeons in the world were looking back and forth at an x-ray and a stick of wood.

Branka's vitals were being monitored on a machine that most likely was delivered in the trunk of a brand new 1957 Chevy. The German doctors made sure there were electronic paddles and that they worked before they started the long operation. Everyone was ready to get started. Dr. Hinz asked Lana to tell him they were going to anesthetize him and would do their very best to save his leg. She told him and he nodded okay.

Then Branka told Lana, "If I don't make it would you please send the money I received from Horst Wolf to my mother Natasha. Miloslav and Jaro know her address. She takes care of my niece who is only four years old and both will need money. Thank you, Lana, for helping me."

Lana told the doctors what he said as she wiped tears from her eyes.

"We will do the best we can, Lana," Dr. Hinz said. "Josh, please tell the Cubans to be prepared to assist if we need them to help stop the bleeding, to pull on the wood, and to put their finger on a vein or artery when needed. Also, if the storm causes us to lose power, I want that emergency generator on immediately."

While a log was being removed from a man's leg in a run-down Cuban hospital, a delegation of Cubans and Ukrainians held open the trunk lid of their car and explained to a terrified mortician the need to dispose of the two dead Russians resting next to the spare tire.

It was starting to rain.

Chapter Twenty-Nine

Shark Dog Crew

With a hurricane coming from the east, the captain of the 623 Blue Water power boat *Shark Dog* decided to look for a protected bay before the brunt of the storm hit. Everyone on board knew what had happened at the beach house from paid informers at the Colony Hotel. It worried Melville Oliver a great deal and caused Justin Clay and his girlfriend Sami Brooks to second guess the whole adventure.

Melville was sixty years old, overweight, short—so short he had a wooden box he stood on to steer. He also wore a wig that wouldn't fool a three-year-old child. The patch of blond hair didn't match his silver sideburns.

Justin was a BMW salesman in Miami and did well but usually spent way above what he earned. He was tall, tan, handsome, and wore his Tommy Bahama shirt unbuttoned to show off a single heavy gold chain. It was easy to see he really used his LA Fitness gym membership and liked to expose his chest. His hair was too long, too slicked back, and too dyed.

Sami was a well-dressed, tanned, beautifully proportioned, blonde slut. If she had a job, she hadn't shared it with Melville or Justin, who introduced her as a college student. It was unlikely she had ever walked by a college, let alone showed up for class at even a junior college. She was arm candy and a great sleeping partner. Justin was pleased with her, and in the event she left, he would find another just like her.

The Blackwater men laughed off any notion this was a misadventure, saying the attackers were stupid and they would take the beach house with little effort.

A year ago, when Melville, Justin, and Sami were staying at the Colony and found out about the money hidden at the beach house, there were only four inexperienced college kids who were going to go after the money. They had no weapons, no military experience, and no one to teach them. Now they had two military heroes, their military-trained girlfriends, and a full arsenal of weapons and explosives.

The four professionals on Melville's boat claimed that the heroes were flyboys and not combat soldiers. The Blackwater men were professional soldiers turned mercenaries by reason of various infractions that cost them their military careers. One, named Jimbo, had raped a young female helicopter pilot after they were shot down in Afghanistan. He denied it and said it was consensual, and she couldn't prove the allegation. They were in the desert for five days and she lost the chance for a rape kit to be utilized. Later, after he was cleared, Jimbo told his friends, "I thought the reason girls were in the field was to fuck us and keep our spirits up." They laughed, and then he filled out an application for Blackwater.

"We have three hurricane holes to hide in around this island. We can go up to the mouth of the San Pedro River below the Colony hotel or further north to Esteo del Pino. These two areas have no services—just a place to get out of the wind. If, however, we go way around to the top of the Island to Piedra Bay, we will be practically in downtown Nueva Gerona—bars, food, and women. That's for the other men, Sami—I'm sure you'll keep Justin on a leash."

"It sounds like you've made the decision. From our present position, it will take us about ten hours. If the boat is damaged or any of us are injured by the storm, there's a medical facility there," Justin said.

"If we decide to attack by land—we are just a couple of rental cars away," Jimbo said as he patted one of the hand grenades attached to his opened flak jacket. The four mercenaries had formulated a plan, and they didn't want the other three involved except as a diversion. The boat owner was emphatic that he didn't want anyone killed. They planned to split up and attack from both the sea and the land. They had brought along some professional gear that would allow for a full nighttime assault. It had to be a surprise and a well-coordinated attack—and the "don't kill anyone" request would be completely ignored. For now, they intended to bar hop and chase whores in Nueva Gerona.

The *Shark Dog* moved into the shipping channel and set a course that would take them to the other side of the island. Melville knew in a few days he would have to repeat the trip and deliver four very mean and talented soldiers close to the beach house. They had no idea that two and maybe three very talented Ukrainians would be joining forces as defenders of the beach house. It would not be a pleasant surprise.

***

The lights flickered a few times in the operating room as the storm intensified and put pressure on old power lines and poorly built structures. Communism promised free housing to everyone, but putting that wet dream to work meant waking up to the reality of large rectangular building with no air-conditioning, no washer and dryers, and a structure that began to fall apart as soon as humans moved in. Beyond the shoddy workmanship, they were butt ugly. The hospital wasn't constructed much better. It had been damaged by a serious hurricane, and repaired with Band-Aids and bailing wire. They needed to run a jack under the waiting room and run a new hospital under it. Branka, however, was just glad any facility was there to give him a chance of saving his leg.

Dr. Hinz had been part of several surgical teams that dealt with impaled objects. One such group of doctors had operated on a man involved in a horrific car crash. A metal fence post had penetrated his abdomen, then traveled through his thigh and impaled his calf. He lived.

In all the cases Dr. Hinz had seen involving the thigh, the femoral artery was a key as to whether a patient would survive. If it had been severed at the scene of the accident or shooting, even if a tourniquet was used properly, the patient would most likely lose their leg or die on the spot. Branka's injury was straight forward. His artery wasn't compromised and he had great care from the very beginning. Keeping his leg intact wasn't a clear outcome.

"Let me have that electric saber saw," Dr. Hinz said. He hit the switch and it noisily came to life when he tested the trigger. He then trimmed the tree limb from the bottom fairly close to its entry into the thigh.

"I want the distance we pull it through to be as short and smooth as possible." He checked the area where one of the nurses had sanded the wood smooth near the wound.

"Here is our mission. When Dr. Kunze pulls the wood towards him, we need doctors on each side of the wound to hold blood vessels and cauterize them. The bark and grain of the wood is going away from him so we reduce splintering. The entire inside of the wound will need to be treated with antibiotics, then shunts put in to drain and observe for infections. We hope to repair muscles, blood vessels, and any other tissue that can be repaired. Are you ready, Herman?"

With a tap from a hammer on the lower side of the thigh and a steady consistent pull, a huge bloody tree limb came free and was dropped into a long metal tray held by a nurse who almost fainted when she saw it. It was out.

***

"They won't dock off shore and paddle to the beach house. These are seasoned soldiers who have most likely screwed up or they wouldn't be mercenaries now, but they have good skill sets. If I was in charge of them, they would be attacking in two places at once and you would never see them until they were right on top of their enemy," Miloslav Sirko explained to Lana.

Lana had taken a break from the operating room after the major blood vessels had been repaired and muscles bound back together in a flurry of skilled workmanship by two great surgeons. It had taken several hours. Branka was alert, talkative and feeling no pain for now. Lana had been the translator for Branka when he was awake, which was most of the time since most of the anesthesia was given as a spinal block. He did sleep some since he was groggy. Miloslav and Jaro had agreed to work for the Americans and the Cubans and had come back to the hospital to discuss it with Josh and Lana. Luis and Julio had convinced the mortician to cremate the two Russians and to send the ashes to Horst Wolf. He would not be pleased. They also had come to the hospital to find out the status of Branka.

"He is recovering well. I think they have saved his leg and life, but the healing process well be long and infections are always going to be a concern. He is young and in great physical shape, so that might tip the scale in his favor for his leg regaining function." Lana spoke directly to the two Ukrainians in their language, then back to English for the rest of the group as she stood outside the operating room entrance.

"Lana, we need you back in here. Branka wants to talk to the doctors," Josh said.

She put on fresh gloves and entered a much less hectic operating room. Branka was sitting up in his hospital bed, his leg still totally numb. Lana translated his questions to the doctors.

"Branka, you will experience considerable pain as your injury begins to heal. The pain, which we will control, is a good sign nerves are still intact. Muscles, tendons, veins, and arteries have been repaired. A good deal of antibiotics are being given to you both orally and topically to curtail infection. We will bandage your wound, but you will have shunts front and back for drainage. You should be able to leave the hospital tomorrow, but you need to stay off that leg for at least two weeks," Dr. Hinz said. "We want you bending it and raising it several times a day so atrophy doesn't set in, but it needs to heal before you put pressure on it—let's say the earliest would be ten days and then with crutches. I will send some home with you."

Josh and Lana agreed to take him to the hotel with the extra burden of a wheelchair with a straight leg extension added. Miloslav retrieved all his equipment from the hotel and found a place to bunk in the beach house for the night. Josh and Lana had asked the Ukrainians to work as mercenaries with them at the house, and they enthusiastically accepted. Branka agreed to stay at the hotel for a few days before moving to the beach house; Jaro would stay with him. The German doctors would come by to check on him to assess the wound. They would be leaving in a week but left word with a local Cuban teaching doctor to look in on him. His healing process would take a long time even with physical therapy and consistent care. His life and leg had been saved.

***

Jimbo and his Blackwater friends had found a bar, planted themselves, and swore they wouldn't leave until the hurricane blew over. Restaurante Rio sat directly on the river, and Jimbo and his crew had docked the *Shark Dog* dingy at a small extended wooden dock they assumed was owned by the restaurant. The winds had not yet reached the velocity required to be called a hurricane, but it had produced enough foul weather to be named Tropical Storm *Angela:* the first of the season. A few local women came in and sat at a table not far from the bar. The men from the *Shark Dog* crew headed there immediately.

One of the women was young, well built, and beautiful. She was Zamira Molina, the daughter of the Mayor Ramon Molina. As Jimbo pushed hard to take Zamira to a local hotel for a night of pleasure for him and total disgust for her, his repulsive language and posturing became unbearable for her. A local policeman was near the entrance to the Restaurante Rio, and she waved to him to come over.

"Sir, I am telling you to leave the bar and go back to your ship." He had seen them dock the dingy.

"No, I'll set out da storm here," Jimbo said and struggled to his feet while his friends tried to pull him back down. Zamira sought protection by moving directly behind the cop and crouched down low. "You're da island rent-a-cop." Jimbo was drunk and his words were slurred. "Not 'fraid of ju." Jimbo reached for the back of his waistband where he had a 9mm Sig Sager lodged against the crack of his ass. He pulled the unsanitary weapon and pointed it at the policeman. His friends tried to grab the weapon, but it fired striking the cop on the outside portion of his upper thigh and traveling through to Zamira's arm and left shoulder as she had positioned herself low behind him for protection. Blood began to come quickly from the wounds. The bartender, a veteran of bloody knife fights and shootings, leapt across the bar with a fistful of white hand towels. Towels were placed against bubbling red fountains to serve as makeshift compresses. Zamira's friends jumped to the aid of their friend who immediately threw up from the shock of being shot.

The cop yelled at the fleeing men, "Stop! Stop! He pulled his 9mm Russian Makarov automatic and sent parabellum rounds toward the fleeing men who dodged the bullets as they flew down the steps to the dingy. Dragging his wounded leg, leaving a trail of blood seeping from under the bar towel, he leveled his pistol at the departing dingy and fired the last five rounds in a good pattern at the men bunched in the small boat. Groans and one scream sliced through the steady rainfall as they left.

In a matter of minutes, an ambulance and Zamira's father slammed to a stop in front of the bar. First aid was given to both of the wounded by one of the teaching doctors who had been assigned to stay in Nueva Gerona to care for Branka. There was blood loss and shock, but the wounds weren't life-threatening. The bullet had not tumbled when it struck either victim, going in a straight line, penetrating without hitting bone, exiting Zamira's shoulder with a small and barely detectable hole. Had the round tumbled, mushroomed, or ricocheted, the outcome would have been very different. A call was made for all available patrol boats, but none were available until the storm subsided. By then the *Shark Dog* had disappeared into low-hanging rain clouds.

Chapter Thirty

The Safe: A First Attempt

Eli and Gina woke up next to each other nude and covered in sweat. It was hot, and no air was circulating. Eli got up and turned the overhead fan on high by pulling on the chain twice. After opening two windows to let in some cool morning air, it smelled of salt, fish, and recent rain. They began to cool down and felt much better.

Eye contact and light touching seemed appropriate for a while. Eli traced Gina's mouth and then her nipples, navel, and gently massaged her vagina and tugged lightly at her pubic hair. She rubbed him softly in his groin and quickly found a fully formed hard member in her hand. Just to make him want her more, she massaged the head and stroked the length of the shaft. Every time he tried to move on top of her she stopped him and made him wait. Finally, she climbed on top of him and put him inside of her. She was wet, and Eli was in agony. Time, responsibilities, the future, the past—nothing mattered. She controlled the slow strokes and smiled broadly as she locked her eyes on his. When she thought he was about to climax, she would stop and lean down and kiss him lightly on the mouth. Finally, her thrusts became hard, fast, and deliberate. He moaned and cursed and moaned and cursed until he was completely spent. Both loved to start their day exactly the way it started on this day.

Everyone staying at the beach house decided to go to the Colony to eat breakfast. There had been no effort to bring in perishable foods even though the refrigerator was working. It stunk. No hands went up when volunteers were sought to clean it. Pete and Mary were coming over later in the day to work on it and also to get the house in order. Eli had given them money for a long grocery list. He didn't hold out much hope for getting many of the items requested. They were coming in the house as all the others were headed to the hotel for breakfast. Eli took a quick glance at the sacks of groceries carried in the house. He was impressed at the amount of fresh vegetables, meat, fruit, and dairy products. Eli reminded her to attack the smell in the refrigerator before she loaded anything.

"Use a gallon of Lysol!"

At breakfast, they were joined by Branka who had a rough night because of the pain in his thigh. He was using crutches with Jaro's help. The entire group, eleven in all, was at the Colony Hotel at the same table for the first time. As they were ordering their meals, a doctor from the hospital in Nueva Gerona dropped by to check on Branka. He had moved from the crutches to his wheelchair earlier, so the doctor wheeled him to an adjoining room and examined his wound. There was some redness, but no serious infection, and his temperature, while slightly elevated, was at an expected range. The doctor pushed him back to the table where his wheelchair was positioned to extend his leg out of the way.

"Did you hear about the shooting last night?" The doctor directed his question to everyone at the table. Very little excitement ever occurs in the sleepy town of Nueva Gerona so he couldn't wait to tell them.

"Some sailors from the powerboat *Shark Dog* shot a cop and the mayor's daughter. Both going to be all right. Clean wound. Went straight through both of them. The boat went off in the middle of the storm. When the coastal patrol gets finished helping people affected by the storm, they will go after them."

"Was there any gunfire exchanged by the cop?" Miloslav asked, imagining he would have returned fire with such a minor wound.

"Yes, the policeman fired as they were going down the steps to their dingy. He managed to drag his bleeding leg behind him and fire the rest of his clip into the dingy as it motored away. He's an excellent shot and believes he plugged a couple of them," the doctor said.

"Wow! I believe that's the same powerboat that was nosing around the beach house. Now, with wounded crewmen and our formable forces outnumbering them, they may decide to leave," Eli said.

No one could be sure about their departure, but the decision was made right there to start the recovery process.

After breakfast, a broad plan would be put in place to assign certain individuals to rotating guard duty and concrete removal chores. The windows in the boathouse would be blacked out while they worked at night. They finished breakfast in record time, and everyone but Jaro and Branka headed to the beach house.

In an hour, the first piece of concrete was placed in a black garbage bag by Eli and Gina, who did it in a symbolic movement and with broad smiles. They had located the button signifying the middle of the hatch by using the measurements made by Bernie and Carmine 57 years ago. A concrete chisel had found it quickly but wouldn't be suitable for removing much concrete. The button meant nothing had been disturbed in all those years. From the button to the edge of the circle or the radius, Eli placed a pencil tied to a string and made a circle representing the hatch cover. A few inches of concrete had been poured and smoothed over the surface.

"It's time for the big boy!" Eli said as he watched Luis and Julio walked toward the shed to get the compressor. In a few minutes, Luis carried a heavily constructed Ingersoll-Rand pneumatic air hammer. Behind him, Julio pulled a small compressor with rear wheels. It had a pressurized air tank with "California" written on it in big letters. It was electric powered, instead of the more powerful gasoline-powered models but would be fine for this operation. It would also be quieter—much quieter at only 60db. Outsiders would not hear an obvious, "breaking through the concrete to find the dough" sound. Eli had posted guards before he started but felt uneasy. So he waited momentarily before using the air hammer.

"Gina, please check on the guards."

"All of them?"

"Please. That damn powerboat has to be headed in this direction."

"Okay, but if you get down to the hatch cover, don't open it until I get back."

Gina made the rounds where she found Miloslav manning the aircraft shed. Once it was checked, she found Cande by the Bull Dozer blade in the woods. Much of the foliage had been cleared by the explosion that wounded Branka. She checked the roof where Lana and Kelsi were using the night vision binoculars furnished by Branka and Jaro. Josh was on top of the boathouse with the rifle and night scope. There was no boat in sight, and five people were watching closely for any light or sound in the distance. Gina went back inside to report to Eli.

"Nothing moving. Got five people watching."

"Good. Let's get started." Eli hit the power switch and first broke the concrete around the circle he had drawn. After a couple trips around he found the edge of the hatch or at least the separation between the original concrete and the pour that filled in on top of the hatch. He stopped periodically as he pounded through more and more concrete, then he and Gina would remove the busted up pieces and put them in black plastic bags.

"Have you thought how we might get this money home? I know we've discussed it a dozen times, but nothing was settled," Gina asked.

"We said we would buy a boat—two boats. One we would set on fire to the north of the route we intend to use to leave, and, while the patrol boat investigates, we'll slip out of Cuban waters to the US. Come into an obscure port where we aren't likely to be searched, and transfer the money to safety deposit boxes or another home safe," Eli said.

"What I have heard is there isn't exactly the Miami boat show to pick from here. A bunch of fucked up fishing skiffs. Not much to pick from, and even then it's unlikely they will sell them," Gina said.

"I wish we had your mom's boat here," Eli said.

"You want me to call her and have it brought over?"

"No! Don't want her tangled up in this mess."

"You'd better get back to jackhammering."

Eli started the compressor and air hammer up and attacked another section of the concrete. He was removing the concrete as though it were a pizza, one slice of stony substance at a time. Each big slice meant more garbage bag with ground up pieces in it. Two hours of work left only the layer directly above the plastic hatch cover. He asked Gina and Kelsi to come in to view the last thin layer that had to be removed. It had busted through in a couple places so white plastic was visible.

***

Melville, Justin, and Sami had tried to save the Blackwater soldier. The 9mm slug from the cop's pistol had entered his upper back, moved through his neck, then tore into his chin and out the frontal part of his brain. He had been bent over in the boat when the policemen opened fire. He had been hit in two other places, but the brain shot killed him.

Jimbo had been hit twice. One through his left hand which took away his middle finger and another bullet caught his upper right shoulder, and then traveled and lodged next to his right clavicle bone. The pain was constant and he loaded himself with what morphine he could find.

"We're headed back to Key West to get you medical help," Melville informed Jimbo.

"To hell you are. I didn't get my ass shot to run home empty-handed," Jimbo said.

"You're in no shape to fight a force much larger than yours. It's my fucking boat and I'm going to try to get us out of here before we're all arrested as accomplices—thanks to you shooting a cop and the mayor's daughter.

Before Melville could take the wheel to direct the boat out of Cuban waters, Jimbo had a Kalashnikov assault rifle pointed directly at his head.

"I'll blow your fucking head all the way back to Florida. Set a heading for the beach house." He got to his feet and marched Melville to the bridge. He watched closely as he turned the boat in the direction of the Colony Hotel.

"You have to know they expect us to cut and run. We're being hunted, and no one would dream we would go back where the patrol boats could trap us. I think the Americans and Cubans are busy digging up the money because there isn't anyone left to take it away from them. Well, they should never count me out. We will attack when they least expect it." Jimbo staggered to a cushioned chair and placed his AK47 in his lap as he took a huge draw on a bottle of rum. The pain from his wound could be seen in his face.

As the powerboat made its turn, the body of the dead mercenary, wrapped with a diver's weight belt loaded with gray lead ingots, was pushed off the aft swim deck. It bounced a few seconds on the surface, then sunk as the wake from the twin diesels churned the water into a boiling white eruption.

Chapter Thirty-One

Branka Wants a War

Branka was feeling better as was evidenced by his demand to join his friends at the beach house. He had lain out carefully across the back seat of one of the rental cars as Jaro drove. There were visible grimaces across his face as they hit bumps and rocks in the road. Not only did he want to join everyone, he wanted a shooting position on the roof. Julio and Jaro took time out to carry him to the roof and placed pillows and mattresses in a way where he could lie flat and look through his night scope toward the water. With his gun and ammo at hand, he seemed to be in his element.

Jaro relieved Josh on the roof of the boathouse so he could assist with the opening of the vault. Luis joined Cande in the woods, and Julio nestled next to Lana in the captain's walk on the roof of the beach house. After a few minutes, Julio moved to the roof of the boathouse to assist Jaro.

Branka was the only one of his comrades to have been awarded the Order of Courage First Class by the Ukrainian President. While wounded in three places by pro-Russian militia insurgents, Branka Balanchuk rushed a bunker and machine gun nest. The insurgents had killed five of the men in his company from the bunker. One of his hand grenades took out the bunker, but twelve soldiers rose up behind it, and Branka took them all on with his AK47. He ran out of ammunition and successfully fought two survivors hand-to-hand, killing them with his knife, after having received his fourth bullet wound. Near death, his friends carried him to a helicopter. The crew on board saved his life by stopping the massive bleeding and reviving him several times before he got to the hospital. A little log through his leg was not going to keep him down. Given a little recovery time, he would be chasing young girls again. If there were a medal for landing beautiful women, he would have a chest full of them.

Miloslav and Jaro had done their basic commando training with Branka and were very capable soldiers. Because of a dismal economy in the Ukraine, they all swallowed their pride to work for the Russians. If they could survive this assignment and get a share of the money, their future and their family's would be secure. A quarter of a million dollars was worth a million or more in their home country.

With guards in place, including Julio and Luis joining on the roof, and an air hammer raised, there was no more waiting for the four Americans who had waited almost a year for this moment. Eli leaned over to Gina, smiled, and kissed her for good luck. The hammer hummed and crackled as it removed the thin layer of concrete covering the plastic hatch. Each time Eli raised the device, three people would start cleaning up the debris. He held the hammer in a manner as to not damage the plastic below the concrete. Once it was clear of shards of old concrete, Eli took a small chisel and worked around the edge of the seal all around the hatch door. Two fold-down handles on each side of the hatch had to be pried open with the blade of the air hammer. The moment required that all four people had to look each other in the eye and grin with a gleeful happiness usually reserved for a kid on Christmas morning.

"Here we go!" Eli said.

Josh and Eli pulled straight up with all their strength on each handle. Nothing. It did not move. Eli and Josh discussed drilling it open or possibly jamming a crowbar on the edge of the hatch.

"Move aside, boys. Obviously, neither of you has ever owned a boat," Gina said.

She reached for both of the handles at once and began to unscrew them from their locked positions. Gina gently raised the hatch cover and let it rest on the side of the concrete which was about five inches above the hatch cover level. Everyone peered in but could see nothing but wood.

"I'll take care of that." Eli lay flat on his stomach and slid his hands to the outside of the wood structure. It was a wooden post placed there to block metal detectors from picking up the metal safe. By twisting at the top he was able to roll the big column away from the opening. Kelsi held a flashlight and pointed it into the dark hole.

"I can see the safe," Kelsi said.

She also saw a wooden ladder next to the column directly below the entrance.

"Eli, let's maneuver it into place," Josh said. Both were prepared to go into the sunken room.

"You think there will be booby traps?" Kelsi asked. She held a light for them as they climbed down the ladder.

"I remember from the sketches that Bernie left us that there was a light switch and an electrical outlet in the room," Gina said.

"Do you remember where?" asked Eli.

"To the right of the safe on the wall."

Kelsi handed the flashlight to Josh as he followed Eli into the chamber. Once in front of the safe, he began mumbling to himself. The light switch was flipped up, and miraculously a double neon light blinked on and off and finally stayed on.

"Twenty-two left, fourteen right—what's next?" Eli stood staring at the huge safe. It stood almost seven feet tall and it was obvious the boathouse had been built around the giant safe. Eli saw the manufacturer's name, Schwab Corp., in raised letters above the door.

"Eighty left," Gina said. Both had memorized all combinations so the information wouldn't be written for someone to steal it.

"Come down and help me," Eli said. She did, and Kelsi called Josh up.

"Josh, Jaro wants you outside," Kelsi said.

Once he was outside, he learned that Branka had radioed in that there was movement seen in the tree line and in the water. Josh ran back inside and stuck his head in the safe chamber.

"Eli, we've got visitors!"

"Shit! Will we ever get to open that safe in peace?" He sent Gina up the ladder first and came up behind her, moved the ladder, and closed the hatch door. Once out, he pulled the rug over the hole. It didn't hide the large indentation above the hatch.

The four safe crackers in the boathouse ran to join Branka and Lana on the roof.

"Where are we needed?" Eli asked.

"Don't know yet. Possible scuba diver coming in from the ocean side. We picked up a warm spot a couple of times. Appears to be headed for the boathouse. Maybe—Eli, you support Jaro there. Milo is by himself in the shed. Josh, can you help out there?"

Kelsi and Gina were armed and positioned on the captain's walk area on top of the beach house. It was like a little fenced-in rectangle mainly built as a whimsical architectural appendage and link to the past when family members and sea captains would look out for ships. Julio radioed everyone and told them what was happening so the two didn't get shot by friendly fire. The three Ukrainians had military headsets with built-in radios. Everyone else had handheld communication devices.

Branka handed his night scope to Gina. "Try to pick up the image in the tree line."

Gina stretched out and propped on her elbows and focused the powerful infrared binoculars first on the two people by the Dozer blade. Then she traveled up above them. Nothing else could be seen. The woods to the right of them seemed clear as well. Quickly she scanned the road and was about to hand the instrument back to Branka when a reddish flash interrupted the green images on her night scope. She checked it again; there was someone by the wall next to the road. She watched as the image went over the wall and was now on the ocean side.

"Gina keyed on the mike switch on her radio. "One intruder inside the rock wall at about 300 to 400 yards."

"Roger that," Luis said as he moved out of the tree line toward the wall.

"Help me to turn in that direction," Branka said as Kelsi and Gina pulled him and his mattress near the edge of the captain's walk in the direction of the image. At about 200 yards out Branka took the shot as the warm image moved towards him along the rock wall. Branka could see through his scope his shot was successful. Nevertheless, he put a couple more rounds into the motionless body.

"Move me back towards the ocean," Branka said. Once there he watched the water for the diver to surface. The others watched all sides now.

"I see an image along the airstrip," Josh radioed from on top of the boathouse. The individual was at the edge of the gravel runway about 500 yards out. A few gas cans had been placed along the edge of the airfield with hopes they could be ignited by tracers from the AK47s. Earlier in the day, two inner tubes with gas cans were tied to a small wooden platform attached to the tubes. The best rifle for long distant shots was the Remington used by the now departed CIA agent, but the 7.62 tracer rounds wouldn't fit the weapon. Branka had just used it to take out the man by the rock wall. Both the top of the house and the roof positions on the boathouse had AKs and tracer rounds. These guns weren't known for their long range accuracy, but in the hands of a good marksman, a 200-to-300-yard shot was possible—beyond that it was only luck if you came close to the target. Some gunsmiths said you should expect a 24-inch drop at 200 yards. Others reported good groupings at 300 yards. It was hit and miss and depended on the ammo, the condition of the gun, the experience of the shooter, and whether he was shooting single shots or on full automatic. The knockdown and penetration power of the AK was unquestioned, but hitting those gas cans to light up the target was going to be a problem. The newer AK that Eli and Luis bought from the dealer might be the best option. The older one they purchased probably had been dropped on its sights and would be the less accurate of the two.

Branka was positioned to ignite the gas cans in the ocean when the diver got near them, so he wasn't going for the man on the airstrip. He held the better AK which could chamber the tracer shells. Milo had the old beat up AK and was in the process of climbing on the roof of the airplane shed to try his luck on the gas cans once the intruder passed them. There were gas containers at 400, 300, 200, 100, and 50 yards. The Cessna airplane was off the strip on the right side about

25 yards out. No one had to tell Milo and Josh to be careful and not damage the plane. Josh took a position prone on the ground to the left of the strip next to the shed.

"Milo, do you still see him?"

"Not in my gun sight, Josh. I only have iron sights on this thing and they look bent, but I can still spot him with my binocs—he's about 400 yards out, creeping along the inner edge of the airstrip. Can you see him in your sights?"

"No, the angle is bad from here on the ground. I can't see past the third gas can."

"Okay, let's plan to set off the 100 yard can once he passes it. He will be backlit and your sight will be overpowered for the moment of the explosion, but it should clear quickly for a shot. Is it a plan?"

"Best plan I've heard all day."

There was a crackle on everyone's radio. "Two divers near the boathouse—another behind the dozer moving fast on our position there. We're being hit from three areas at once!"

"Holy shit!" came from several people.

"Another—in a boat crossing offshore!"

"Fuck me! What's happening here?" Eli yelled on his radio.

"Bring it on!" yelled Branka.

Chapter Thirty-Two

Shark Dog Attacks

Julio called for calm. "The boat is a diversion! Go after the people you can see." Jimbo had demanded Melville run the fourteen-foot skiff back and forth like a madman to take the attention away from the divers. His big powerboat was anchored at a nearby cove out of sight.

"I'm trying for the gas cans floating near the boathouse. I need a shooter to take out the divers," Branka said.

"I'm your man," Julio said as he aimed the bolt action Mauser 30.06 in the direction of where he was told the divers had surfaced. He was perched on the top of the boathouse but could only see darkness. If Branka couldn't light up the sky, they would come ashore unharmed.

"Come on, you Russian whore—light the men up," Branka muttered to himself as he pulled the trigger on the old soviet weapon. The rifle spitfire and a tracer went in the water a foot or so in front of the inner tube. He adjusted the sights and moved it up a few inches.

He first patted the assault rifle on the top of the weapon and said, "My old Russian girl. I apologize for calling you a whore." An orange tracer came to life like a rocket from the barrel of Branka's famous Kalashnikov as he squeezed the trigger with no more force than it would take to squeeze a lemon. Branka knew that Mikhail Kalashnikov was also a poet at heart and only wanted a good defensive rifle. His design had been counterfeited so many times 50 percent of the 100 million weapons around the world were fakes. His hope was that this was a real one.

As Julio aimed his weapon, he was temporarily blinded by the red-orange explosion over the water. He looked away, let his vision heal, and drifted his sight over the now illuminated surface. Two figures were trying to put out fires in their hair, slapping and dipping under to douse the flames. One surfaced about 100 yards out. Julio's big bullet caught one diver in the chest. The second shot found the back of the skull of the other diver who was thrashing in the water trying to escape. Both were floating on the surface waiting for the gentle waves to wash them ashore.

Julio had no way of knowing that Justin and Sami had been forced to scuba dive into a death trap. Jimbo had planned the entire multipronged attack. It wasn't going well. He was out-gunned and had now found most of the firing positions were elevated and well manned. He wasn't finished, though and felt he had a few tricks that might reduce the odds. His fellow soldier in the woods heading towards two armed combatants was about to find the odds were against him.

Luis and Cande had moved back to the ocean side of the dozer blade when they heard on the radio a shooter was moving on their position.

"He must be really stupid or doesn't have infrared capability," Luis said.

"You have the Thompson. All I have is a pistol and a shotgun," Cande said.

"Get your shotgun ready—he's not far off." Luis could see he was moving through the trees at a fast rate, oblivious to any danger ahead.

Now, Luis could see his face, helmet, flax vest, and automatic weapon. He would ask him to surrender.

"Halt! Halt! Drop your weapon! Raise your hands or die where you stand."

Startled, he froze in place for a second and then opened up with his automatic weapon in the direction of the voice. Limbs and bark flew above the couple and the ringing sounds of bullets hitting the dozer blade sounded like spastic church bells. When the man began to change his magazine, Luis and Cande opened up on him with buckshot and automatic rounds. He fell in a heap and was dead before he hit the ground. They called in the encounter. Now there was one more fighter by the airstrip and the crazy boat person.

Jimbo was in terrible pain. Morphine and alcohol did little to stop the festering pain of having a bullet lodged in his shoulder blade.

His missing finger angered him more than it hurt. The strap holding a rocket-propelled grenade launcher across his back rubbed against the lodged bullet making movement a walk through hell. He had brought all this on himself. The girl at the bar, the cop, and now he was responsible for most of his crew's death.

Milton wasn't dead yet, but crisscrossing like an idiot in a small boat in front of one of the best shooters of any military in the world didn't insure a long life expectancy. Branka didn't know that Milton was forced to zig-zag at gunpoint by Jimbo. To Branka, he was another combatant, not a very bright one, but a target to be eliminated. Also, he was irritating everyone who had a weapon. There were times when no less than five weapons were aimed at him at once. It was bizarre no one had fired on him. Maybe he was just too crazy to shoot.

Milo and Eli had lost sight of their combatant around the 100-yard marker—somewhere just beyond it, they thought. Milo had Jimbo focused in his infrared binoculars when he saw him rise and fire the RPG.

"RPG! Run like hell!' yelled Milo as he dove off the right side of the shed. Eli took off to the left. Neither made it more than a few paces when the rocket-propelled grenade entered the doorway of the fuel shed and blasted straight through the glass window at the back of the small building. A millisecond later it exploded on the road in front of the beach house.

"What the fuck!" Jimbo said out loud.

Rifles from the house and boathouse showered down rounds all around him, but they were shooting in the dark. Now tracers were fired from the beach house and from Milo, trying to light up the area. It was difficult to see the gas can in the dark as well. Jimbo had taken the opportunity to move across the airfield into the tree line after the errant RPG blew up in the road. With four more rounds left, there was still a chance he could do serious damage. As he moved laterally using old island pine trees for cover, the first of the gallon gas cans erupted, lighting up the entire area like the sun had come out. No one was sure which tracer hit it, and no one cared. The area was a blaze of light. There was no combatant in sight—he had vanished.

Jimbo wanted a clear shot on the house and boathouse, so he moved with the protection of the trees at an angle that would take him directly in front of the dozer blade manned by Luis and Cande, who were now experienced battlefield soldiers. Lana, Gina, Kelsi, and Branka radioed in about the new movement in the tree line.

Suddenly Jimbo stopped and turned toward the old metal remnants of the dozer. He loaded a shell and moved the launcher in the direction of the old dozer blade. A constant wave of bullets whizzed by him from all of the elevated soldiers watching the horror that was about to happen. The tree line was close to 500 yards from the roof of the big house so the shots were all missing their targets. The two guards jumped on the blade from the opposite side and hugged each other, not knowing what was about to unfold. Even though in all probability the explosion would not penetrate the dozer blade, the concussion from being that near when a RPG went off would most likely kill them. Many times in the past, artillery shells had gone off near soldiers hunkered down in their foxholes. They were found dead without a scratch on them, but the concussion had broken every bone in their body.

Jimbo was struggling. He had no middle finger on his right hand, excruciating pain near his shoulder blade, but he placed the round in the RPG and raised it to fire at the images he had just seen on his night vision Yukon monocular unit. It took time. With only the light from the stars and an infrared capacity, he saw two distinct figures. Now they we gone, hiding most likely from the blast on the other side of the huge dozer blade. He fired and didn't realize how close he was to the giant metal scoop. The back blast picked him up and threw him, rolling him and bouncing him next to the road. Blood was pouring from his nose and ears—he could hear nothing—no sounds at all. Hobbling and dragging his rocket he took bullets in his vest and the back of his leg from guns being fired from the top of the beach and boathouses. Tracers lit him up several times. Once he reached the other side of the blade no one was there. While he had shouldered his RPG getting ready to fire, Luis and Cande had moved further down the tree line. They knew he couldn't hold a scope and a RPG at the same time so they took off. The back of his thigh was leaking blood at a fast rate.

Jimbo thought to himself, *if I'm going to die I'll take as many of those fuckers with me as possible.* With the last of his strength, he lifted the rocket launcher and propped it on the upper edge of the dozer blade and pointed it broadside at the house. Awkwardly, he loaded one of his last three rounds for the RPG 7. He clicked off the safety, unscrewed the plastic safety cap on the tip of the explosive device, and found the house in the sights. With 500 yards to cover, it wasn't an impossible shot but damn difficult. If there was a miss, it would automatically self-destruct at about 950 yards. Insurgents had been known to measure off that distance and plan airburst over enemy positions. As he adjusted the sights, he saw a strange strip of red-orange light move toward him like a large mechanical snake. Sometimes the colors were green then back to red. They were tracers, both American and Russian, and Branka was walking them right up to where Jimbo was hiding. The fiery serpent would be on him in a second, so without sighting, Jimbo pulled the percussion trigger causing the first stage of the rocket to blast out of its holder. First, it seem to be level, then it rose and rose until it just barely cleared the roof of the big house and headed out to sea. At that very moment, Melville was doing another weird crossing maneuver right as instructed by Jimbo, who had told him he would kill him if he didn't keep up the diversion. He looked at the trail of the rocket and noticed it was headed right toward him, so he got off the throttle.

"Holy Mother of God!" he yelled and dove overboard as the rocket was nearly on him. At exactly 950 yards from where it started, the timer on the rocket triggered the explosion overhead. The boat came out of the water and landed upside down and started sinking fast. It popped up quickly as it had flotation material built into the boat under the seats and in the bow and stern. The vessel was full of water but it floated enough for Melville to grab on. Jaro came off the roof of the boathouse and told him to swim it in. Melville did just that for a while but was old and not in good shape. He yelled for help. Jaro dove in and swam out to help him. Everyone wanted to save the boat since there wasn't any kind of watercraft on the property.

Jimbo waited too long to duck down from the tracer trial that was snaking up to his position. A tracer struck him on his forehead just after he fired the RPG sending a burning strontium compound round deep into his brain. Briefly, bright red light emitted from his eyes and ears.

The battle was now over, and again the people at the beach house were going to be forced to explain several dead bodies. This time, all the people on the boat were wanted by local police. Eli decided to have their Cuban friends call the local police and let them deal with the bodies. He felt certain they were tired of carrying bodies around in the trunk of their rental car.

One person was still alive and everyone was anxious to question him. The police would surely arrest him and take his boat. The group needed a boat.

Chapter Thirty-Three

The Safe Opens

Julio was on the phone with the police who were bringing a truck to carry off the bodies. They weren't pleased, and Julio sensed they had wanted to kill the entire crew of the *Shark Dog* for the cop shooting. The Mayor was willing to execute any survivors.

On a couch in the boathouse, intense interrogations and negotiations were taking place.

"You do know the Cubans won't let you take your boat out while you're in prison?" Eli asked.

"Why do you think I'll go to prison? I didn't shoot anyone," Melville said.

"Accessory to murder. You drove the getaway boat. You sheltered the assailant. You made no effort to contact authorities. And—you hired these goons to begin with. They're your employees," Josh argued with his best lawyer voice.

"Melville, you're fucked. You're going to need lots of dough to hire a good Cuban lawyer. Got a lot of money?"

Melville held his head in his hands and sobbed.

"What about my boat? Will they take it? I have very little money. Spent most all of it buying the boat. Maxed out my credit cards."

"I want to know everything about that boat. What did you pay for it? How much do you owe? Tell me everything we need to know about it. Age? Engines? Last overhaul? Leaks? Fuel? Is it a chick magnet? If you're honest, we might give you something for the boat to help you with your lawyers," Josh said.

Melville spilled out everything he knew, including the boat purchase which occurred just one week ago. He was more than willing to sell. Milo, Jaro, and Gina had taken the skiff out to pick up the big powerboat. Gina would pilot it back and hoped it would handle like her mom's big boat. She would also be operating in the dark. Everyone knew that Cuba had the first rights in confiscating property used in the perpetration of a crime. Josh and Luis suggested they offer compensation for the vessel to the Cuban government. Prices were kicked around, and Melville agreed to sell his interest in the *Shark Dog* for $100,000. An account would be set up for him in Havana so he could pay his lawyers. He would give them a bill of sale and it would be up to them to negotiate with the bank and pay off the $200,000 note. They would also offer the Cuban government $100,000 so they would release it. All these transactions depended on money being in the safe. They were spending money they hadn't seen yet, so it was easy to throw around random numbers.

When the big boat docked at the boathouse, Melville went on board to point out some unique controls to Gina and handed the paperwork over to Josh. He would call the bank listed on the paperwork as soon as it was open, explain they were purchasing it and wished to pay off the note. They would want money to make the transfer. Josh and Eli would visit a local bank when they opened sometime that day. Hopefully, they would fax the paperwork to the Colony Hotel to be signed and returned.

An hour had passed when the police arrived, along with the mayor and two Cuban military men. They brought along a small pickup truck. They would collect bodies, but good weapons left by the insurgents were traded by the group for old ones. Two AK47 were traded for a shotgun and an automatic .22 rifle. The RPG and two rounds were hidden.

Eli said, "I hope they can get all the bodies in that little truck."

"They'll stack 'em like cordwood," Josh said. The five bodies still lay where they had fallen except for the two divers who were pulled onto the beach. The police collected all the passports and papers of the deceased crew. They didn't ask specifically about the weapons; they only asked where they got them. They said they asked around and had borrowed them and would return them shortly to their owners; they would keep a few but didn't mention that to the police and military. With Julio and Luis there, the questions were directed to them and their answers were taken as gospel. The explosives Luis and Eli had stolen were buried near the shed in plastic bags. Later they would be moved to the deep woods and then back to the quarry.

Melville was handcuffed and brought into the beach house for questioning. He gave a statement and used Josh as a lawyer and translator. They learned one of the crew had died from gunshots fired by the wounded policeman, and they had buried him at sea. They asked about the boat, and Josh started negotiations on the purchase and compensation. Josh drew up a bill of sale between Eli and Gina and the Cuban government. They wanted $200,000 since it was a big boat. The mayor interceded with the Cuban Government over the phone; the official was not pleased to be roused out bed at 4:30 in the morning. Not once did they ever ask about the source of the money.

"Tell them it's okay. We will transfer the money to whatever government account they want," Eli said. The Mayor wrote down the bank numbers for the transfer and the telephone number to verify the transaction before the American group could leave the island. It was all relayed to him from some party headquarters in Havana. When too much questioning ensued, either Luis or Julio took over the phone. Julio cleared large deposits of cash in the bank.

"Can we get a clearance to take the boat through Cuban waters?" Julio asked for the Americans.

"As long as they're not busy, we will clear you and let the patrol boat know you will be passing out of Cuban waters. Please tell us when you are ready to leave, and it will be arranged," the Mayor said after getting the instructions from the Cuban official on the other end of the line.

Satisfied with the information they received and carrying a truckload of dead bodies, the Mayor and his little army dodged the huge hole in the road made by Jimbo's RPG and headed towards the hotel where they turned north towards their headquarters.

Branka was brought down from the roof of the beach house and placed in a bed to rest. It was now about five in the morning and still dark. Later in the day, a checkup with the German doctors would be scheduled around their dive trips. Everyone was tired—more like wasted, but the safe really needed to be opened to see if everything was in place.

A less energetic group would have been hard to find, but they all assembled in the boat-house, pulled the rug back, opened the hatch, and moved the ladder in place. There wasn't much room in the vault, so only four people went in: Eli, Gina, Kelsi, and Josh. The rest lay around the hatch hold looking in. No one was on guard. If someone attacked, they would be waiting a while for return fire.

"Eli, I'll call out the combination and the times you turn the tumbler. You're the official open-upper guy," Gina quipped.

"OK. Fire away."

"Twenty-two right—go around the number four times and then stop on twenty-two."

"Got it."

"Fourteen left three times and stop on it."

"Done."

"Eighty right two times and stop."

"Yes—now what?"

"This is tricky—go back left slowly and it should start to tighten, then open."

"Here goes." He barely moved the tumbler knob and became aware of the heat in the vault, Gina's breath on his neck, and the excited presence of Josh and Kelsi. They had become great friends, and their faces were animated and their bodies tense. The marker's chrome knob passed the number 78 and then 75. So far it had not tightened. At the 70 mark, he seemed to feel it was somewhat tighter. As he approached 60 he was sure it had tightened. At fifty-five it clicked and stopped.

"Here goes nothing," Eli said as he pull the handle downward and watched the door open for the first time in 57 years. There was a mild hiss from being sealed air tight all those years.

"It's a walk-in safe!" Gina said as she moved in front of Eli to explore. There were pull-out drawers on each side from the floor to the ceiling with just enough space for one person at a time to walk. About six feet in, there was a small room with big drawers from the floor to the ceiling. As Gina walked to the rear, she nonchalantly pulled out a drawer at about face level. It was full of US hundred dollar bills stacked neatly with paper wrappers denoting their total value. Most were thick $10,000 packages.

She then walked to the large drawers on the bottom of the little room. Kneeling, she pulled one open with a lot of effort.

"Holy shit! It's full of gold!" Eli came in and kneeled beside her.

"These are the common gold coins and there must be thousands in here. In 1959, they were worth only about thirty bucks. Now they are over a thousand each."

Josh and Kelsi followed them in, pulling out drawers and cursing little happy curses.

"Mother of God, this is unreal!" Josh said.

"Fucking amazing!" Kelsi said.

After everyone had gotten over the shock, Josh asked if he could take it to the sorting table. Eli and Gina agreed and continued to explore the room. Eli kept pulling out the metal drawers until he found the gold collection drawer.

"Here it is. See how each coin is marked and enclosed in a plastic sleeve? Written on it in Uncle Carmine's handwriting is a brief description and their value in 1957 or 1958. They have both a bullion value and a numismatic value. This one from Great Britain was worth three thousand, two hundred and fifty dollars in 1956. Here's another one from Germany worth fifty-seven hundred. It's safe to say they're worth at least twice that now," Eli said barely able to breathe from the excitement and the lack of good air in the vault. There was a musty, aged smell in the vault. Old money and dust.

"I need to get some air," Gina said, and Eli agreed with her. They walked past Kelsi and Josh who were in and out carrying money and stacking it on the table. Eli and Gina made their home in two metal folding chairs for a few minutes to watch the money pile up and to catch their breath.

"Do you think it's fair to give Julio and Luis the same as the newcomers?" Eli whispered.

"No, they will get what Josh and Kelsi get. Everyone will get a bonus. Tell them we will pay them the extra when the three Ukrainians have left. They're staying at the hotel tonight and will leave in a few days. We can join them for dinner tomorrow," Gina said in a low voice.

Shortly, the table was beginning to fill up with stacks of hundreds. It was time to start dividing the money. Eli yelled to the people peering into the vault.

"We need duffel bags, plastic sacks, and whatever you might have to pay you."

He could hear a lot of rushing around. Some went upstairs, others to the storage shed, and Luis and Julio went to the airplane. In a few minutes, people started showing up with suitcases, duffel bags, garbage bags, and even a large waste basket.

"I want to talk to you before we pass out the money." Eli had climbed up the ladder far enough to be partly out of the vault.

"Many people have been killed in this world for much less money than you will have. Each of you will get a bonus. Some more than others. No one will get less than 100 gold one-ounce coins. So for you Ukrainians, that will be over $350,000 US. Are you happy with that amount? All of you will be rich when you get back to Russia."

Jaro and Milo said they were beyond happy and didn't care what everyone else got since they were latecomers to the game and had only been there a few days. "There will be no trouble from us," Jaro said and Milo nodded.

"Will you come visit us in the states?" Eli asked.

"If you come to the Ukraine," Milo said.

"What about your friend, Mr. Wolf?"

"He will not be a friendly person. I will not be surprised if he came here to see what happened. If he does—he will not be alone," Jaro said.

"I don't guess we can ever let our guard down, can we?" Eli said as he took two duffel bags and a plastic garbage can for the three Ukrainians and let Josh and Kelsi start filling it. Kelsi took a duffel and counted out 300 gold coins.

"Throw in five or six extra for each person in case we miscounted," Eli yelled at Kelsi.

The gold coins, mostly US St. Gaudens, were counted and added to the Ukrainians' duffel bags. Gina asked which bag was Branka's. It turned out to be the small plastic trash can. His luggage was at the hotel, so they grabbed whatever they could.

"I'm throwing in a couple of the ten thousand dollar bundles for Branka's medical expenses. Are you guys ok with that?" Gina said.

"Of course! You're very generous," Milo said.

"We're sorry he got his leg injured, but had we not blown him up, he would have killed us," Gina said and smiled.

"You know him now, and you're right—he would have killed all of you. He is the best soldier in the Ukraine," Jaro said.

"You guys weren't too bad yourselves," Eli said.

Now it was Julio and Luis's turn.

"Julio, are you ready to be paid?" Eli said.

"Sure—what's that!" Outside a screaming whistle could be heard followed by an explosion.

Chapter Thirty-Four

Horst Wolf Comes to Fight

"Take me to the roof and give me that RPG and the AK with some tracers." Branka was now awake and fully ready to fight. It would be safe to say he loved battle. He was so skilled and wired for combat, other places bored him. You could invite him to a cocktail party, but unless a fight broke out, he was not going to be your most talkative guest.

Jaro and Milo rushed him to the roof while they carried their weapons. Josh and Eli quickly found the roof of the boathouse. All the girls ran to the roof of the house to be spotters of shooters. Kelsi was the first to respond.

"Powerboat—thirty or forty feet in length. Two Zodiacs coming in hard—three—no—four men each. Two men on deck. One has a RPG. He's loading!"

Julio took the Remington 750. In what seemed to be only two seconds, he fired. The round struck the man with the RPG in his chest. It was at least an 800-yard shot.

"Holy shit! Julio, you're showing up your Ukrainian buddies," Kelsi said.

"Lucky shot," Julio said.

"The man on the boat is picking up the rocket thingy, and he's trying to aim it. I don't think he knows what he's doing," Kelsi said as she tightened the focus on the night vision monocular taken from Jimbo.

"Rocket thingy?" Luis laughed.

Julio was also watching him and almost broke out laughing. "Oh no! What a fuck up!

Julio watched through the rifle scope and Kelsi witnessed it through the night vision Yukon. Having trouble holding it steady, the man pulled the trigger as the weapon was aimed directly at one of the Zodiacs about 400 yards from shore. The rocket took off on a path so perfectly aimed at one of his boats it would not be possible for an experienced RPG man to duplicate it. The men in the boat were so tuned to the enemy ahead of them they never saw the round coming and most likely felt nothing as it landed squarely between the four men, exploded and killed all four instantly. Now there were four AK47s since two were taken from the last attackers, and Eli had his Tommy gun. These guys coming in must have been rent-a-soldiers because they had no respect for the people they were attacking. Once they crossed the 100-yard range Julio told everyone to fire. Tracers and bullets showered the men with about 200 rounds. They didn't have time to shoot back. Their bodies floated next to a sinking rubber boat.

This little war had to be the work of Horst Wolf, and most likely he was the one who blew up his own men.

"I wish to sink Mr. Wolf, if nobody minds," Branka said.

"Sink it!" Cande and Lana said at the same time.

Branka was in a prone position and asked if Kelsi could spot for him. She had the night vision Yukon on the boat. It had a yardage readout which indicated 835 yards. She read it out to him and said, "He moving out!"

Branka looked at the iron sights, adjusted for movement of the boat and fired.

"Look at it go!" Cande yelled.

The rocket left a beautiful red-orange tail as it gained altitude and then started its arch downward. It struck the boat right above the inboard engine housing. The stern was mostly destroyed and now it was dead in the water and sinking.

"You got him!" yelled Josh and Eli from the top of the boat-house.

"Let's make sure," Branka said and asked Kelsi for another reading.

"Nine hundred thirty-five yards. He's dead in the water."

Branka made adjustments to his funky flip-up sights on the RPG launcher. It was never intended for this purpose. *If I can just get the target and altitude correct, it will detonate at nine hundred fifty yards automatically,* he thought.

He fired, and everyone held their breath. The whole crew was tired of fighting. This should have been a time for celebration, but Horst Wolf had to try one last stupid move. The beautiful colors of the burning rocket lit the sky. It was on target. *Would it really blow up at 950 yards? Maybe 980 or 100 yards?*

It was early morning, but the sun wasn't up yet. Only a preliminary hue suggested there would be a newly birthed sun in a short time. In the distance, they could see a little area illuminated from fires onboard the now missing deck and cabin of the powerboat. The bow of the boat rose up and dove straight down aft end first where the water had rushed in from the first RPG strike. A few boards and fiberglass kept burning on the surface. The RPG had done exactly what it was supposed to do. Kelsi watched the water for a while but saw no infrared bodies. It was over for what everyone hoped was the last time.

Hopefully, now everyone could get some sleep but not until each had their money. It was the thing that kept them going—the reason they fought so hard. It was the freedom and power which would set them apart from others. Eli and Gina resumed giving out money, and Julio, Luis, Lana, and Cande wanted to see and feel their money before they slept. Jaro and Milo fell asleep as soon as they lay down next to their duffel bags. Everyone was sure all the fighting was over—except Branka. He was on alert. Something bothered him, and he kept the binoculars and the rifle scope trained to the ocean even when his friends brought a garbage can full of money and placed it down next to him.

***

Horst Wolf was a fifty-year-old German with thinning dark hair, broad shoulders, and the owner of a 45-foot Viking power boat, bow in the air, burning, and sinking in front of his eyes. He was a bad man for a multitude of reasons, but he didn't rule an empire by sitting behind a desk. Scuba diving had been a passion for many years and he was damn good at the sport. At his home in Russia, he constructed an indoor pool that was 15 feet deep. For practice, he would throw all of his scuba equipment on the bottom of the deep end of the pool and dive in after it. Once on the bottom he would calmly stand a tank upright, turn on the air valve, put a regulator in his mouth, clear it of water by blowing through it, and then slide into his buoyancy compensator. Next, he put on his personal gear, cleared his mask, and would swim on the bottom for a while. This wasn't good enough so he would do it blindfolded. This training came in handy a few minutes before his boat was blown out of the water by one of his former employees.

"I can't fucking believe that is my beautiful boat burning and sinking," he muttered to himself.

When the first RPG round hit the rear of his boat, Horst grabbed a scuba tank with a regulator attached and rode it to the bottom at fifty feet to a sandy bottom below a coral head. He had no mask or fins and didn't need them. Even though the salt water stung his eyes, the moonlight let him know where he was. One of his favorite dives was a night dive when underwater lights are turned off. Rubbing the sides of barrel sponges would cause a fireworks display of bioluminescent organisms which most divers never see. This night he didn't have time for playing around. He moved upward toward a dark object on the surface. It was the skiff that he had anchored some 100 feet from the mother ship just in case he needed it. Inside were some survival food, water, clothes, and a micro Uzi 9mm with two large 32 round clips. He came up on the starboard side of the small vessel so his infrared image couldn't be seen by the night vision binoculars or rifle scopes. It was there, hanging on the gunnels of what amounted to a lifeboat; he watched the Viking 45 footer find the bottom of the warm Caribbean waters.

***

Snoring emanated from every room in the beach house. Tired young people who had been shot at and attacked from far too many factions needed their brains to rest and heal. Most felt like it was Christmas day, and their dreams were centered on the things they could buy with a sum of money most still couldn't fathom. All slept, including Eli and Gina who had made a pallet on the rug near the vault. If the Cubans, under the direction of Julio and Luis, would let the boat pass without inspection, they most likely could dock in Miami Beach next to Gina's boat without incident. If they came in at night, they could unload their treasure and within the next few days check in with the harbor master, since it would have to have the registration changed over to Eli from Melville. Hopefully, some of that paperwork would happen during the day.

Branka was still watching—like an owl spotting a mouse. He watched the horizon moving very slowly in sweeps. At a few hundred feet to the right of where the boat sunk, there was a flash of red in his night scope.

"Holy shit—something is there!"

He looked around and nobody was nearby to talk to. He got back under his night vision goggles and looked again. He could see the red, tiny as it was, appear at the end of a small boat. The red person seemed to be loading items in the boat—maybe scuba tanks, a gun, fins— they were just blurs next to the red illumination and he couldn't make it out since the light from the morning sun only gave him an outline of what looked like a small boat about 1200 yards out. The 750 sniper rifle was lying on the far right side of the captain's walk some 30 feet away. Branka began to pull his body along until he could reach out and grasp the butt of the rifle. Once in his hands, he slid and dragged his leg with a great deal of pain back to his mattress and night vision equipment. The Remington 750 had three cartridges in the internal clip awaiting their transfer into the firing chamber. He pulled the bolt back and slid one round into the ready position. The safety was off so he placed the gun on a rolled up part of the mattress and looked for his target. The boat appeared to have been started since red around the hot motor could be picked up as an infrared signature on both the rifle scope and the Yukon night vision unit.

"I've got to stop this fucker," he muttered to himself.

Twelve hundred yards would be a tremendously difficult shot. He knew this better than anyone. He was shooting at a downward angle and the bullet, a 30.06 200 grain round would begin to fall a lot at that distance. He wished it was a 150 grain or even 180 grain so it would have less drop. *Who bought these cartridges? Were they going bear hunting?* He aimed about one foot above the rear section of the boat as it moved away. Now it was 1250 yards—1300 yards. He took the shot. It was so loud it completely destroyed the peaceful night; people actually fell out of their beds. The red image sat up to operate the motor. He fired again—this time he was focused on the red image at the rear of the boat. He saw it fall off the boat on the port side and float. He floated there for a long time.

"I hope that fucker is dead—but I'm not taking a chance."

Branka dropped his elevation, so he was reasonably certain he could strike the body in the water. He pulled the trigger again and the body rose up in the water for a second and fell back into the same motionless state. He looked around and saw that most of the crew was standing next to him. Julio picked up the night vision monoculars and spotted the limp body. The skiff was on auto control and headed out to sea.

"Do you think it was Mr. Wolf?" Julio asked.

"My guess. I think I'll get some sleep now," Branka said.

"We'll help you to bed—and thanks for staying on duty," Luis said as he and Jaro helped Branka down the stairs to his room. Kelsi carried his trash can full of money and set it next to his bed. He was at peace but slept with a Kalashnikov whore on the pillow next to him.

Chapter Thirty-Five

A Great Surprise

Pete and Maria showed up at the beach house mid-morning in the old jeep. The word was out that fighting had been occurring in the area. They wanted to check it out and see who was still alive. The little truck stuffed with bodies passed in front of their house with the police following behind. It was also time for them to clean house, but they had a better suggestion.

"How about we cook you breakfast?" Maria said.

The occupants of the house and the boat-house drifted in yawning and were treated to bacon and eggs and pancakes. Maria had purchased the supplies in town.

"Pete, you and Maria will get a bonus today that will knock your socks off!" Eli said. "We'll tell you how much when we figure it out."

Pete smiled. "I have coffee ready," he said and began to set out cups on the table.

Branka used his crutches to get to the breakfast table and sat with one leg pushed out away from the table. No one had showered in a few days. If body odor were a green gas it would have made a cloud above the crew.

Eli had some announcements. "Later today we will all go to the local bank here and make deposits and transfers to our home banks. If you don't have banks in your home countries, I suggest you go online and open them. This way your money, or at least some of it, can be passed through without you getting caught with over ten thousand dollars in cash on you when you go through customs in your respective countries. Hopefully, we have enough rental cars to get everyone to town."

After breakfast, a migration took place toward the hotel and showers. Eli and Gina were moving their cash and coins to the *Shark Dog.* Luis and Julio helped them and were told they were getting an additional $250,000 for all the help they got with dealing with the government. They were going to put most of their money in their Cuban accounts but were certain they could take quite a bit of money to Havana and put it in safety deposit boxes. They felt sure everything deposited in the accounts would be taxed.

It took many trips to get the balance of the $25 million and the thousands of gold coins on the big yacht. It was all stacked in the master stateroom and looked like a movie was being filmed about a heist on an ocean liner.

"Let go the hotel and fax those forms, then round everyone up to go into town," Eli said.

Gina gave the two housekeepers $100,000 each for taking care of the beach house. Many of the guns were loaded in the cars so they could be returned to those who asked for them back. At the hotel, the crew smelled much better for the trip to town. After the papers were faxed to the boat dealer, they were assured the completed forms would be sent to the hotel in a couple of hours. Gina and Eli took a quick shower together, changed clothes, and formed a caravan with the others into town. Julio had called ahead, and the bank was ready for them.

On the way they stopped and passed out guns and drove over to the big metal shed. There they returned the AK47. The man was surprised it got back to him. Eli now had a couple of AKs and his prized Tommy gun locked away in the vault. The Thompson would be moved to an excellent hiding place in the master bedroom head before they left. Eli found a panel on the floor of the marine head to access the pipes going to the toilet, with ample room for a nice Tommy gun. It could be pushed completely out of sight even if someone removed the panel.

The bank took the US dollars, made the CIC conversion and wired the funds to every bank account. Cande had her $250,000 sent to Spain, Lana's went to Russia, and the Ukrainians shared an account in Kiev. They would divide it later. Luis and Julio deposited $400,000 each in their Havana bank accounts. Josh and Kelsi put all but $5,000 in their accounts in Florida.

At last, Eli and Gina made their deposits. Julio had cleared this with the government for a fee. It was the same as money laundering in the US, but in cash-strapped Cuba, it was just business as usual. It cost Eli and Gina $50,000 per million to have the money transferred to Eli's California bank and Gina's Florida bank. It showed up as a clean transfer of funds. They both did $5 million each. It went through perfectly. Both rented safety deposit boxes which they filled with gold coins. After everyone was paid, they still had over $10 million on board plus a couple million in gold. A great deal of effort was used to hide the money and gold on the *Shark Dog*.

The evening was steak and lobsters at the hotel as most everyone was leaving the next day. The doctors were still seeing after Branka, and he was getting along well for someone who had dragged his injured leg all over the rooftop to get a good shot. He would go home in a few days with his fellow countrymen.

The following day, Julio made the call to the coastal patrol to allow the *Shark Dog* an unfettered passage out of Cuban waters. He and Luis loaded some of their money on the plane, and after saying their goodbyes and promising to meet back there in a few months, they took off for Havana. They were part owners and wanted the old placed fixed up. Although it was much more of an adventure than Cande and Lana had signed up for, they were willing to come back to see a civilized beach house.

With only Pete and Maria left at the estate, Eli and Gina held hands and walked from the back patio to the beach. The coastal patrol had picked up Horst Wolf's skiff but never found his body. There were bloods stains but nothing else in the boat except an empty gas tank for the outboard motor. The boat did have two bullet holes in it from a large caliber weapon. The other men that were killed in the raid washed ashore later in the day; that is, all except one. They expected him to wash ashore any day now. The only person to ask about the bodies was Branka. He wanted to see all the bodies as they came in. He wasn't told about the skiff since the report was given to Julio and Luis.

The couple walked to the house and told Maria and Pete goodbye, gave them a hug, and accepted the sandwiches they made for them for the trip. They talked briefly about the things that needed to be done for the place. Since money wasn't a problem, they said they would start the process of subcontracting the repairs.

"I wish Josh and Kelsi had come with us," Gina said.

"They want to stay in Havana a couple of days at the National Hotel. I think they're going out to dinner with the other four crew members," Eli said.

On the way to the boat, they walked through the boathouse, stopped to put the rug back over the hatch, and moved a little furniture around. They had stalled long enough; it was time to shove off. Eli untied the ropes and pushed the boat away from the dock and then joined Gina in the wheelhouse. She had no problem reversing out of the dock. As she pulled in view of the beach house, she honked at Maria and Pete who had walked out on the patio to wave to them. It was late afternoon, sunny, and hot. The main salon was air-conditioned, and if the doors to the bridge were closed, the cool air would eventually cool it as well. Gina had to navigate around some outer islands and then cruise control could take over. In forty-five minutes she was in the clear. The *Shark Dog* was on auto and sandwiches were laid on a dining table along with a cold beer. Eli sat next to Gina and kissed her before she had a mouthful of turkey sandwich. Gina looked him in his eyes.

"I love you, Eli Swartz!"

"I love you, Gina Spada!"

"I don't like anybody very much!" came from a person standing behind them. He held a very small Uzi submachine gun. "I'm Horst Wolf and you must be some of the people who killed all my men."

Chapter Thirty-Six

Horst Back to Life

"You're supposed to be dead. How are you still here?" asked Eli.

"I'm not stupid. I may be less accurate than I should be with an RPG—okay, I'm a lousy shot with the rocket gun, but I'm very good at fooling night vision glasses. I floated one of the dead commandos to the opposite side of the skiff. He hadn't been dead long and still had a warm signature for the infrared scopes. I loaded him in the boat first; I got in after him, started the motor, and headed out. I knew Branka would never abandon his post and wouldn't give up until he found my body. When he fired the first shot, I was lying flat on the bottom of the boat and my dead buddy was propped up by the motor. The second shot came and I pushed the body overboard and let him shoot at it one more time. Later, I guided the skiff into a protected area near shore, unloaded my gear and swam around and approached your *Shark Dog* from the stern. I sent the skiff out to sea since I now have a much bigger boat. Let's talk about how we are going to get through the Cuban coastal patrol with this big old tub."

"I suggest you jump overboard as soon as we see them, and then we will come back and get you. Promise!" Gina said.

"Ha! At least Americans have a sense of humor. We Germans are told it is missing in our gene structure."

"You Germans don't know how to have fun," Eli said.

"Where is the money hidden on board?"

Eli and Gina had no intentions of telling him where it might be. The ship had a safe and there was $100,000 there. The rest was sewn into the internal guts of the queen-size mattress in one of the three cabins on the boat. The gold coins were in sealed freezer bags below the engine department in the sump area. It was nasty, oily, and smelly. It always had water in it when they were underway, but if you were docked for long periods of time the sump pump would clear most of it out. If it rained, then more water would seek the lowest level.

"Mr. Wolf, we knew we would encounter the Cuban coastal patrol here and possibly we would be boarded in Florida as well. So fortunate for us, and not so lucky for you, we had friends who convinced the Cuban banking system to wire the money to our accounts in the States. Would you like a sandwich instead?" Gina said.

"No, thanks. I've already eaten. You may have wired some of it, but the amount of money you guys inherited far surpasses what would be allowed in any country—even a corrupt one like Cuba."

"Your thinking is flawed, Horst because the more that is sent, the more they make. It cost fifty thousand dollars for each million. It's money laundering, we know, but it's a hell of a lot better than having a Nazi wannabe stealing it on the high sea," Eli said.

"You sure you don't want a turkey sandwich instead?" Gina said.

"I'll take a cold beer. Then we, that would be you, are taking this boat apart board by board."

***

Branka sat at the hotel bar drinking vodka on ice. The hotel manager walked by and spoke to him.

"How's the leg, Mr. Balanchuk?"

"Much better. It had a big hole in it and will take many weeks to heal properly."

"You've had an exciting time here on your stay. I hope you now get to relax a while," Martinez said.

"Not much good at relaxing—don't know why."

"Did you hear they found the skiff drifting offshore?"

"No, I didn't. What was in it?"

"Nothing. Just an empty gas tank."

"No mask, fins, scuba tank, gun?"

"It was totally empty."

"Strange—and thanks, I will try to relax some."

Martinez walked off to pester some other unsuspecting guests while Branka tried to replay the movie in his mind of his encounter with the man and the skiff. Something wasn't right. Even though it was a misty part of his vision then, and even more so now, he did see the red image loading something in the boat. Not just once, but numerous items. He couldn't make them out, but he was sure something should have been in the boat. *Completely empty—couldn't be.*

"Jaro, can you and Milo join me at the bar? I'm sorry to interrupt your Road Runner cartoon—this is important!" For 57 years, Cubans couldn't watch American TV and now that the ban had been partly lifted (at resorts only) people would constantly glue themselves to the new flat screens.

Jaro and Milo knew Branka would have some kind of battle plan against an enemy, either real or fantasy. When a battle was not going on, and he didn't have a weapon in his hands, Branka was thinking about a battle. General Patton would have loved him, Fidel would have asked for his hand in marriage, but thank God there was always a war going on someplace. It was getting too peaceful at the Colony Dive Resort.

The two Ukrainian cartoon addicts sat down next to Branka and ordered vodka straight up. For the people of the former Soviet Union, vodka was like orange juice in the states. The minimum drinking age for vodka is "none" in Russia. If they can hold it up and guzzle it down, they're old enough.

"Here's what concerns me." Branka could tell he didn't have their attention. He slammed his fist down on the bar just as the bartender was about to place their drinks in front of them. Without spilling a drop, the bartender withdrew the drinks until he felt it was safe to place them down. Looking intently at Branka, he eased the glasses in place.

"As I said, something concerns me. I believe I saw the man we assumed was Horst Wolf loading items into the skiff. Scuba tanks, mask, fins, and a pistol or small machine gun. When the patrol boat picked up the skiff, it was clean—nothing in it. I have a theory. Of the people we killed in the water and the ones Horst killed himself, all have washed ashore except Horst and one other man. They weren't far from shore, so you would expect the ocean to carry all of them in. Horst and one guy are missing. Why? I will tell you what I think happened. It's crazy, but he was smart enough to pull it off."

Branka proceeded to explain what he thought happened, which was almost identical to Horst's explanation to Gina and Eli. Once he was finished, they asked what they could do.

"We need to call Julio. Do we have his number?" Branka asked.

"I have it, but I don't have service most of the time. It works at the beach house for some reason," Jaro said.

The hotel manager was making his trip back to the office at that time. "Martinez, can we borrow your phone for a minute?" Branka asked as he took Jaro's phone to get the number and dialed it in the hotel manager's phone.

It took a while for Julio to answer as he was busy flying the plane. "Hello, is this Martinez?"

"No, it's his phone—it's me, Branka. We believe Horst Wolf has tricked us, and I'm going to guess he's on Eli's boat. Do you have enough gas to chase them down?"

"It has a 700-mile range, and I topped it off with the gas we had put on the airfield. What do you suggest I do? This isn't a MIG29, you know."

"Pete and Mary came by here for lunch and said they left about 45 minutes ago."

Julio banked the 172 Cessna and headed back across the island and out to sea. Normally, he would admire the hues of ocean color, from the light blues and greens in the shallows to the dark blue where the Caribbean slid off to unimaginable depths. He loved to scuba dive, and now that he had a beach house, he could come over often. He couldn't think about that now, though. His friends were in trouble.

"I'll fly low and see if they are in trouble, Branka. If he has a gun on them, they may not be able to signal us. I'll call Martinez's number when we spot them."

Luis, Cande, and Lana were very concerned. These two were now their very good friends. They had planned so many good times in the future together. These criminals seemed to be coming back to life.

After about 20 minutes in the air, Julio spotted the boat dead ahead. He called Martinez's phone, and Branka picked it up immediately.

"Branka, I have them spotted. I'm going down for a closer look." Julio pushed the yoke downward and leveled off at about 50 feet above the water. The plane shot past the *Shark Dog* not fifteen feet over the water.

"Don't go out yet. When they come back, just go out and wave like nothing has happened, or I will shoot your ass and that's a promise," Horst said.

On the way out, Eli whispered to Gina, "Make the fucking sign."

Gina looked confused and then remembered the closed fist with a finger going back and forth. As the plane neared, they waved and just when they were close enough both did the gesture of the finger in the closed fist so that Horst could not see their actions. They waved again as the plane buzzed overhead.

"What the hell was that sign they were making?" Julio asked.

"I couldn't see much since we're going so damn fast, but it looked like the sign for fucking," said Cande.

"Why would they do that?" Lana asked. "Do you think they were telling us they are screwing on board? My God, we all know that's happening!"

"It's not that at all," said Luis, who had been quiet during these passes. "They're being fucked! They've been hijacked!"

Julio whipped the plane around and made a pass that only allowed a few feet between the wing and the deck. He repeated it several times trying to draw Horst out in the open. On the fifth pass, he got his wish when Horst ran out on the deck from the bridge and fired part of a clip at the Cessna. The plane took several hits. None hit the gas tank or engine but a couple came through the cabin into the cockpit ceiling barely missing Cande. Enough of the passes; Julio had found out what Branka had suspected. Julio headed back toward the island. As he turned, his phone rang again.

"Julio, this is Branka again. The patrol boat is docked at Iguana Cay not far from you. They say there's a small airstrip there. Maybe you guys can direct the patrol boat toward the *Shark Dog*? Here are the quadrants." Branka called them out, and Luis wrote them down.

"Anybody ready for some action?" Julio asked but knew the answer.

He did a steep bank and kept calling by radio for the patrol boat. An officer on the Cuban boat answered after a few minutes and asked if the callers knew some guy with a Russian accent named Branka. Everyone laughed. In a short time, Julio touched down on Iguana Cay. He taxied as close to the boat as possible, and they all jumped out. They still had their pistols with them. Julio introduced everyone, but the Cuban boat crew knew who he and Luis were and welcomed them aboard. Lana and Cande were wearing very short shorts, the kind which allowed a small portion of their very attractive butt cheeks to escape from the fabric, making the girls very welcome among a bunch of horny Cuban sailors. In a few minutes, the patrol boat was at full speed in the direction of the *Shark Dog*.

***

Branka paced back and forth on his crutches, dragging a useless bandaged leg behind him. The doctors had seen him today and said there was very little infection, but bleeding was still an issue because he would not let the leg rest. They applied new dressings.

"Sorry, doctors, but the bad leg will just have to be attached to an active soldier."

The doctors just threw up their hands. If the injury had been a broken leg, they could have made a cast with a boot under the foot. No such luck with Branka's wound. Much of their concern concentrated on the delicate microsurgery they performed on veins, tissue, and muscles so carefully and skillfully put back together for the commando.

Branka called the local airport in Nueva Gerona to inquire about aircraft rentals. The lady on the phone spoke very little English and no Russian.

"We have no airplanes. They are finished. One small helicopter. Very expensive. You want to talk to them?"

"Yes! Connect me."

In a few minutes, a woman answered. "May I help you, comrade?"

Branka recognized the accent. "Do you speak Russian?" he asked her in Russian. She answered in Russian.

"Where are you from?"

"I am from a small village outside of Kiev. My name is Dasha Hordiyenko. Where are you from and what is your name?"

"I am Branka Balanchuk from the city of Kiev. I want to rent your helicopter and a pilot. I don't care what it costs."

"I give you good price, and I will fly you. It has been slow this week. Yes, I know about you and your medals."

"Please fly to the Colony Hotel and land in the back parking lot."

"I'll be there in 20 minutes or less."

Branka asked Jaro and Milo to get his equipment from his car trunk.

"I need my AK and my flak jacket. Maybe my Kevlar helmet."

They brought it for him and helped him get to an empty parking lot. It wasn't long before he heard the helicopter. They were hoping to go with him, but it was a two seater. He pulled himself and his bad leg in. He found room for his crutches and placed his bad leg in a bent position, causing enough pain that a normal person would have fainted. He glanced over to see his pilot and was awe-struck. Dasha was the most beautiful girl he had ever seen. Green eyes, sun-streaked hair, movie star face, and legs that appeared longer than his. She caught him staring at her legs.

"Down, boy! I assume you have work to do."

"Take me out past Iguana Key and look for the coastal patrol boat and a 63-foot power boat called *Shark Dog*. Please."

He waved at his friends as she took off, and they made every gesture possible to acknowledge they noticed how pretty she was. Branka didn't date much, not because he didn't care for women: he was just very, very particular. He challenged himself to only accept the company of beautiful women. His standard of going for only the most attractive ladies resulted in spotty success and kept him single. He was only 25 years old, so it wasn't critical. He had to ask:

"Dasha, are you married?"

She answered through the headphones they both wore to hear over the noisy engine.

"No, are you?"

"No, I think I was waiting to meet you."

"Whoa! You're a fast talker. Shouldn't we go to dinner first?"

"We should. Will you have dinner with me if I live over what I'm about to do?"

"You are cute, a war hero, and our families live close to each other. Have any money?"

"Yes!"

"Then it's settled. I'll go to dinner. How likely are you going to be killed today?"

"Very! How do you feel about being shot at?"

"Shot at—no problem. Getting hit—big problem."

Chapter Thirty-Seven

A Final Fight

Julio and Luis stood with the captain in the wheelhouse of the *Frank Pais,* named after a teacher in Santiago de Cuba who led a revolutionary force that actually did more to take out Batista than did Fidel and his band of ragtag rebels. Unfortunately, Batista had him whacked before his forces could take out the Cuban President.

The patrol boat was a Russian Zhuk class vessel, probably forty years old and due to be decommissioned ten years ago. It was 78 feet long and featured four twin-mounted 12.7 mm machine guns, Russia's version of a 50 caliber, which most likely weren't functional. It had been reported that only five or six of these boats were operational. It could be less.

Rafael, the Captain, believed he had picked up the *Shark Dog* on radar. He explained it might also be a whale or a pod of dolphins; he couldn't be sure. The radar screen belonged in a museum. Julio thought the objects they saw might be dirt on the screen. However, after an hour, they spotted the vessel going about twenty miles an hour. The Frank Pais could do thirty. While they had the boat in their sights and were closing in to overtake them, a helicopter flew overhead in the direction of the *Shark Dog.*

***

Dasha was stone-faced as she maneuvered the small Capri G2 helicopter over the boat. The Cubans had picked up this modern quarter-of-a-million-dollar helicopter from a drug bust. Branka told her to drop fast on the back stern deck and he would roll out. She should take off like a scalded banshee with the bottom of her craft toward the boat. If she wanted to wait to haul his body back, she was told to put her little craft down near the coastal patrol boat dock on Iguana Cay.

Branka leaned over and kissed Dasha as her aircraft touched down on the deck.

"Do we have a date?" Branka asked.

She looked shocked but managed a smile.

"Yes. Please come back."

He rolled out and took a position on the aft deck roof. Once he hit, the pain from his injured leg felt as though he had fallen on a downed power line.

It had been a perfect place for Dasha to drop down. Instrument sensors, antennas, and radar receivers were protruding on the higher cabin roof, but she put the little chopper in the exact spot to miss all the things that might have caught her blade. In a flash, she gunned the bird, went sideways and gained altitude. A stream of 9mm bullets followed her up. A few of them struck the undercarriage but didn't damage anything that might bring down the aircraft. Dasha noticed a round came through and ripped a hole in the center of the passenger seat, then exited through the ceiling. She had now been shot at and didn't care for it.

Branka thought he knew where the shots had come from but couldn't get Horst in his sights. Horst had seen the helicopter drop down but didn't know if anyone got off. With Gina as a human shield, he walked toward the stern deck. Gina tried not to look up when she approached the rear of the boat. If someone had been placed there, she didn't want to expose them. Horst was looking everywhere but didn't see Branka on the roof. He had told Eli to stay at the wheel but kept looking back for him. The commando let Horst pass through. Horst was extremely cautious and took almost five minutes to reach the stern of the boat.

Branka was directly above him and yelled, "Drop it, Horst, or you die!" Gina broke free and it was just Horst and Branka.

"Fuck you!" Horst said and without looking up he began to spray the Stern deck roof with 9mm parabellum. Branka answered with a more powerful burst from his AK47. Both men were hit but not seriously. Gina found her way to the swim deck and cowered down there.

Branka was hit in his left hand; two rounds hit his vest but only knocked the breath from him. Another creased his Kevlar helmet. He wrapped his hand with a bandana he had in his back pocket.

Two rounds entered Horst's body from an elevated position. One tore through his collarbone and out the front of his chest. Another drove through his neck muscles, barely missing an artery. Big wounds, but not fatal unless he bled to death.

"You dead, Horst?" Branka said and quickly moved to the roof above the main cabin.

Horst fired where he heard the sound. Branka quickly sent a burst toward where Horst had been shooting and heard a moan. There were shuffling sounds below, and Branka could hear Gina protesting. Suddenly Horst came out in the open, shielded by Gina, who was struggling to break free. His Uzi was held against her temple.

"Throw your weapon down. I'll shoot her right now if you don't!"

"Okay, but don't hurt her," Branka said as he saw something Horst didn't.

Branka threw his weapon in front of Horst right at his feet; it bounced off the fiberglass deck and appeared it would strike him about the middle of his knees. He reacted by stepping backward awkwardly to avoid getting hit by the heavy weapon and loosened his grip on Gina, just enough for her to break free. She dove on the aft deck just as Eli came around the far corner of the stern cabin, firing his Thompson. It blew Horst off the boat into the water. He was dead before he made a splash. It was over.

"Sorry it took so long. The gun was stuck under the floor where I hid it in the head. Finally had to rip up another board to get it out. You okay?"

"I'm fine. Just really, really fucking tired of this shit. Is it really over?"

"As far as these guys go. Can you believe that crazy ass Branka? Has a log stuck through his leg, and he jumps out of helicopter to try and save us."

"I love the man!" Gina said as she helped him down from the roof of the stern deck cover. Eli ran over to help.

"Hope you will have time to let your leg heal, Branka," Gina said.

"I believe I met a nurse that will help me."

"You haven't had time to meet a nurse," Eli said.

"She doesn't know she's a nurse yet. I will train her."

"What does she do now?" asked Gina.

"Helicopter pilot—she needs a new occupation."

In a few minutes, the Cuban patrol boat came alongside the *Shark Dog*. Horst was floating on the surface. Some bodies sink; those are usually the lean ones full of muscles. Fat ones, full of indulgence and gluttony, hang around longer than they should. Horst was one of those. The Cuban Navy men on the patrol boat fished out his body. A call out on their radio from their station on Iguana Cay reported that a small helicopter was waiting for Branka. He climbed in the patrol boat with Julio and Luis, who had briefly gone on board the *Shark Dog* to make sure everyone was okay. They waved to Eli and Gina, who now had a free shot out of Cuban waters.

Eli was glad they were cleared to go, but there was the issue of possibly being boarded in US waters. They had a plan, but it was shaky. Cherie was coming out to meet them in the *Caribe Fantasy II*, an old boat suffering from a missing master cabin mattress, soon to be remedied with one of the most expensive sleeping pads in the world. A replacement mattress would be passed over to the *Shark Dog* just so no questions were asked.

There was little chance a local boat only out for a few hours would be searched or even called to the attention of the harbor master, Coast Guard, Dade County Sheriff, or one of the numerous unmarked DEA and Homeland Security boats. However, the *Shark Dog* was a boat reported by Cuban authorities as harboring men who had committed various crimes. It was cleared now for departure from Cuba with new ownership, but it was highly unlikely these new developments had been reported to American authorities. They were not yet buddies again. It was a marked vessel itching to be searched and impounded, not necessarily in that order. The smart thing was to call ahead and report the change of ownership and the resolution of criminal activities aboard. Eli did that and found out a few things.

"Gina, dear, here's what I found out about reentering from a foreign port. Any boat that has been to a foreign port has to report in to customs, and the people on board are only allowed to leave the boat if given permission. Once the customs officer has inspected and checked for items that need to have duty paid on them, and once they have checked our passports, and other paperwork required, then and only then, can the people on board be admitted back to the US. It isn't really a drug issue, a human trafficking issue, or a terrorist issue. No, none of those things. It's a paperwork issue."

Eli and Gina met Cherie about twenty miles off the coast of Florida and handed over a mattress and a Thompson submachine gun.

"I have a place for the Tommy gun in a rope locker that has an extra interior compartment. What the hell are you guys doing with a submachine gun? It's illegal, isn't it?" Cherie asked.

"We know. So is sneaking in ten million dollars," said Gina.

They wouldn't search the vessel under normal circumstances. Unless there was a fire, marine accident, or some obvious breach of maritime law, the boat would slide back in her slip near Cherie's back porch.

After calling in for instructions, the US Customs Office told them where to dock for inspection. They were on board within an hour but had to get a Spanish-speaking officer to call the number given to them for the Cuban authorities. There was a little confusion when they found the boat registration wasn't completed or the ownership transferred. Finally, the customs people were able to get enough forms signed to satisfy their lust for newly signed documents. They were released, and Gina piloted the boat to her dock opposite the *Caribe Fantasy II*. Cherie met them both with a large margarita and beer-battered shrimp.

They now had $5 million each in the bank, over $10 million in cash in a mattress to divide, and more gold coins than they could count. It might be a battle to keep it all, but they could afford the best estate and tax attorneys on the planet and most likely would need them to be able to keep all the inheritance. More than all of this, they had friends—friends so close that they had risked their lives with and for them. Gina and Eli would have gotten married that day if anyone asked them to. They knew they would be life partners.

It's possible Carmine Spada and Bernie Swartz knew that their elaborate plan to leave the money to survivors of the family, once Cuba reestablished a relationship with America, would build character and develop relationships. Or maybe they thought it might do the opposite if the characters of the recipients were weak. This group of friends may have had their flaws, but the specter of greed and corruption never arose among them. They fought certainly because they all wanted a share of the money, but most everyone felt each of them would have died to save the person fighting beside them. The test would come now to see if honorable uses of their new found riches would help or hurt them.

Eli and Gina had always talked about forming a charity to help Cubans, but rather than give money away, they thought why not start businesses that will help the average Cuban worker by giving them jobs that pay a living wage? Before they left the island, Julio and Luis agreed to help find a business that could be formed on the Isle of Youth that would bring either tourist dollars or farming income to the downtrodden island. Kelsi and Josh agreed to help. Branka, Milo, and Jaro all wanted to find a place in Cuba and were willing to help with a project. None of the Ukrainians wanted to spend another winter in their native country. They would go home to visit in the summer. To this point, the money had not corrupted anyone, and the friendship of the group hopefully would help bind them together and guard against unwise decisions.

As Gina and Eli enjoyed their margaritas and looked out over both powerboats, they discussed with Cherie some plans for the future.

"We have a reunion planned in Havana in one month. Julio, Luis, Cande, and Lana are going to host the meeting at the National Hotel. They don't plan to rent the entire place like the mobsters did in 1946, but instead, they plan to use the same meeting room used then to discuss ideas for starting some Cuban businesses," Eli said.

"What we all want is to do the best we can to help people with the money Bernie and Carmine left us," Gina said.

"Kids, I'm sure you will do more good than they ever dreamed anyone could. Believe me, Carmine and Bernie would be very proud." Cherie clinked her glass against Gina's and Eli's margaritas and took a long sip of her drink.

"How are we going to get all that gold out of the bilge water?" Eli asked.

"Honey, that sounds like work for a man. I'll cheer you on with drink in hand."

Eli leaned over and kissed Gina in front of her mother.

"A pretty face allows you to get away with so much."

"Have I tied you up and made love to you yet?"

"Oh, my God, isn't this where I came in?"

Cherie laughed and knew there would be grandkids in her future. She decided to share a quote with her daughter and soon to be son-in-law. "Kids, I want you to keep this thought in mind as you count your new found fortune. It was Ralph Waldo Emerson who said, 'Without a rich heart, wealth is an ugly beggar.'"

"Mother! What in the hell does that mean?"

"It means you will be corrupted by it if you don't have a giving heart," Eli said.

"You two are so damn smart," Gina said, "but let me conclude this conversation with another little tidbit: 'A successful man is one who can make more money than his wife can spend. A successful woman is one who can find such a man.'"

Eli looked at Gina. "Have you found such a man?" he asked.

"That I have—that I have indeed."

The End

Charles L. (Chap) Harper

Chap Harper is a native Arkansan and retired insurance executive who moved from California to Hot Springs where he shares a cabin on Lake Hamilton with his wife, Susan. Writing was something he did even in his youth, and in 2012 he published his first novel, *Once Upon a Reef*, which drew heavily on his love of scuba diving. In 2015, he published *Once Upon the Congo* with Smoking Gun Publishing. *Beer, Bait, and Ammo*, a thriller set in the South, was published in 2016, also by Smoking Gun Publishing. *Under Cuba* is Chap Harper's latest novel and was inspired by the author's recent trip to Cuba.

Other Books by This Author

Once Upon a Reef - 2012
Once Upon the Congo - 2015
Beer, Bait, and Ammo - 2016